DIABLO RETURNS

TIM FORD

ISBN: 978-1-989506-52-3

Published in Canada by Pandamonium Publishing House™.
www.pandamoniumpublishing.com

Cover Design: Alex Goubar
alexgoubar.com

CONTENTS

1

Charlene's entourage, or as I call them, circle of fucking Neanderthal assholes eventually left. When she turned around, she saw me just staring at her, my eye contact was piercing to say the least. Charlene was caught like a kid with her hand in a cookie jar. Her face went beet red. She nervously smiled, and slowly walked towards me. Her shoulders slouched, headed tilted down ever so slightly said everything. Sheepishly she asked if I saw who she was talking to.

I said, "Yeah, your old boyfriend, or is fuck friend, Matt Burns, he was the one with his arm around you, correct?" I asked, or really demanded, what the fuck he wanted, and what all was he saying

"Matt is one of those guys that is just a hugger. He just asked what I was doing here, I said me and my boyfriend just got back from a wonderful vacation in Reno. That was about it, nothing else really, and yes, I let him know I have a boyfriend, one that I love very much." Said Charlene with a nervous giggle.

It hurts me that we had such a great time away, and I know she is holding something back from me. For now, I will drop it, but you know I will be watching her a little more closely, and also maybe put feelers to see what he is up to. As we were waiting for our baggage, I sensed every cop in the airport watching me a little too close for my liking. Maybe we should have stayed in Reno for a little longer. It was almost midnight. I didn't feel like calling anyone to pick us up, so I grabbed a taxi back to my place.

On the drive over, the city seemed to have changed a little, it just had a different kind of feeling. A feeling that made me a little nervous. The taxi dropped us off in front of my apartment. I truly expected to see a cop's card on my front door asking me to call them as soon as I can. I looked around before heading upstairs and saw no one watching us, either friend, or foe. Charlene went straight into the bedroom to get changed for bed, while I headed to the answering machine. Rachel left a message that Jerry got her a deal on a Sportster and for me to call her. Donnie also left a message asking if I want to go out for beers and shoot pool Monday night. That message was like reading a fortune cookie, can't wait to hear the tales of Barry being robbed, hopefully also shitting his pants. After Charlene got dressed, she came out, said she had an early day and was tired, needed to sleep. She gave me a kiss goodnight. I said I would be in shortly. But my mind was racing, fucking Matt Burns now knows she lives in the Bay area. Why is it whomever I give my heart to, it comes back to bite me?

Charlene set the alarm for seven; I didn't even hear it go off. Not even sure what time I even got to bed at. When I finally woke up, she left me a note on the kitchen table thanking me for a wonderful time. Love Charlene. I just looked at it and threw the note in the garbage. I grabbed some breakfast and then headed for Donnie's bike shop. As I walked in Donnie shot me this huge smile and said let's go outside and talk. "Everything go well?" I asked him

"Financially yes. For Barry and his two bodyguards not so well. We had to kill all three. They weren't giving up their cash without a gun fight."

"Barry was a fucking hot head cheap bastard, doesn't surprise me. Do I want to know anything else?"

"No, you don't. Joseph has your cash. I already paid off Jerry."

I knew better then to pry, like I was always taught, what I don't know, won't kill me. I thanked Donnie, he asked how Reno was. I said outstanding. Keeping this whole Charlene was a whore for Matt Burns to myself, for now anyways. I said we are still going to play pool tonight. He said sure, why not. I then decided to hit the gym seeing how I had all kinds of positive energy. And yes, it had to do with a dead dude.

My cousin Jerry gave me this big hug and asked how Reno was, out-fucking-standing. "I heard you grabbed Rachel a bike."

"Yeah, I did, 1972 Sportster. Twenty-two hundred. Great deal. Just pay me when you get your cash from the Irishman."

"Thanks, I will see him at some point today. Donnie and I are going out and shooting some stick, come join us."

Jerry said that works for him. We then worked out together; I showered up and said I would give him a shout later. Great workout, cash coming in, what a perfect Monday and then you turn the corner to go home and an unmarked cop car is parked outside your place. Deep breaths Mitch, you have done fuck all wrong. The fuckers were blocking my driveway, so I gave a little beep on my horn. They both jumped, useless and lazy fucking cops. I had to yell at them to pull ahead so I could pull in my driveway. They pulled just enough ahead for me to pull in and then they backed up to block me in. Time for the games to begin. I get out of my car as do they. I nod to them, and they ask if I am Mitchell Strongbow. "The one and only; who wants to know?"

"San Francisco homicide. We need to talk Mister Strongbow."

"Sure, where?"

"We can go up to your apartment or you can come downtown with us."

"My apartment is cool."

We go upstairs and I am positive I had no weed or even a roach in the ashtray, I better be positive.

"What's up guys?"

"Tell me about your relationship with Barry Goldstone."

"Why is he dead?"

"What makes you think that?" as both cops just look at each other now, and yes, both each raise an eyebrow, at the same time, with just a little smile.

"You said you were homicide cops…" and brows drop, smiles are gone.

"We are not sure. Barry is missing; when was the last time you had contact with him, and what is your history with him?"

"I had a child with his stepdaughter, fucker never liked me. I ran into him on Thursday at the bank, first time I have saw him in years."

"I see, and where were you this past weekend?"

"I left for Reno Friday morning with my girlfriend and came back last night. I still have our plane tickets in the bedroom, the hotel receipt, even a police ticket for public urination, would you like to see them?"

The one detective said yes, so I went in and showed him the tickets and the receipt. He then asked what my girlfriend's name was and her address.

They thanked me for my time. I could tell they were a little shocked with my cooperation. I also believe other cops have told them what a hard ass I have been in the past. I hope me being upfront didn't draw anymore suspicion onto myself. Fuck em, nothing to hide, or fear on this one. I grabbed lunch and then headed to the Drunken Leprechaun to see Joseph. And if the cops are following me there, well that is also where I am employed. Joseph was sitting in the front in a booth reading the newspaper. I asked him if anything was newsworthy. He lowered the paper and said grab us a coffee and then meet me in his office. I did as instructed and met Joseph in the back. He said he had my cash with a great big smile. "I was questioned by a couple dicks about an hour ago. You think I should take the cash now?"

"What did they ask you exactly?"

I told Joseph everything including my perfect alibi.

"Good job lad, I will teach you how to execute the perfect crimes and how to get away with it also. Take your cash now. If the cops were serious about you, they would have taken you downtown for a serious interrogation."

Yeah, Joseph was in a good mood. He asked how Reno was with my girlfriend. I said we had a really good time, I got to know her really well.

"That is good to hear, Mitchell. Keep the woman in your life happy and you will be happy. She seems stable, but she has a bit of a troubled past, doesn't she?"

"Yeah shitty marriage to a pro football player. He was shot dead by the cops in a 'roid rage."

Joseph squinted his eyes a bit, I know that look. "You seem bothered by that, why?"

"I just hope she doesn't drive you crazy and shot by the cops, lord knows that heathen Thom fucked you up enough."

I showed Joseph my arms and said, "Look no needle marks. This chick doesn't even smoke pot. We all have issues."

"Make sure she knows nothing of our business dealings, I mean nothing. And if she demands and whines, dump her ass and move on, you seem to do well with the pussy."

"I let her know that I do bounty hunting and P.I work, could be called away at a moments notice."

"Good boy. Now I do have a buyer for the goods. I need you and Donnie tomorrow to fly with me to Boston. I will pay for your flight, meals and give you two grand, sound good?"

"Yeah, I am in."

"I will be happy when your prison pal gets out, I hate flying commercial. I must get these jewels out of the Bay Area. They have yet to become a heat score but when and if they find the bodies, all hell will break loose."

"What time and I assume I will be packing a weapon?"

"No weapons on the plane just for the ride over, wear a suit. Meet me at O'Brien funeral home for seven A.M. You are now an official member of the funeral home business. We are sending a John Doe to Boston. I have the jewels in the casket with the John Doe. My cousin Seamus the "Shark" Finn will take possession of the casket.Then you and Donnie can enjoy the sights of Boston and head home the next morning. I will be spending a couple days with my cousin. He is getting married next month, and I am in the wedding party. He wants to go over wedding stuff."

"Sounds good, you are grabbing Donnie, or do you want me to?"

"You can pick him up. I still haven't talked to him about this, you want to tell him what is going on. If he can't go let me know and I will ask Connor."

"That's cool, we are going out tonight to shoot pool and have a few beers."

"Do me a favour, stop by and see him now then. I hate loose ends."

So, like a good soldier I stopped by and saw Donnie and told him the plans. He said that doesn't work for him, Connor will have to do the run tomorrow. Donnie said he will call Joseph now and let him know he won't be able to do lunch tomorrow, Donnie once again said nothing ever over the phone, but you can always get your message across. I went home and made sure my one and only suit was wearable. It really wasn't, so I took it down to the laundry mat and had them do a quick press for me. The laundry mat was not far from Lucy's old house. What a fucking blood bath that was. I hope her Mom is rotting in hell. I can't go down to Chinatown without getting some grub. I looked at my watch and realized Charlene gets off work in thirty minutes. It might be a nice surprise to get her some food as well. So, I hauled ass to Charlene's place. She was more than happy to see me. We ate, fucked our brains out and then I told her I am going out of town and won't be back until sometime Wednesday.

"Business?" was her only question, I said yes.

"Are you still wanting me to move in with you, Mitch?"

"Yeah, dead serious, I really meant everything I said in Reno. Give your notice, I am ready to up our relationship."

Her whole face changed. "Mitch, I really love that you want more of a committed relationship. Please don't get mad at me, but I am not sure I want to move in with you right now. I have not lived with anyone since Dave. I thought it was just the booze and weed talking."

I just stared at her and couldn't believe what I was hearing from her. "No, I was dead fucking serious, Charlene. Listen, I have to meet Donnie and Jerry. I will give you a shout once I get home" I gave her a kiss on the side of her cheek, she kept saying please don't be mad. I didn't say a word as I left. Fuck I was pissed, nuclear pissed. Every other door I passed in her hallway I muttered *fucking cunt*. Did her seeing Burns suddenly give her cold feet?

I headed right to the pool hall where Donnie and Jerry's bikes were already parked out front. They could tell I was not in a great mood. Both looked at me and asked if I was fighting with Charlene. That made me laugh.

"That obvious?"

They both said yep.

2

I was into my fourth beer when Donnie said Joseph won't like you smelling of booze first thing in the morning. Switch to soda. I called Joseph a fucking cunt and grabbed a coke. The boys went back to my place, and I paid off Jerry for Rachel's bike. Jerry said when I get back, we should hook up with Rachel and go for a ride together. I said that was cool. Three Strongbow's ripping around California on their Harley's. There hasn't been three Strongbow's ripping around since Jake was alive. The boys left just after ten. Charlene called a couple times, fuck her, I was in no mood to talk, or to hear her blubbering whimpers and cries. All this grief that has overcome her, all on her shoulders. Seeing at how I had a busy upcoming couple days, I unplugged the phone. Set the alarm and tried my best to fall asleep. The Chinese food was repeating on me and the anger I had towards Charlene didn't help. I tossed and turned before finally falling asleep. Woke up, had a long hot shower and while in there was hoping Rene was awake at her Dad's funeral home and yes, I would fuck the shit out of her right now. I grabbed a quick bite, got dressed and headed to O'Brien Funeral Parlour. I got there with fifteen minutes to spare. As I ring the doorbell Joseph answers it and looks at his pocket watch. "I am early, you said seven."

"I know lad, and you also look respectable and on time, good stuff."

I went into the front room where there was a casket sitting on a trolley. Connor was already there and came over and shook my hand. Frank just nodded at me, didn't want to shake my hand, just nodded at me. Hmm, maybe he knows I fucked his daughter and doesn't like it. Fuck him too. I saved his daughter from those two punk animals. Joseph gave me my plane ticket and said I would be driving in the hearse with Frank. He then handed me a 9MM and said any trouble along the way. Shoot first, shoot to kill. "I thought you said no guns?"

"No guns on the plane" Joseph and Connor are going to follow us all the way to the plane. We will be stopped by airport security. Joseph said I am to stay with the coffin the whole time while it is being loaded onto the cargo haul of the plane. Then I am to head to my seat and let him know all is secure. The four of us all took a side and rolled out the casket. All four of us, also like hawks, were looking all around to make sure we weren't being watched. Kind of funny.

We put the casket in the back of the hearse. I jumped in the front with Frank. The whole drive over Frank was quiet, and you could feel tension for sure. I asked how Rene was. "She is doing well. Concentrate on looking out for any threats please."

I clenched my jaws, did a little angry snort out my front nostrils and thought to myself if anyone tries to hijack and rob us, I will let them kill Frank, or I will kill him myself. Fucking prick. We arrived at the airport with no issues. Pulled up to the restricted area. Showed our paperwork for the casket and were escorted to the plane. I did as instructed and stayed with the casket during the whole loading of the casket and made sure it was secure and the lid locked. As I turned around, Frank and the hearse were nowhere to be found. Says everything doesn't it! I then showed my ticket to the airport official, and he let me board with the crew. It was cool, I was also the first person to be seated. About fifteen minutes later the rest of the passengers started to board. Joseph asked if there were any issues, I said none other than Frank being a total dick. Joseph just laughed, patted me on the chest and called me a horny bastard. Then him and Connor took their seats. Fuck, I was locked up for two years, of course I am horny, and Rene was more then willing. I also realized with Connor coming instead of Donnie, I will be touring Boston by myself. Oh well, will give me a chance to clear my head about Charlene, I hope.

And then it happened, you know when you are thinking of someone and then you run into them. Well, the next person being boarded was the hot Indian teller from the bank. I just had a vision of her and thought I should have at least taken her phone number. I stood up and waved to her. She looked at me with total shock, shook her head and started to laugh. She came down the aisle and I gave her a hug and asked where she was going. Headed to Boston she said, as her sister just had a baby girl on the weekend. She asked what I was doing heading to Boston. "Delivering a dead body."

She started to laugh, asked if I was serious, told her it was the truth. I asked where her seat was. It was on the opposite side of the plane and back twelve rows. I looked at the guy beside me and pulled out a fifty-dollar bill. "Switch seats with her and the cash is yours."

"Sure man," was his response.

Her name is actually Anita Gray, she was pleasantly shocked that I was willing to pay for her to sit beside me.

"Thanks Mitch, that is very sweet of you." We had the whole flight to get to know each other. And did I think of Charlene? I only did when Anita asked how Reno with my friend was.

"It was good, had fun, got drunk, lost money in the casino, saw some good shows."

Anita then looked into my eyes and asked, "And just what type of friend were you there with, a wife or girlfriend?"

"Never been married, I wouldn't call her my steady girlfriend, just someone who I like to take off with and have fun. And what about you? Anyone special in your life?"

And right now, up in the sky I am once again redefining my relationship with Charlene. "No, like you I have never been married. I just ended a relationship with someone about a month ago."

Now paying that guy the fifty bucks to switch seats was a double win as Joseph walked by and glanced back at me talking to Anita on his way to the washroom. Fuck it, time to have fun with Joseph.

"Anita the guy who just stared back at me was my boss Joseph. This is not a cheesy or sleazy way to get to first base. But if you kiss me when he leaves the bathroom, I will buy you dinner in Boston."

She just smiled and didn't even wait for Joseph to leave the bathroom before she came in and gave me this long kiss, tongue play of course. My eyes were closed but I knew when Joseph did walk past when all I heard was, *Jesus Murphy*.

When Anita broke away, I started to snicker, and she asked what was so funny. "Didn't you hear my boss just say *Jesus Murphy*?"

Her eyes lit up and she said yes, then she started to laugh as well. "I will be honest with you; I don't know my way around Boston at all. You will have to choose the restaurant as I can't break a kiss agreement and not buy you a promised dinner, total breach on my part, what kind of fellow native would I be?"

"What hotel are you staying at. That will help choose where we eat?"

"No idea, but time to spin Joseph's head even more. One sec, and I will go and ask him." She started to snicker as I headed to the front of the plane. Joseph had that look on his face and Connor was beet red from laughing.

"Listen boss, Anita wants to know what hotel I am staying at."

"You told me less than twenty-four hours ago how Charlene is your girl. You are quite happy with her, correct?"

"That was twenty-four hours ago, not so much now. Had a scrap before we left."

"You cock will be the death of you, lad. You will be staying at the Copley Square Hotel under the name Willie Hertz, you brought your phoney I.D, correct?"

"Of course, I did, what room number?"

"Room three seventeen. I already paid for tonight. You want to stay extra nights, you pay your own, fair?"

"Yeah, that is fair, nice hotel?"

"Very nice, a happy crew is a productive crew"

I went to the back and told Anita I am staying at the Copley Square Hotel. She raised an eyebrow and said nice.

"My sister and her husband live not that far away. They are near Fenway. I know a good restaurant not far from there. What time will you be done with work?"

"Well, we lost three hours time correct?"

"Very good Mitch, yes three hours."

"This is almost a seven-hour flight, add the time, damn we won't land till six. I should be done by eight, nine the latest. Come to the hotel and I am sure it has a bar if I am not back. The name for the room is under Willie Hertz, not my name."

Anita squinted her eyes, did an inquisitive smile and asked who Willie Hertz is, "as you said Joseph is your boss's name."

Fuck how do I answer this one. My vibe tells me either way she won't care as she is really digging me. "Willie is a name I sometimes travel under."

She bit her lower lip, gave me this mischievous smile. "You know my ex-boyfriend was a bad boy. He too travelled under an alias from time to time. Are you a bad boy, Mitch?"

My turn to smile. "You tell me, what do you think?"

"Yes, I do, and to be honest, I have zero problems with that at all. Now as far as the time when you are finished work tonight, that will be kind of late for dinner. How about drinks tonight then you can buy me breakfast in the morning?"

I think I know where she is going with this. Really looking forward to seeing how the night plays out. In a seven-hour flight you can learn a lot about someone, including Apache, full blooded, wonder what my deceased relatives would think? And for me, I was curious about her ex so called bad boyfriend. Hank is his name, and he currently resides in Folsom prison for the next twelve years. It appears Hank was a high-end vehicle car thief. His partner ratted him out, Hank managed to fire one shot at his rat partner before the undercover cops busted him. Hank then ratted out the people who he would sell the vehicles to. To me Hank is not such a bad ass, he is a fucking rat, him and his partner. But I kept that opinion to myself. I did let her know I did a deuce in San Quentin for Lucy's death. Now she did bat her big brown eyes and asked what I was really doing in Boston. "Delivering a body believe it or not."

Her response was hmm, and a big smile. As soon as the plane landed, and we started to exit the plane Anita said she would slide by my hotel around nine as Joseph was giving me the hurry up signal. She pulled me in and gave me this long kiss. As we finally broke away, I said thanks for pissing off my boss even more. "Fuck your boss, that was legit on the house big guy."

Being the gentleman that I try to be. I let Anita go first, plus her ass totally turns me on. As we exited the plane, we showed security our documentation and were allowed to go to the cargo haul door and wait for the casket. Seamus already had a hearse waiting for the John Doe. It took about thirty minutes. All of us looking all around for any trouble from the cops or fellow crooks. These diamonds have caused at least three deaths, I wonder if anyone else was killed during the initial theft? Joseph now signalled for Seamus' men to open the back and the two of them helped us load the casket in the back. Joseph said he and Connor were going to go with the body and they would drop me off at the hotel. Man, this was a kick ass over sized Caddy hearse. Joseph introduced me to Seamus' men. They were quiet, shook my hand but you could tell the trust wasn't there yet. Or maybe that I was not a fellow Mick. Connor asked what was with the chick on the plane. I said I met her in the bank when I was depositing a check the other day. And just for Joseph to hear. "I am also hoping later tonight to make a deposit in her pussy, mouth and ass."

Joseph looked at me and shook his head in disgust, said I need the good lord in my life. Seamus' guys laughed. I asked Joseph when is he back?

"I should be back Sunday." I then asked Connor. "I have to be back tomorrow night as I will be running the bar."

Connor then asked if I am going home tomorrow.

"I am not sure, depending on how well Anita and I hit it off. I need a break from Charlene to be honest."

3

The boys dropped me off with my luggage right in front of the hotel. I am sure the doorman didn't expect a hearse to be dropping anyone off. It was almost eight. I checked in under Willie Hertz. I let them know I am expecting a female named Anita if they could let her up. This was a cool looking older hotel. Once again Joseph has impressed me. I went upstairs and grabbed a shower. Got changed into my jeans and a t-shirt. I don't think I will ever get used to wearing a suit. Right before nine there was a knock on my door. A female knock for sure. Confident and fully hard, I opened the door and there was Anita. I gave her this long kiss and when I broke free, she asked if I did eat yet.

"No, and I am starving. You?"

"Yeah, I did, what are you craving?"

"You mean other than you?"

She laughed and said she might be desert afterwards.

"Well then, I will need my strength. A killer steak would hit the spot."

"I knew you were going to say that. There is a really good steakhouse a block from here."

We walked hand in hand to it. Anita was a vodka on the rock's kind of girl. I just wanted a beer. I love going to different cities and trying out their local draught beer. The steak was cooked to perfection, just enough pink. And what was my steak of choice you ask? Bacon wrapped Filet Mignon, medium. Fully loaded baked potato. I was stuffed. We left there just before eleven after we asked our server where there was a kick ass bar. He said two blocks east there is a bar that has open mic every Tuesday night. A couple guys from Aerosmith have showed off their talents there before joining the band. I love Aerosmith as does Anita. So off we went. The place was packed, I was totally shocked to be honest. But then you heard how talented the musicians were. Fuck, they were all good. The only thing I didn't like was the fact my back wasn't against a wall. Especially in a foreign city. I could also tell a couple patrons give us the eye. It wasn't that we were complete strangers; it was our skin color. I am used to picking up hostilities in a crowd, you don't survive San Quentin without this sense. We were on our second drink when I noticed this one guy at a table with a bunch of his buddies just staring at us with this angry look on his mug. They looked like they were in university or something. Not nasty looking, but there were I would say at least eight of them, enough to be trouble. Anita also picked up on them and asked what their fucking problem was to me. "I don't know, don't pay the one asshole any attention."

I see this one guy get up and head towards our table. He was doing the patting of his mouth with his hand doing a mock Indian call. Fuck the last guy that did that with someone special with me he took quite a beating. I flew at the guy and threw a left jab, right overhand punch and kicked him in the gut as he went flying backwards. As much as I would have liked to see him lay there in pain, I knew someone at his table would come at me Sure, as fuck this ginger with curly hair came charging at me. Him I squared right in the nuts. The rest of his table was stunned as I yelled anyone else. I also know from working at the Drunken Leprechaun, the bouncers are going to be on top of me any minute. I spun around in a full circle and threw a back fist. Lucky for them, they hadn't reached me in my kill zone yet. Three bouncers came like a second later, one helped the assholes on the ground. One called me on, the other told me and Anita to leave as the cops have been called. I stared at the one who called me on while answering the other one that we will leave without problems. I went over and got Anita, and off we went.

The whole time while walking back to the hotel room I kept watching behind us to make sure none of the loudmouths' pals were following us. She loved me fighting and kept telling me that the whole way back to my hotel. I didn't relax until we were inside the hotel. Then I gave her a long kiss. Checked my hands for any damage and all was good. I knew the first guy I cut his mouth wide open or popped his nose as I did have blood on my right hand. You come back to reality and realize you are in a hotel room with a gorgeous brunette. You can feel the sexual tension and intrigue start to build. Just enough booze was drunk for both of us to lower our inhibitions. For me it is no guilt involving Charlene. For Anita, not quite sure, will soon find out. And part of my excitement is not only is she beautiful, but I have never been with a fellow Indian. Anita is already sitting on the side of the bed. She smiles at me and asks me to come closer. So, I walk closer to her. I am now standing directly over top of her. She tells me to remain standing as she now raises her eyebrows and starts to unzip my fly.

She says, "Lets see what you have for me dessert wise." She delicately pulls up my now fully erect cock and says nice. She then opens her mouth and starts sucking on my cock. After a couple minutes of a nice intense sloppy wet blow job, she now takes my pants right off and tells me to lay on my back on the bed. I look at her and ask if she is also going to take her pants off. She laughs and says right now I am bleeding more than that goof at the bar. I smiled and said she doesn't need to say any more. So, I laid flat on my back. My knees bent and my feet flat. Anita jumps in right between my legs and starts sucking and stroking. This girl is good at sucking cock. In fact, she can go deeper then Charlene can. She was like a machine, dam stroking, sucking, killer seductive eye contact. It only took maybe five minutes before she found my sweet spot and I was ready to blow my load. I let her know and her strokes went faster and faster and as soon as I started to shoot, she took her mouth off my cock, closed her eyes and rubbed the head of my cock all over her face as I started to cum. And once the last ejaculate shot, like a trooper she put my cock back in her mouth and swirled her tongue around it until I was soft. She then went into the bathroom and the next sound I heard was gargling. I couldn't move, she totally drained me. Anita sat on the bed and said, "I have to get going now. My sister was anything but happy I just showed up at her place and took off for a date. I knew I said you owed me breakfast but that would just piss her off even more. When are you going home again?"

She just made my decision a whole lot easier. "My flight leaves tomorrow at noon."

"If you would like to make up for the meal you owe me, you know where to find me."

"I would like that, sounds great Anita, thanks." I got dressed and went downstairs until her taxi arrived. I gave her a kiss goodbye;

glad I heard the gargle happening and said I would be in touch. I went back upstairs to my room and just laughed, what a crazy night. Normally I am the one leaving the chick's place. I phoned downstairs and said I needed an eight A.M. wake up call. At least I don't have to pay for another night's stay. All and all, I think I like Boston. There will always be meatheads who not only deserve, but also get a good beating from me. The bed was nice and soft, the booze helped me relax and Anita drained every bit of energy I had left. I don't even remember falling asleep. Nothing worse than being woken by a phone in a strange bed and having no clue where the phone is or where the hell you are. After the third ring I rolled to the left side of the bed. You sort of remember telling the switchboard to wake you up, but it wasn't switchboard. "Hey you horny bastard, you alone?"

"Yes, I am alone Connor, what's up?"

"Change of plans. I will be by in twenty, get dressed." I looked at the clock and it was ten after seven.

"I will grab a quick shower." I staggered to the showers; my legs were still weak from last night's amazing blowjob. As I was washing my balls and dick, I still pictured Anita going to town on me, so fucking hot. If Connor wasn't on his way over, I would jerk off. I just got out of the shower and was starting to towel dry my hair when there was a knock at the door. I walked over in my robe, looked through the peephole at Connor. What a goofy looking fuck first thing in the morning. I let him in and asked what's up.

"Joseph wants us bringing the cash back to San Fran today. We have another John Doe and the cash will be in the casket. Where is the Indian chick?"

"She went back to her sister's. When is our flight, at twelve noon?"

"Yeah, same flight time as yesterday. So, did you bang her?"

I smiled and said, "No I didn't bang her, but man she blew me and let me shoot all over her face. Fuck, that girl can suck cock."

"God damn Strongbow. Good for you man."

"I assume Joseph wants me back in the suit again?"

"Have to look the part. As soon as you're dressed, I have to call Seamus' funeral parlour and they will come and get us."

"You think we have time for breakfast, it isn't even eight yet."

"Yeah, I think so."

We went downstairs and ate breakfast. Connor asked what all went down last night. I told him about the fight and the reason why Anita only blew me is she had her period. I also let him know she is a cool chick, works at my bank and that is where I first met her. "So, you are telling me that you barely know her and if it wasn't for her period you would have fucked last night?"

"Yeah, no doubts in my mind. I will drop by the bank in a week or two and ask her out, and then fuck the shit out of her." We finished our meals by nine. Went back upstairs and Connor made the call. I packed up the rest of my stuff and then checked out. Went out front and waited for Seamus men to show up.

"So, tell me about your cousin Seamus," I said.

"I am glad I am family, scary guy. He didn't want to meet you even though Joseph said you were solid. Old school IRA gangster. His new bride is half his age, she is smoking hot, you would like her Strongbow." Before we knew it that great big caddy hearse pulled up out front. We both got in and then headed to the parlour. Seamus guys seemed a little more relaxed and asked me about a couple guys from San Quentin. The one was a relative of Jimmy Duggan, who was deported back to Ireland. I said Jimmy helped me out, then I got thrown in the hole for a month, came out, and the bastard was gone. Can't say I knew the other guy. We showed up to the funeral home. The four of us wheeled out the John Doe. Put him in back of the hearse and then headed to the airport. It was funny listening to these two guys slam other drivers on the road, especially with their accents. Now Connor has been in the states for a long time, but around them, his Irish accent was coming back full force. The drive there was a hell of a lot more fun this time. We pulled up to the security gate, showed our paperwork and were issued to the plane. This time Connor went inside the cargo haul and made sure everything was secure and good. Before the guys left, they shook my hand and said good working with you. Connor and I then went back into the terminal as we had at least ninety minutes before boarding. We grabbed a coffee and kept an eye on our plane. "I asked about him and Meg."

"I will end up marrying her. Her parents are not such huge fans of mine. They want more for their daughter."

"Are you fucking serious? You spoil her rotten. I have never known you to have anything on the side. You guys go to every single 49er and Giants game. Man, I hope one day I have as much as a solid relationship as you two."

"And what's up with you and Charlene? I thought you two were pretty tight."

"So did I. She was married before. Do you remember a ball player named Dave Rockford?"

"No shit, fuck I remember him. The cops killed him, right?"

"Yeah, they did, and in Reno, I asked her to move in with me, she said she would. Come back home she says she thought I was just high when I asked her. She said she is not ready for that type of relationship. So, fuck her, moody cunt."

"I also see the way you look at Nyah Quinn. Would you do her?"

"She is truly the apple in the garden of Eden. Sean would kill me. She is beautiful and I have never been with a black or half black girl before. Never had an urge. But just something about her drives me crazy. I think part of it is the whole positive vibe. And Sean has the dead vibe. Maybe in time. Why has she talked about me?"

"Yeah, she thinks you're hot, she asked me what you were in prison for. But I agree. Sean would kill you. Not worth it and Joseph would allow Sean permission to kill you. All these girls are like his own daughters."

"I have to ask you, Mitch about Natasha, Lucy and Kerry."

"And what would you like to know, Connor?"

"What were they like in bed?"

"Why, Connor… you kinky bastard. Lucy would take gold as nothing was off bounds with her including us bringing other chicks into the bedroom. Natasha would get silver, but we were teens, I am not sure how she would be now. She was game for anything between us, an amazing kisser. Now I also did a threesome with Kerry and Jane Cooper, one of the reasons Tash and I broke up. She would get bronze; her tits were amazing. Still can't believe she is dead, fucking Fraser. And I am not being a pussy or getting all mushy, but do you know who the one female is I love more then any of them?" Connor thought about it and then answered he was not sure.

"My daughter Katrina. I love her more then anything in this world and that little girl doesn't have a clue who I am, fucking sucks, man."

"That brutal Mitch, one day she will know who you are. Why don't we travel to New York and as they said in the Godfather, make Natasha and her husband an offer they can't refuse?"

"I hope one day that her mom will tell her. I am willing to try court and force them. Rachel being a lawyer said to keep my nose clean especially with me just out of prison and look like a model citizen and not give a judge a reason to say no."

"A bullet in the back of the skull is cheaper and less stressful. Your call man, I am here for you though." I thanked him and then we heard our boarding call. That was nice of Connor. Great conversation with him. For most of the flight home I was really deep in thought.

4

Right from the Katrina situation, not sure how I want to engage with Charlene. I don't feel guilty letting Anita blowing me. I would have fucked her too. But I sure as fuck ain't stupid and I will never mention what happened. Suddenly, I had a weird vibe, a dark vibe. I also commented to Connor that I have these weird vibes.

"Frank is going to meet us, correct?"

"Yes, he knows what time we land and he will be there"

"Normally when I have these bad vibes shit goes down, and I mean bad shit. Cops hate me, they would love to kill me. If for whatever reason the cops are waiting for us. They will shoot to kill. Don't force them to kill you. If we can get away from them, lets try it. Now if it is other bad guys. Let's fucking killing them all. Frank will have weapons for us, right?"

"Yep, including an AK 47, that is all yours, Mitch."

"Why waltz when you can rock and roll, Connor? Good stuff." Force of habit I looked at the area surrounding the airport as we were descending. Any unusual amount of cruisers although if it were the cops they would be in unmarked vehicles. In theory anyways. We had it arranged that we would be the first ones off. We cleared security and within ten minutes we saw the hearse headed to us on the tarmac. What I was not expecting was Rene all dressed up in a suit exiting the hearse. She looked at me and smiled, she went a little red which made me smile. Connor asked where her Dad was.

"He has really bad flu and is in bed. Relax I have done this before,

Connor. Hey Mitch, how are you?" I gave her a hug and said I am doing well and nice to see her. Connor and I brought the trolly into the plane and lifted the casket onto it. Fuck whoever was in it was freaking heavy. Connor almost dropped his side. That would not have been good as you are watched the whole time by airport security. Lazy fucks should've come over and helped us. Rene stood at the rear of the hearse as we wheeled over the casket and eventually put the casket in. Rene drove with me sitting beside her and Connor at the window seat. Not my choice but Rene insisted, and Connor needs the window for air. Now, here is my biggest concern. I have had this bad vibe. Connor is more interested in his head stuck out the window. I am not sure if Rene knows what else the funeral home is used for, and does she know there is a lot of cash in the casket.

If I just say, "Hey Rene, did your Dad tell you to make sure you pack weapons?" Fucking dog and pony show all of the sudden. Just like I was taught in Special Ops you improvise, but no rear-view mirror in a hearse. Connor was blocking the mirror on his side. He is lucky he is Joseph's nephew, or I would smack him as soon as the casket is dropped off. Rene kept talking so I couldn't even listen to the sound of a racing engine. Well, this is one hell of a heavy car; I can always take control of the wheel and force someone off the road. But luckily for me or us I guess, there were zero incidents. I still wish Connor would have been watching to even see if we were followed at all by the cops or crooks. They could be plotting and planning our moves for next time. We ushered the casket inside the house. I looked at Connor and asked if we are done. He said yep, all good. I told him thanks for chatting on the way home and I would see him Thursday night at the bar. If he needs me, he knows how to get a hold of me. I gave Rene a hug goodbye and said it was good seeing her. Before I left, she asked if I wanted to go for a beer. Connor in the background just nodded his head yes and had a huge smile. I looked at Rene and said yeah, a beer would hit the spot. She asked if Connor wouldn't mine locking up the place once he is done. Connor said that was not a problem. He then asked about Frank.

"Let him sleep for God's sake or he will have you waiting on him hand and foot." Rene and I jumped in my car and headed to one of her watering holes. It was a bit of a dump, but she said the wings are killer and the draft is always fresh and cold. So, we each got two pounds and a pitcher of draught, girl didn't lie, both hit the spot big time.

"So, how is school and how are you doing?"

"I am actually doing good, and I am glad I had a chance to see you before I move."

"Oh yeah, where are you moving to?"

"I am moving to New York next week."

"New York, good for you, what are you going to be doing there?"

"I hooked up with a studio up there and doing makeup for different TV series. My one girlfriend from here got me set up with an interview a couple weeks ago. They liked my work and offered me a job. I think that is why Dad has the so-called "Flu" to keep me home."

"That is outstanding, hon. So happy for you. Does Dad know we ever did anything, as he was cold as fuck to me on Monday?" She laughed and said yes sort of which made me laugh, I asked what does sort of mean?

"Dad says he doesn't like the look of you. He asked if you always behaved yourself around me. He was being a dick ever since I told him about the job. So, I said I like when he misbehaves around me, in fact Dad, I encourage it. Yeah, it didn't go over very well at all. Sorry, Mitch." Now for me personally, I don't know if Frank has ever killed anyone, fuck as far as I know he maybe a retired contract killer for the IRA, and Joseph rewarded him with this gig.

"That's all right. Yeah, I thought something was up, glad it wasn't me getting a wrong read."

"I feel I can be straight up with you about anything, I like you Mitch and I want to make up for the last time we fucked. I was not into it at all. I want to give you a going away present and I really want to show you what I am really like in bed. You in big guy? Give me one last chance to redeem myself?"

"Of course, I am in. I can't fuck you at your place as I will be working with your Dad now and then. It would have to be back at my place. That work for you?"

"Yes, it does, let's go back to my place and I can get a change of clothes and my car unless you want to drive me home tomorrow."

"Yeah, I will drive you home." We finished up our pitcher, I drove Rene home and she grabbed her stuff and then we headed to my place. The whole drive over she was completely different. She was rubbing my cock through my jeans telling me what she wanted to do with me. This is the girl that I first had the sexual vibe off of. And then you are tested at how truly coordinated you are. Rene pulled down her pants and put my hand over her cunt. I started to finger her, she was soaked and moaning away.

Shift up or down, hand on the steering wheel and giving her a quick orgasm via three fingers playing with her pussy. Talk about a hot ride in a hot rod. It was kind of neat her pulling up her pants before getting out of the car. Now I haven't been home in a couple days. Not even going to check the answering machine till tomorrow. Or maybe if Rene is passed out. Lord knows how many calls from Charlene or the cops regarding Barry. As soon as we got upstairs, Rene straddled me and was necking with me as I worked our way to the bedroom. As soon as we were in there, I was still necking with her while lifting her t-shirt above her head. I then with one hand undid her bra, fuck I am getting really coordinated. I broke away from kissing her and then lifted her high enough so I could suck on her tits. I would have lifted her even higher to munch on her pussy through her jeans, but her head would smash through the ceiling.

So, I lowered her just enough to cradle her and then lay her down in the bed. I then started to undress myself while the whole time just smiling at Rene as she was now taking her jeans and undies back off once again. Rene now spread her legs and I jumped into between them. I didn't insert my cock in her as I wanted to suck on her boobs and finger her once again. After a couple minutes Rene had another orgasm. Once she caught her breath, she said she really wanted to suck my cock. I smiled and then snickered in my head as my balls have been sweating for seven straight hours on my cross-country flight. Fuck it, I love having my cock sucked, I don't think she will be as good as Anita but who cares. The sight of my cock in Rene's mouth was such a turn on. I give her an A for effort, yeah not bad but I really need to fuck her hard. So, I flipped her to the bottom of me and guided my cock into her now soaked and pulsating pussy. She put her hands on my ass for me to move harder and faster, like she was reading my mind. After very little time I heard two noises I didn't hear last time. Her wet pussy making that fart noise, and the girl likes to moan. She did have some decent hip movements and before I knew it, I was ready to cum. I asked where she wants me to shoot. Yeah, birth control never comes up until you are at the point of no return. She was breathing heavy, and I believe she said to cum in her. Too late now if I heard her wrong as I am starting to shoot. Rene is still grinding her hips into me which makes me shoot even more harder and volume. I collapse on top of a now drenched in sweat Rene. It took me a couple seconds to catch my breath even though Rene was slapping my ass, saying I am really heavy. I eventually rolled off her and just stared at the ceiling.

Rene asked if that was better. "Fuck girl, so glad you wanted to prove yourself, damn." I went and got us a beer, rolled up a joint and smoked in and then said I really need a shower. I asked Rene if she wanted to join me which she did. Nothing more sensual than washing each other. In Nam, the whores in the bathhouses would scrub you clean, you felt amazing getting a month or two worth the dirt off your body. Been hooked ever since. As soon as we towelled off, I laid her flat on her stomach on the bed. I then broke out the baby oil and put it all over her ass and then started to massage it in. Not sure if she is into anal or not, but the first time I met her I fantasized about it, she has a killer ass and hips. Loved hearing her moan again as I was rubbing her ass cheeks nice and hard. I slowly slid my right thumb inside her ass and with my left hand I started to finger her pussy. This chick gets off on being fingered hard. After a couple minutes I was now starting to move my thumb in and out of her ass and still not met with resistance. I eventually got up on my knees and positioned my cock against the tip of her ass. Fuck it, hear goes nothing. I put some baby oil on the shaft of my cock and lots on the head of my shaft. I slowly started to penetrate her ass with just the head. No hip movement, just an inch at a time. Rene was still, other then her moans and groans, so fucking hot. Once the head was fully in, I started to re-massage her ass cheeks and started to add more of the shaft of my cock into her, once again a little at a time. Eventually my cock was all the way in. Time to pull back slowly and start some hip movement. Super deep moans now were coming from her. Her ass was so tight it didn't take long before the excitement got to me, and I shot a monster load inside her ass. Tiz a weird feeling when you pull your got out of an ass that is soaked with oil and cum. It still has the pressure and makes this weird sound when you pull it out. Rene just laid there so I went and got her a towel and cleaned up all around her ass and pussy. She rolled over and she had a couple tears rolling down her cheeks which kind of freaked me out. "You all right? All you had to say was stop and I would have stopped."

"No just bad memories, Lance one night when drunk didn't want to stop when I said no. Like an idiot he fucked me in the ass as hard as he could. No you where very respectful Mitch, thanks."

"I am so glad I killed that fuck, enough talk about him." We grabbed another quick shower, dried off and then went into the living room naked, smoked a couple more joints, had a beer or two and then we both went back into the bedroom and slept. No way could I keep my eyes open a second longer. I was out stone cold. Rene woke me up the next morning and said she would cook me breakfast, but I have zero groceries.

"Yeah, I haven't been around much lately. How about we go one more time, quick shower, get dressed and I will take us out for breakfast, then drive you home." She said that worked for her. As we were getting into, I heard my door buzzer go off. Something tells me I better put my cock away and answer the buzzer.

I asked who it was, "Mitch, it is Rachel, Natasha is here with me. Can we come up?" My ears must be fucked up from the flight, I thought she said Natasha. I electronically opened the door from the bedroom. I let Rene know my sister is here and I will meet her in the living room. I got dressed, went into the living room, and my heart skipped a beat, it was like I just saw a ghost. Beside Rachel on the couch was Natasha, guess my hearing isn't fucked up after all. My stomach dropped and I asked if everything was O.K. With Katrina.

"She is wonderful. I feel really awkward talking to you about something Mitch, but Rachel said I should." Rene now made her way out of the bedroom wearing just her bra and undies. Rachel just looked at me, smiled, and yes giggled while shaking her head. Natasha went beet red in the face, but at least she smiled.

"Rene, you remember my sister Rachel, and this is my ex girlfriend, and my daughter Katrina's Mom, Natasha." Natasha said she was sorry and didn't want to interrupt anything. I am pretty sure I know why Tash is here and it has to do with Barry. Time to gamble a little.

"Listen, I am just taking Rene out for breakfast. You girls can join us, or I can meet you back here in a couple hours, say noon, or we can do lunch somewhere." Both Rachel and Natasha said they would come back here for noon. They left and Rene said, "Fuck that was awkward. When was the last time you saw her?"

"I think it was three years ago. Yeah, awkward could be an understatement, baby. Let's go downstairs. I wanna give you a Pamdora's Box t-shirt to wear in NYC."

"Thanks, Mitch; I will wear it proudly." So, we went downstairs and introduced her to Janine, grabbed her a Pamdora's Box and a Grateful Dead t-shirt for her. Any chick that lets me fuck her in the ass gets two free t-shirts. We went to the Drunken Leprechaun for breakfast. We had a great conversation about starting all over again in life. She said as much as she loves the Bay Area, she had to leave to feel independent. Said Dad was strict and that also included a lot of verbal abuse which bothered me.

Anytime she would start to date someone, he would call her a whore. I am thinking what kind of Dad says that shit? She said I always have a place to crash if I come to Brooklyn. She also said when she does come back for a visit she would like to hook up, go out for beers and fuck our brains out. "I would expect nothing less." She was a cool chick. Sorry she is leaving but I fully understand why.

I drove her right to the front doors of the funeral parlour. I told her to call me once she is settled. She gave me this long kiss goodbye and thanked me for everything. "By the way, my ass really hurts," she said and then started to laugh.

And judging the way she was walking; girl was telling the truth. As I now headed back home, that same knot and bad vibe I had on the plane was back full force. Fuck, why wouldn't have Rachel called first this morning to warn me. And then it hit me, I turned the ringer off the phone before heading to Boston as I didn't want to hear from Charlene. I think I better check my messages as soon as I walk in and as far as Tash goes. Fuck see what all she wants. I doubt it is to tell me that she is going to allow me in Katrina's life. No wonder she brought Rachel with her. I am still pissed at her. I turned my ringer back on and then started to listen to my messages. Eleven from Charlene alone. Begging for me to please contact her so we can talk. Not sure why she is crying hard in some, fuck she is the bitch that changed her mine about our relationship and it moving forward. And yes, one from Rachel saying Tash wants to talk with me and asked her to come along. You could tell that Tash was also present just the way Rachel was talking. I cleaned up the apartment and lit some incense as I can still smell pot, and I think maybe Rene's ass. Right at twelve on the money the buzzer went, I looked down from the window in the living room and saw it was Tash and Rachel. I took a deep breath and then ran down the stairs to let them in. Rachel gave me a hug and Tash got all awkward and wasn't sure what to do. So, I just said come on up. Like a good hostess I offered them a coffee or tea or drink. They both said coffee would be good. I put the kettle on, checked the milk in the fridge which has now become cottage cheese. So, I said I have no milk and would be right back. Thank goodness the corner store is on my block. I ran all the way there and back. I was back just as the kettle went. I made coffee for the three of us. "So, Tash what brings you here today?"

"Barry my step-dad is missing, and I need your help in possibly finding him."

"I am not sure if you know this or not, but two detectives already interviewed me about his disappearance. I never liked the guy Tash, but that was eight years, why would they ask me about him?"

"My Mom said Barry ran into you at the bank and you really upset him. So, when the police asked my Mom did anyone have a vendetta against him your name was pretty fresh on her mind."

"I just teased him, that was it. The teller also picked up on how angry Barry was towards me. I didn't start shit. Check with the teller, her name is Anita by the way."

"I believe you; you were anything but his favourite. So, can you help me look for him or find out what might have happened to him? I can pay you."

I don't say it, but I thought to myself let me get to know Katrina and tell her I am her Dad. But this is way too hot, and I would get us all killed by Joseph and Donnie. "I really don't have a clue and I really want you to understand where I am coming from, and Rachel being a lawyer will back what I am saying. I am a convicted felon, Tash; let's say I did get lucky and find him, and God forbid he is dead. The cops would have my ass back in prison. They won't believe I got lucky. I am an ex-con, an easy target, especially with your mom saying I am person of interest."

Rachel told her I am telling the truth. I would become a prime suspect especially with Kurt Wilson and the cops having a hard-on for me. Tash didn't know that Kurt was now a cop and that he beat me as soon as I got out of San Quentin, and it cost the cops a black eye and twenty grand cash. Tash thought about what we both said, she teared up as Rachel rubbed her back. Rachel then said, "But Mitch, if you hear anything can you let me know and I will call it in as an anonymous tip?"

I was nodding my head yes and letting both girls know that works for me, but that would never happen in a million years. "So how is Katrina doing?"

"She is doing very well. Almost completed grade three. Missing her front teeth. She also has her first crush." I laughed and said who.

"Fonzie, off Happy Days."

"I don't have a clue who that is, what is a Fonzie?"

"He's a leather jacket wearing biker hoodlum on Happy Days."

"Just like her Mom was back in the sixties."

Her face went beet red as Rachel now started to laugh. "Sorry, I had to Tash. And I must ask you and please be honest with me. Does Katrina know anything of me?"

As soon as she looked down at her feet, I knew what her answer was.

"No, Mitch. What do you want me to say? That her real Dad was just released from prison? Rachel has told me that you are doing really well, and I am happy for you. Deep down, I know you are a good person. In time I promise you that I will bring you up to her. Just give Stan and I time."

"Time to see if I fuck up and land back in prison? Remember, I saved your cousin Amy's life during the riot."

"My family is very thankful that you saved Amy. Abby and my Aunt Muriel cannot thank you enough. And as far you fucking up and going back to prison, I don't think that at all. Mitch, she still believes in the Easter Bunny and Santa, and she is a Jew. She still checks under her bed and the closet for bad people. And with her Granddad missing, this is not the time. I swear she will know about you sooner than later." I looked at Rachel whose eyes were big and pleaded for me not to explode in a fit of rage.

"That's fair, but I will hold you to it."

"I know you will, that is why I said it not only to you, but also in front of Rachel."

Time to throw a bone her way and make her happy that I am interested in finding Barry. "I know Barry was also into hot stuff. Did he rip anyone off lately, and please don't tell your Mom or the cops you contacted me about him. If anything, tell the cops you were talking to me about Katrina, please."

"I know he does a lot of shady business deals. Mom has said there has been no threats or damage to the store or house."

"That was my next question. You think he might have a girlfriend and they took off and got all fucked up?"

"I actually asked my Mom that, and she got really mad at me. I believe he has had different mistresses in the past."

"I bet you dollars to donuts he is in some hotel in Acapulco with some whore right now drunk off his ass." This made her cry as her voice quivered and said I was more than likely right.

"Sorry, Tash. I didn't say it to hurt you, just looking for a positive scenario."

"I know Mitch, I am sure he will come home, and my Mom will end up killing him for making us all sick."

"Can I at least come by and watch that?" She laughed which made me happy, Rachel smiled and just shook her head. Tash then asked about the t-shirt store and what else have I been up to.

"Did you like the name?"

"Yes I do, I love it like I loved Pam. Your whole family would be proud of you turning thing around."

"Thanks, I hope so. I also work part time at a funeral home picking up stiffs from the morgue. And I bounce at the Drunken Leprechaun on weekends. No idle time for me. Janine, my manager, runs the t-shirt store. She is the reason we make money. I also own this whole building. I have a 68 Cobra Mustang, another Harley, a truck and a canoe that Rachel and I went fishing in last week. Life is good, no more heroin, sticking to the gym, I like the odd drink and toke to be honest. You know I never realized how important living is until you are that close to death. I have had too many close calls. No more." She lit up with a nice smile and I got a semi hard-on.

Fuck this was the girl with the golden smile and glow that first attracted me. Now I am cold sober, no weed into me yet and I sense she really digs me right now. The same smile, playing of her hair when we were teens. We just stared at each other. If Rachel wasn't here right now, I would try and seduce her. It was like a Star Trek tracker beam, as neither one of us wanted to stop staring at each other. Then my door buzzer went. It was like someone woke me up startled from a great dream. I even flinched. I pushed the receiver and asked who it was.

"It's your girlfriend Charlene, remember me?" Tash looked at me and shook her head, whatever inroads of seduction I was laying was just blown up with one hundred pounds of TNT.

Tash looked at me and said, "So, Charlene is your girlfriend, and not Rene?" Not sure why but I did this goofy look, stuck my hands out and went, "Well…"

She burst out laughing and shook her head in disbelief. Rachel just gave me the same look that Mom would give me when I was caught coming home hours past curfew. "Be right back, girls." I ran downstairs to let in Charlene who started to bust my balls right away. "I have company, we will talk about us later on, I promise."

"You have a girl up there Mitch, is that way you have been avoiding me?"

"Two girls actually, show some respect in my place. We will talk later, drop it now and come upstairs, or go home, I ain't in the mood for your bullshit." That half Italian and half Irish temper of hers that made her great in bed, but difficult for her to back down from a fight. She gave me the death stare, nodded her head yes, exhaled and walked upstairs, a heavy walk at that. Rachel and Tash now were standing up and had their jackets on. Rachel said hi to Charlene, as

Charlene just looked at Natasha. Both just squinted their eyes at each other, oh fuck I better step in here. "Charlene Borden, meet Natasha Hotz, who is also my daughter Katrina's, Mom."

They both said hi with zero emotions. Rachel also picked up on this and said they should get going. Natasha did give me a long hug and thanked me. Not sure if she did this just to piss in Charlene's corn flakes or not. It did feel good hugging her once again. And for the first time since my Mom and Pam's funeral, I didn't want to let go. And for once it wasn't a sexual thing, it was a real-life flashback to a time in my life I took for granted. A time I so yearn for. I just stared at her after we broke free, time stood still, it was just Tash and I in that room, no Rachel, or redheaded monster named Charlene. Once I came back to the land of the living, I said I don't want you coming home to Katrina empty handed. Let's see if I have any t-shirts she would like. Charlene, have a seat, baby. I will be back."

Rachel didn't say goodbye to Charlene, nor did Tash. I introduced Tash to Janine and told her is my daughter's Mom. They hit it off really good. I asked Janine if we had any Fonzie iron-ons and she said yes. Two different kinds. I asked Tash what size Katrina is, and Janine got her set up. Told Tash to grab a shirt for herself also. She said thanks and then looked at all the designs on the wall and through the catalogue. I could tell when her face lit up she found her design. I walked over and it was Janis Joplin. "She loved you, Tash."

"Thanks Mitch, she had so much talent, what a shame." After she grabbed the t-shirts I asked when is she heading home. She said unless something happens, next Sunday. So, do I take a bold step and ask her out? Fucking right I do.

"You need anything let me know, don't be afraid to ask hon, I am here for you." Fuck I love when Rachel gives me that look. You know, *I can't fucking believe what you are doing right now.*

"Thanks, Mitch." She gave me another hug and I kissed the side of her neck. Once again, she went beet red with blotches on her neck, so fucking hot. Rachel hugged me and said she loves her new bike, thanks. I asked if she wanted to go riding tomorrow. She said that be wonderful. I told her I would give her a call later on. She wished me good luck with Charlene. I gave her the thumbs up and then headed upstairs. Well, if Charlene wants a knock down drag out battle, she will get one from me. She was sitting on the couch with her legs crossed but her toes were moving a million miles an hour. I went and grabbed a beer, fuck I really needed one. I asked if she wanted one and she said no. Fuck her.

I went into the bedroom that still smelled of Rene's ass. I grabbed my bag of weed and rolling papers and came out into the living room and sat back and rolled a joint. I lit it up and blew the smoke towards Charlene who now called me an asshole. "You know I have asthma, thanks." So, I went and opened up the windows and lit a couple candles in the living room and in my bedroom, yep, it smelt like sex. I then sat down and asked what's up baby.

"I don't know Mitch, you don't answer my calls, you walked out on me remember?"

"I walked out because you really let me down. You think I ask every chick to move in with me?"

"I thought it was the booze and weed talking for you in Reno. I love you, but I am not ready for that kind of intimate relationship."

"Obviously I was, and you're not. So where does that leave us?"

"I really don't know to be honest. I love the time we spend together, I felt like the walls were closing in when you asked me to move in again. Maybe in time I will, but not right now."

I laughed at her, "Do you really think I am going to ask you again, set myself up for you to slap me? Fuck no."

"So, does this mean we are done, Mitch? Is this why your ex was here?"

"Tash flew in as her stepdad is missing, she wanted me to see if I heard anything or to ask around about him. I didn't even know she was in town. Rachel brought her over. And as far as we go, I have to think about us."

Charlene started to cry and said she loves me and doesn't want to break up. But I have to slow things down.

"I am slowing things down between us Charlene. I am doing just that."

"By ignoring my calls?"

"I was in Boston for fucks sakes, got in late last night, straight to bed. I wake up to Rachel and Tash at the door. For someone who wants to cool it you certainly get pissed with not enough contact."

"I was worried about you; I had a bad vibe. Mitch, I fucking love you so much, you don't know just how much. I don't want it to cool off, I am just not ready to commit to living together. I am just starting to find happiness and peace with myself. Do you know how much I blamed myself for Dave's death? I still get nightmares. I never told you this, but I take medication to help me deal with his death. I want a relationship with you. It is going to take time for me to get to that point of being ready again to offer my best. Right now, I am honestly not there."

Fuck I wasn't expecting to hear all of this. Man do I feel like a selfish asshole all of a sudden. "I am sorry. I didn't realize just how bad you are still hurting. No, that is cool. But I won't ask you again."

"I should have been honest with you in Reno, I am the one who is sorry. From now on I will be totally upfront and honest with you." She looked at her watch and said she had to get back to school for the afternoon. I walked her to her car. Gave her a hug and kiss goodbye. She asked if I wanted to come over for dinner tonight. I said yes, I need a good home cooked meal. I went upstairs and had another beer and pondered all the madness that took place this morning. Fuck me large. I lost Lucy, fuck I also realized I lost Lucy the first time she stuck a syringe into her arm. She is better off without Dave; I will never understand chicks. Later on that afternoon, I had a phone call from the one and only Herschel "Hershey Squirts" Adler.

"Strongbow, you crazy fucking Indian. You are always a hard guy to locate."

"Herschel, you crazy fucking Jew. How did you track me down?"

"You forget I have friends. How is life boobie?" "Life is good man, you?"

"Wonderful, I am getting married this Saturday. You and a date are invited. Are you interested?"

"I would be honoured, man." He then gave me the address where he lives. He lived in a secluded area in Carmel Valley. He said no neighbours for miles. Peace and quiet, he can shoot movies and have outrageous parties without the cops being called. Sounds like an area I would enjoy. I called Connor and said I have to attend a wedding on Saturday and could I have the night off. He said sure just don't let his uncle know. So that night at Charlene's, I asked would she attend the wedding with me. She of course remembers Herschel and said she would be honoured. I spent the night, we fucked our brains out twice. It was good, really good. I gave her a kiss the next morning and headed home, man this girl wears me out. I grabbed a quick nap then hit the gym and had a killer workout. After the gym Charlene and I talked about what wedding gift do you bring for a porn producer? So that was my task that afternoon. Fuck, if any city in the USA would have a kinky gift, it would be in San Francisco. Salt and pepper shakers shaped like cocks made me snicker. So, I grabbed the shakers and also a blender. Herschel loves his mixed fancy drinks. Even in prison he would try and fancy up prune wine. He even brought in these fancy little umbrellas for his glass.

The rest of the week was good. On Thursday Rachel and I went for a ride down to Monterey on our bikes. We grabbed a beer and some lunch. She said she was overly impressed with the way I handled myself around Natasha. "See sis, I told you I have grown up. Prison does that and I meant every word I told her. How are things with you and Mike going?"

I could tell by her smile all was good. "He really treats me like a princess, Mitch. I am really happy." That made me happy hearing it. Friday night was working the door at the Drunken Leprechaun. I did catch Nyah looking at me a little longer than normal. She also was pretty excited to see me back. I would smile and thank her and then feel the cold blast of arctic air on my back aka Sean Quinn. If Sean wasn't such a head case killer, I could have fun with him, just not worth my life. The band was really good tonight. A Yardbirds tribute band. Charlene showed up around eleven that night drunk right off her ass. She came staggering over acting all lovey dovey. My back did go up a bit as far as I know she was just going home after work, packing a suitcase for the weekend as we are spending tomorrow night at Herschel's.

"Where were you, baby?"

"I went out for drinks with some of the girls from work. Why baby, you look mad, don't be mad. I love you." She then just got up and went to the bar to get a drink. I watched her and then Connor called me over.

"Your girlfriend is wasted, not going to serve her. Send her home in a taxi, Mitch. She is starting to get mouthy with Nyah who refused her."

"I will drive her home; I don't trust these perv taxi drivers."

"Mitch, you have to come back quickly. I am not having last call with only Sean working. I am putting my neck on the line giving you tomorrow night off." I thanked Connor and headed straight to the bar Her eyes were almost rolling. She was so drunk.

"Hey baby, let's go back to my place."

"But Mitch the party just started, baby."

"Nyah just announced last call. That is why she can't give you a drink." She looked at her watch, but she couldn't tell time. I took her car as no way would I risk her throwing up in my Mustang. She was all over me in the car, she is slurring telling me how much she loved me. As soon as we got back to my place she was passed out. So, I threw her over my shoulder and carried her upstairs. Put her on the couch on her side with a pail of water beside her. I hailed a taxi back to the bar and was gone maybe thirty minutes total. I walked right over and thanked Connor and apologized to Nyah. And then I had a bit of a horrifying thought. I should have shut off the ringer. This will be the time Rene calls and wants one more for the road fuck. The rest of the night was quiet, Charlene was the only drunk that was cut off and thrown out, oops. Normally I have a couple drinks with the bar staff, but I figure I better go home and tend to her. I came home and she was still in the same position. Now the hundred-thousand-dollar question. Do I carry her to bed and risk her getting sick in it? Or let her sleep on the couch? Fuck it, I carried her into the bedroom, took off her jeans and shirt and then I did something I have never done before. I stuck my fingers in her pussy and then smelt them. If I smell cum from inside her, this will be it for us. I pulled them out and was not really sure if I wanted to smell them or not. I have fucked around with two different chicks this week, being a bit of a hypocrite. But seeing her talking to Burns the other day, I have some serious trust issues. I stared at my two fingers and said fuck it, sniffed it. All was good, just a normal pussy smell. I gave her a kiss on the forehead and then went back to the living room, rolled a joint and cracked a beer. Put on Jethro Tull "Thick as a Brick" and got mellow. I went to bed around three, Charlene was in the same exact position as a couple hours ago.

I was up by ten, Charlene was still out cold. The wedding was at three. At least a two-and-a-half-hour drive. Not sure how long it will take her to get ready. Time to wake sleeping drunken beauty. She wasn't waking up for nothing, just drooling and snoring. Drastic measures. I went and started to run the shower, even though she was still wearing her bra and panties I picked her up and threw her in the shower, a cold shower. She certainly woke up now screaming away, I hope whoever is working downstairs don't think I am murdering her. She came out of the shower just cursing at me, still drunk I might add. I threw her a towel and asked what she remembered about last night. She had that deer in the headlights look as she was still shaking while drying off. "I don't even recall how I got here, Mitch. Fuck, my head is pounding and that is a major league asshole move on your part. Fucking thanks. Why can't I sleep?"

"Because we have a wedding to attend, remember, now get your shit together, or you can go back to bed and I will take someone else"

"Like who? Your ex that just happens to be in town?"

"No, I would invite my sister, I am only civil to Tash as I want visitation rights sooner than later. The cunt has taken away the one thing in life that means more to me then anyone.Now the wedding starts at three, it is going to take us about two and a half hours to get there. Time's a ticking. We have less than two hours to eat and get ready."

Her face matched her hair, fiery red. She said she is coming, stuck out her finger and warned me never to do anything like that again.

And times like these I don't feel so guilty fucking Rene and having Anita suck my dick. I am glad we are not living together. What the fuck was I thinking? She jumped in the shower while I made myself a couple fried egg sandwiches, no way am I sharing a shower with her. I woofed down my meal and she still wasn't out. Fucking plan B I went into the washroom and dropped a super stinky shit. It was bad, like napalm bad. She even said from the shower I was gross, fuck her so I flushed the toilet. She screamed once again and came flying out saying I burned her.

"How am I to know you lose the cold water? I have never flushed the toilet with anyone in the shower." Her eyes then started to get big and full of water. She then raced to the toilet and started to throw up, that stinky shit deserves a medal. As soon as Charlene left the bathroom, she laid back down on the bed. Time for my quicker than normal shower, we are talking fire-base shower, in and out in two minutes, no way she is going to flush the toilet on me. I towelled off; she was just lying on the bed staring at the ceiling. I have zero empathy for her right now. She knew we had a wedding today and yet she still got all fucked up last night. I just looked at her, she was all sweaty, she sat up with one hand on her gut and the other over her mouth. Her eyes were almost rolling, I was fucking dying inside with laughter.

"I am going, I just need a minute."

"I just made some greasy green eggs; would you like some?"

She looked at me in horror and then ran to the bathroom and got rid of some more booze from the night before. I had enough fun, and I certainly don't want her puking in the car. So, I made her some dry toast. Then walked into the bathroom and rubbed her back and let her know I just did, in a very sheepish voice she said thanks. A couple minutes later she made her way into the kitchen. She was nibbling on the toast like a mouse, I then opened up a Coke for her and told her to down it as it will help along with a couple aspirins. She thanked me once again, finished the toast and soda and then she said she would get ready. I went into the living room and smoked a joint before getting ready myself. Then it was time to get on my suit.

Ran downstairs and put the gifts in the trunk and the directions in the front seat. I know from having two sisters the more you say are you ready, the more they seem to regress. So, I said fuck all. Put on Black Sabbath Paranoid, smoked another joint and clock watched. At two minutes to twelve Charlene came out dressed and ready to go. She did say her head is still pounding and the dope smoke is making it worse, can I please refrain from toking on the drive. I said that is fine. I grabbed us a couple Cokes for the road and of course a double paper bag in case she feels the need to hurl. I asked if she needed anything else for the ride. She went into her purse and said this will help. I asked what she just washed down with her soda

"A Valium for the road." What can I say? I needed two joints this morning. I warned her to put on her sunglasses for the ride.

"Mitch, I don't even know where I parked my car last night."

"You didn't. I drove here from the Leprechaun; do you remember even being there?" You could tell she was trying her darndest to recall and nothing.

"Let's go and I will tell you about in on the drive over." Hangover or not, I am playing my music. Long drive, let's start off with Deep Purple, Made In Japan. As soon as we get out of San Fran, I tell her the whole story that happened at the bar. She kept apologizing and said she never meant to embarrass me at work. I then asked what happened as she was supposed to drop by around eight.

"This one girl at work yesterday was her last shift as she got a new job, so we all went out to wish her good luck."

"Any guys go out with you?"

"Yeah, a couple, but that gym teacher never went. I think you scared the living daylights right out of him." Funny last night she said the girls only. Yeah, and she wonders why I will always have trust issues with her. As soon as Space Truckin came on Charlene passed out cold until we were like fifteen minutes away when I started to nudge her. Man, she is hard to wake up when she is out cold. Nothing to help me, no shower to throw her into, plan C now. I put the car in neutral and hit the brakes hard. She woke up terrified. She looked at me shaking like a leaf, she was so fucking scared. "Sorry a wild dog just ran across the highway; God that was close." She just shook her head; I swear I could hear her heart just a pounding out of her chest. I found the final marker on the side of the highway. Rest of the drive will be back roads; this should be fun. Couldn't get any speed built up at all, but it was only twenty past two, lots of time. Lots of annoying rolling hills which made a vein in the middle of Charlene's head pop out. Now, I was getting nervous as she was becoming pale again, fuck I don't need her throwing up this close to Herschel's on either herself or me. So, I pulled over to the side of the road and told her to get out, stretch her legs and drink another soda. I stood against the car as Charlene walked around and drank her soda. After about ten minutes the colour came back to her to face. "You going to be alright?"

"I think so."

"What did you drink last night as I have saw you pound them back and not be even half this sick?"

"Started off with beer, then we got into the Mescal. I believe I also ate the worm; you are right. I can normally handle my booze." That better have been the only worm she had in her mouth last night.

"You do know the worm is full of Mescaline, that is why the booze is called Mescal."

Her eyes got big, she nodded her head yes and then said that makes sense. "I haven't felt this weird in a long time. No more Mescal." We got back in the car, and I drove with enough caution to appreciate her not feeling well. After about five minutes we went up this hill and when we came down into the valley, we saw Herschel's place on the left side. It was a sprawling ranch. Looked amazing. We were both in awe. At the front gates were security. We were stopped, asked what our names were and then allowed to drive onto the property. The main house was about a mile off the road. There had to be at least twenty-five cars off to the side in this temporary parking area. A couple motorcycles also. As we parked the car and got out, I headed for the bikes to see if there were any club stickers on them. Nothing at all. We got our wedding gifts out of the trunk and then headed to where the service was about to take place. It was an outdoor service right by this good size pond with a huge water fountain in the middle of it. The chairs were all set up. There was a place set up for gifts. We were asked what side; we said groom and then were ushered to our seats. I looked at my watch and we still had twenty minutes till the service started. Now who I am, I looked at every single person there. I wanted to see if I knew any friends or foes. Some of these guests were dressed in outrageous outfits or costumes. It looked like an Andy Warhol freak convention. People dressed up as if they were in the eighteenth century, some chicks wearing leather pants and a leather vest, no shirt or bra. White guys dressed up like pimps. Rather bizarre. I always look to see who would be a threat, force of habit. I also realized I didn't bring a handgun or knife with me.

Charlene seemed to be coming back to the land of the living. Thank God. So, you are waiting for the wedding to begin and people ask where do you know Herschel from. I am sure if I said San Quentin, they would hide their jewellery on their fingers, and I really don't know if his friends know he has done time. So, I tell whoever asks, from the Crowbar Hotel. They always look puzzled, and I say it is just outside San Francisco, Charlene always snickers and said she worked there also. Eventually Herschel and his best man walk down the aisle to the front of the altar. He had a violinist play here comes the bride, pretty kick ass rock version if I do say so myself. They always look like coke heads when they play that fucking intense. I turn around and his bride is at least twenty years younger, fuck she has to be my age. She was also Asian, and yes, I felt myself drawn to her. If Lucy has a sister. This would be her. Same height, weight, smile, and eyes. I was starting to have butterflies and felt warm and fuzzy all over. I couldn't take my eyes off her. She walked past us, looked at me in the eyes and smiled. Charlene turned to me and asked if I have met her. I just shook my head and said no. I am dying to hear her name as you know it will be something exotic. She spoke perfect English while exchanging their vows. Didn't expect that. The service lasted about twenty minutes in total, perfect. We all applauded then went up and congratulated the newlyweds. Herschel shook my head and said, "I know this girl, you worked in the library correct?" Charlene said yes.

"I am sorry darling, but I forgot your name."

"Charlene Borden."

Then Herschel gave her a hug. He then introduced us to his new bride Jade. I hugged her and said congratulations. I didn't want to let go. Everything about her reminded me of Lucy including the way she hugged and even smelled. I then heard Herschel clearing his throat and came back to earth.

"Sorry man, just zoned out for a bit."

"Don't worry about it. Listen, guy; go inside and get yourself a drink. Me and my lovely bride have to mingle for a bit." Charlene asked what was that all about with Jade. Do I tell her the truth? What the fuck why not.

"Jade looks identical to Lucy. Just, fucking zoned out." Charlene showed me her fist and said, I zone out with her one more time she will send me to another time zone. We went inside and Herschel has quite the kick ass family room with a killer bar and bartender, female of course, who I am sure also does pornos for him.

I grabbed a beer while Charlene just asked for a soda. "Still hurting, baby?"

"You know it." A couple female waitresses wearing tight black shorts and fishnet stocks and white tank tops sporting a bow tie were coming around with hors d'oeuvres. I certainly had an appetite, Charlene not so much. And then I smelt that wonderful, sweet leaf smell. I wondered where the blue smoke could be spotted. They look at you and not sure who the fuck you are. But they all know why I walked over. The one guy said, "Hey big guy, you want a hit of this?"

"Damn straight." So I got into the toke circle. Charlene sat on the couch and one person asked if she toked, I said no but I make up for her. A couple said I looked familiar, I said the same to some of them, mostly the woman anyways.

"Mitch Strongbow, and this is my girlfriend, Charlene." I could tell a few had heard either my name or the Strongbow last name at least. They then asked did I know Herschel or Jade. I answered Herschel and they asked how. I am sure they will find out by the end of night one way or another.

"I was in San Quentin with him." And I also love to see what the fuck in people's eyes, especially when they ask what for, and I say manslaughter.

"But it's cool guys, I found Jesus on the inside." The one girl said good for me. "Yeah, I found him, then I killed him." They all didn't know what the fuck to do know until Charlene told them I am just fucking with them. They still weren't sure if I was serious or not until I told them I was pulling their leg with Jesus, everything else was the truth. So, my toking buddies, every single female was a porn star, a couple of the guys were also, or cameramen or the guys who are editors. We all seemed to get along. All of us after all had a seedy side. Even my soda drinking girlfriend who I noticed was making steady eye contact with this one brunette, and of course she is a porn star. Goes under the name of Venus Fox. After about an hour of getting to know everyone, this guy said dinner is now being served outside. Herschel spared no expense for his wedding. Every kind of meat you could think of. It was not reserved seating, so we sat with our new friends. Dinner was killer, surf and turf. Bottles of champagne at each table. Charlene felt well enough to have a glass. It was like it was full of vitamins, she perked right up and now felt like partying. After Herschel and Jade said their speeches thanking everyone did the real fun begin. They had a live band playing and to thank their guests for coming to their wedding, Herschel had a table set aside full of drugs. Coke, weed, hash, uppers and downers. I grabbed a joint and asked Charlene if she wanted anything on the table. She was staring at the sugar bowl full of coke. Venus Foxx, whose real name was Lynn was beside us, took out a baby spoon of coke. Broke out a razor blade and set herself up to do a rail. She rolled up a twenty-dollar bill. Did her line, then a glassy eyed Lynn whispered something in Charlene's ear and made up another line. She looked at Charlene and said go ahead. Charlene was nervous and looked at me and asked if I mind.

Lynn now gently massaged me by the crotch and said, "You don't mind do you, Mitch? I will make it worth your while if you let her do a line." I have never seen Charlene high on street drugs. Just buzzed on prescription meds, and booze, that's about it. I leaned into Lynn and asked if she was going to take us both on.

"Absolutely, big guy." So, I gave Charlene my blessing. She bent over and did her line. Charlene came up for air, and Lynn met her with this big, long kiss. Lynn then looked at me and said to follow her. The three of us holding hands went to the side of the house where this huge hot tub was. Other couples were in there naked and making out. It was so hot watching Lynn and Charlene neck, while undressing each other. After about five minutes, I reminded the ladies I was present and don't forget about me. Both girls giggled and came towards me. Lynn started to neck with me, while Charlene started to undress me. Once my shirt was off before girls started to kiss my nipples as I started to play with both their pussies. Once it was time for my pants to come off, they acted like surgeons, Charlene took the belt off while Lynn undid my pants. Once my pants were off, Lynn grabbed me by my fully erect cock and took me in the hot tub while holding hands with Charlene. The three of us headed to the one end that was vacant. Lynn and I both seemed to have the same game plan, tag team Charlene. Both of us reached for her pussy at the same time, it caused us both to laugh. Stupid as this sounds, we actually played *Rock, Scissors and Paper* to see who to play with Charlene's pussy first. By the way, always rocks first, and in hindsight, maybe because I was rock hard, yeah I won. I was fingering her pussy while Lynn was sucking on her breasts. Charlene closed her eyes, just enjoyed both of us having our way with her. After a couple minutes, Lynn whispered something into Charlene's ear, something that made her giggle and get out of the water. Her ass was on the concrete, and her feet in the water, and her legs spread wide apart. Lynn started to slowly nibble at the inside of her legs. She stopped, turned around, looked at me and said, "Okay Strongbow, lets see what you got."

Now, I know without a doubt I could knock out every guy here at the wedding. But Lynn, aka Venus Foxx has had some legendary porn stars in her. It is now my turn to show this expert what I can do. Was I intimidated? Yeah, a little, but I am a Strongbow, I never back away from a good tussle. Time to see if I can get her to moan like she does in porns. Charlene was definitely in a zone, her eyes glazed over, enjoying every minute of Lynn's oral skills, and seeing me starting to insert Lynn from behind made her roll her tongue. By now, a couple guys made their ways towards us. If they think I am available and go both ways, I will fucking drown them. But it appears they just wanted to drown their cocks in Charlene's mouth. Charlene grabbed both guys both their cocks, started stroking them and asked me if this is what I always wanted to see her do. My whole body was shaking as the kinky endorphin train was running full throttle. I couldn't even speak; I just nodded my head yes. She started to suck on one while stroking the other, and then switching back and forth. Her eye contact with me was intense. Lynn was also now starting to moan as she told me to slap her ass hard. I always thought when watching a porn that two guys would cum within seconds of each other on some chick was staged. Well that was until Charlene had the one guy cumming in her mouth, while the other was now starting to shoot on her tits, I must have been feeding off them as I started to cum inside Lynn. She shook her ass like a bucking bronco. I just grabbed onto her hips really hard. My legs now felt like jelly as I watched Charlene now lean in and kiss Lynn. Holy fuck. After they were down, Lynn asked Charlene is ready for some more champagne and another rail of coke. She said yes, then Lynn asked me if I would join them. Of course, partying is just starting now. Went to get dressed, and Lynn said at Herschel's parties, no one gets their clothes back till the sun comes up. Speaking of up, I was on my way to the washroom when I ran into Hershel and his lovely bride Jade. He was just wearing boxers, and Jade was wearing a white latex bustier with no bottoms. Herschel definitely picked up that I found Jade intriguing to say the least.

"Mitch, tell the truth, when you first met me in San Quentin, did you ever think I would be marrying someone as beautiful as this?" I eyed Jade up and down once again, thought of Lucy, and yes, blood started to flow back into my cock.

"If I didn't see it with my own two eyes, fuck no." Herschel laughed as Jade came in and started to stroke my cock. I truly wasn't sure what to do. This is his bride; Herschel is right there.

"You wanna fuck her Mitch?" said Herschel with no real emotion. Was this a game he was playing with me?

"Jade is beautiful, but she is your bride, not sure how to answer you to be honest." Total war going on between my moral values and the lust I have for Jade.

"Tell you what Mitch, let me help you out with your answer. I wouldn't have gotten married today if you weren't my protector in San Quentin. I would be honored if you fucked my wife, now having said this. Not an open invitation from this day forward. And you can't cum inside her." Triple smile time next, I smiled at Herschel, Jade smiled at me, and fuck, Herschel smiled at both of us. He escorted Jade and I to his master bedroom, and yes Jade kept playing with my cock the whole time. Once in there, Herschel pointed to the bed, and told us to have fun. Still not sure if it was the weed, booze or coke, still a fucked up situation if you ask me. But no way am I turning down this Tiger Lily. So, we start to 69, and what is Herschel doing, he has his one hand on his dick, and the other filming us. Not fucking cool.

"Herschel, put away the fucking camera, and if you want to whack off over me banging Jade, that is cool, I respect that. But sit in the chair over there. I don't want your old Jewish goo coming anywhere near me, understood?" Jade laughed, and Herschel said he understood. Sat his old hairy ass down in a chair. Now, where were we? That's right, 69ville. After about twenty minutes of solid sucking, I told Jade I have to get in her. And surprisingly, Herschel was still spanking away, but now he was smoking a cigar. I looked at Jade, and said she picks the position. She smiled, took off her bustier and got on top of me. After she inserted herself on top of me, she started to slowly grind me. I was playing with her breasts while making intense eye contact with her. Around ten minutes later, she was doing full deep thrusts, her wet pussy now drenched my legs, and Herschel, well I guess he busted a nut as he was now cleaning himself up. Jade had me so mesmerized, didn't even hear Herschel. She smiled at me, nodded her head and asked if I was ready? Now if I didn't cum with Lynn and Charlene, I would have came already. I told Jade I am still good to go. At that exact moment, I swear the ghost of Lucy poltergeist right into Jade.

"Okay Strongbow, lets fuck." She then got on the bottom, spread her legs, pinched both nipples and smiled. Jackhammer time. For the next 20 minutes, I gave Jade everything I had. And we are talking full strength fucking, no prisoners. Biting her nipples. Rubbing the top of her clit and then sticking my thumb also in her twat with my dick. Eventually her feet were resting on my shoulders, perfect time to now stick a finger in her ass. And yes, once again I know her moans and orgasms are real, no fake scripted. Just like every porn in the 70s, you finish doggy style and for me, I did remember Herschel saying not to cum in her pussy. And now I am at the point of no return. I pull my cock out and insert just the head into her tight ass and shoot my whole load inside her. I collapse right on top of Jade, it feels like my heart is going to explode, fuck, if I were to die now, I am sure the poltergeist of Lucy would take me to a special place, not quite heaven. Fuck, do you really think they would take me in? And not quite hell, I have spent enough time there. Eventually I rolled off Jade, now I wasn't sure what she would think of me cumming in her ass. But she rolled over, kissed me on the lips for a minute, then said, "That was amazing."

Jade then asked if I wanted to join her in the shower. I looked over to where Herschel was sitting and whacking it, he was gone. I said sure. Tiger Lily turned into a Geisha girl inside the shower. She cleaned every inch of my body, that also included some neck and even foot massage, which was hard considering my legs were pretty shaky. After we dried each other off. Jade put on a silk Japanese robe; it was jet black with a pink dragon weaved all the way through it. She went to her top dresser drawer and pulled out a certain kind of pipe that I haven't saw since Vietnam, a true opium pipe. Jade asked if I cared to join her. Took a deep breath, told myself this is as hard as we go tonight, no needles, stay strong, and enjoy the opium buzz. Still my favorite. I just smiled and nodded my head yes. Jade lit up the pipe, took a couple long slow tokes, laid back down on the bed and slowly exhaled before passing the pipe to me. Four solid tokes for me before I had to lay back down on the bed. I truly felt so warm, like a heated blanket was wrapped around me on a cold winter's night. After about twenty minutes, Jade said we should join the party. I looked over at the clock and realized I left Charlene and Lynn about an hour ago. Fuck, so much for being her protector. Jade and I walked hand in hand to the main party room. Now maybe because I haven't smoked truly good opium in a long time, mixed with the booze, coke, and weed. I was pretty fucked up. I was bouncing off the walls like a pinball into the bumpers. As soon as we got in there, Jade and I plopped our asses down on a beanbag chair. A disc jokey was playing music, some people were dancing, some people were fucking. Whole lot of sexuality in this room. Herschel made his way over to us and said he would swap me two brownies in return for his wife. I asked him if that is all his wife is worth. He laughed and said I have already tried his wife, now try the brownies and let him know in an hour what I think of them. He gave me a wink and said I will enjoy them. Didn't really think much about it. I said sure I would do the trade. Jade gave me a long kiss, said I am an amazing lover, and to enjoy the brownies. I scarfed down both brownies, didn't think much of it. Still really stoned, I thought maybe the sugar would bring me around a little, no such luck.

There seemed to be a lot of noise coming from the one corner of the room, all kinds of hooting and hollering. Curiosity definitely got the best of me. It took all the strength and balance in my body to get up out of the beanbag chair to see what the fuck was going on. Jell-O legged and all, I walked over and saw this circle of guys and girls watching something going on. My stomach now flips as I can't believe what I am seeing. It seems Lynn and Charlene are having a personal competition with each other, and what kind of competition you ask. It appears who can drain the most cocks tonight. I had to rub my eyes as it was like I was seeing double. Both girls were beside each other. Both riding a guy, while having another guy in their ass. But that is not all, of fuck no, wait sham woo fans, there is more. Each hand was jerking a guy off, and yes, their mouth each had a cock in it. How the fuck do you take on five guys at once? I walked around to make eye contact with Charlene. She looked right through me. Her eyes were that of a demon, a possessed demon. I broke out in a cold sweat and had to sit down, or should I say collapsed into another bean bag chair, one with a view of Charlene and Lynn and their lustful sinning. Suddenly I felt like Herschel, is this what it felt like watching me fuck Jade? I couldn't look away; it was as if I just looked at Medusa and turned to stone. The disc jockey just started the song Kashmir. Both girls in perfect harmony were in sync with the song. Their sexual moans were like the perfect background singers. I could also now tell the brownies that Herschel gave me were definitely not the kind your grandma would make. It truly feels like I have been covered up with a warm blanket on a cold winter day. I know this blanket all too well. There was heroin in those brownies, compound with me already smoking opium, booze, weed, coke. I am beyond fucked up, not cool in a house full of strangers, especially ones that keep fucking my girlfriend. I have heard stories of snuff films. Fuck, they could kill both of us. Pretty sure for some people, this would be their favorite movie of all time. I am starting to drift hard, my head is bobbing, and I can barley keep my eyes open. And for those couple of seconds, they are focused on Charlene and Lynn, at least I think it is them, they suddenly look different. They look dirty, evil, taker of souls. Fog, thick blue fog, couldn't see a fucking thing. But my ears certainly hear familiar voices. It was Lucy, she was cursing and in pain. As I stood up, I was now out of the fog, and in a Hue whore house. Nedelko and Tucker were in the largest bathtub I have ever seen. Of course they weren't alone, three boom boom girls were in there with them. I look over to the bed and Minicucci and Dunnet are having their way with Lucy. Cucc is actually playing a little too rough for my liking. "Cucc, take it easy on her, Mama San come and cut your dick off man."

Lucy just smiled at me while Cucc now came at me with a head of steam. "What the fuck Strongbow. I paid her, this whore likes it rough, don't you?"

She may have nodded her head yes, but I could tell she was scared of him. "That's not the point, too many G.I.'s treat her like shit. She is someone's daughter, sister. What would you do if someone treated your daughter, or sister like this?" This truly got not only his attention, but everyone's attention in the room.

The Italian bull now came at me full force throwing punches. I fucking hate fighting a guy naked, especially when he still has a massive hard-on. He gets close enough that he attempts to throw an overhand to knock me into next week. Now I do believe in fate, he stepped on Lucy's underwear with his left leg, well his leg went out on him, and he hit the ground really hard. Suddenly all that tension in the room was replaced with laughter, that was for about ten seconds. Stokes and Oscar walked into the room all serious. "Colonel Klemnec wants our asses dressed and ready to bug out in five. All the Khe Sanh and Quang Tri were just overrun with several divisions of NVA. They are about ten minutes from here. Colonel wants all birds in the air, we are going to bug out to Da Nang."

The boys jumped up out of the tub, Cucc stuck out his hand for me to help him get up. We are truly brothers in arms. I knew I wouldn't be struck by putting myself into a vulnerable position. Within a minute, we were all dressed and ready to leave. Lucy thanks me for sticking up for her. I said no problem. She then starts to cry and asks if there is room on the slick for her. I shake my head no, tell her U.S. personnel only. Those tears disappeared as did the sad look on her face.

5

"Fuck you, Strongbow; you are all talk like the rest of the Yanks.
I hope Charlie skins you all alive." Her vengeance is not only in her
words, but also in her hand, she is holding a Colt 45 pistol. For me
being an experienced battlefield vet, the gun she is holding doesn't
scare me, what scares me more is those fine hair fibers in my ear. It
picks up a shrill heading our way. Do I now die as a result of a boom
boom girl I have legit feelings for, or the RPG that is coming at us at
295 meters a second? I take a breath, smile at Lucy which infuriates
her even more.

"What the fuck is so funny G.I. ?"

"I always knew I would die in a whore house." She scowled at me
until she heard that RPG 10 meters away. You don't close your eyes,
you want to stare death in the face, be a true warrior. Then came the
explosion, it sent me flying through the air. Funny thing, it landed
me right into this chair. After the smoke cleared the room, I stood up.
Looked around and realized I was no longer in Hue, but in Herschel's
party room. And what did my eyes see? Charlene flat on her back,
playing with her pussy as some guy is yelling at her tug on her meat
as he is pissing on her.

I walk towards Charlene and her pissing bandit, must be Italian
with all the jewellery he is wearing. I give him the death glare,
then ask him what the fuck is he doing. "Easy there Chief, wait
your fucking turn, this freaky whore will let you do anything to
her." He curled his lip, that was the last voluntary action for him. I

threw a solid left hook, heard his jaw pop before he hit the ground, knocked out cold. I looked at Charlene who only had a slit for eyes. Told her to get the fuck up off the ground, now. I might as well be talking Chinese to her. My temper matched her hair, fire red. Fuck this. Grabbed her by the foot and dragged her naked body outside, picked her up by the hair and threw her in the pool. At first, she was struggling to stay afloat, and right now. I sure as fuck ain't jumping in after her. You could tell by the hatred in her face she was starting to come back to the land of the living.

"Why the fuck did you do that you asshole?"

"Cause you ain't getting in my car covered in cum. Get your ass out of the pool now, I am leaving in 5 minutes, with or without you."

She just stared at me, pure fucking hatred. "Time is ticking wench, get your ass in gear." She mumbled something under her breath before getting out of the pool. It did take us a couple minutes before we could find our clothes, but I made sure to see if the guy I knocked out was alive. He was still out cold, well he will get a special departing gift from yours truly, damn straight, morning piss goodbye. On the way out, Herschel had the caterer preparing breakfast. Charlene could barely walk, let alone stand being in the sun. You know what, fuck her. Long drive back. I am hungry. Told Charlene to park her ass down as I am eating before we leave.

"You just told me I have five minutes to get dressed or you would leave without me." She was fuming as her speech was slurred.

"I also don't remember giving you permission to fuck every guy here. Now sit your ass down, or I will knock you out, put you in the trunk of the car. And maybe I will spend another night here, where is your friend Lynn by the way?" Charlene vibrated at first, I truly thought her head was going to explode. Her face was fire red, even her freckles were glowing.

"I will meet you by your car, don't be long," she growled at me. Fuck, she was even frothing at the mouth, then again, could be some guys love juice, I'm so fucking disgusted in her. So, you know I ordered steak and eggs, and who sat beside me? Lynn. She asked where Charlene was. I told her I wasn't sure. What I was sure of, I wanted to fuck her one more time before I left. A revenge fuck if you must. At least with Lynn, you didn't have to impress her by buying her drinks, showing off what assets you own. She already had me last night, and that my friends are my best asset. So, after we finished breakfast, I asked her if she wanted a quickie before I left. She smiled and asked where. I wanted to bang her right in front of

Charlene, but I don't want all the drama, just some of it. I took her by the hand, walked up a hill, a hill that overlooked my car. And who would be lying face down passed out, Charlene of course. I started to neck with her, rubbing her boobs at first before I slid two fingers inside her pussy. After a couple minutes she told me to stop, I was shocked, she is a porn star who I fucked last night, so I asked what's up?

"My pussy is killing me, this isn't any fun, and I do this for a living, I can only imagine how Charlene is feeling today. You have one hell of a filly on your hands Mitch. Drop your pants, I will blow you." She made me smile while still offering to blow me, and she was right, Charlene is a one hell of a filly, a wild filly. One that I don't trust. No way did she stay faithful to me while I was in prison. I also have no doubts those two screws that paid her a visit, the ones she lied about at first. She fucked them, whore. Lynn asked me if everything was all right, it seems my rage stopped me from getting fully erect. I told her it must be all the drugs from last night. She said nothing personal, but she needed sleep, like right now. I told her I understood, and apologized. Walking back down the hill with her, she headed to the main house while I headed to my car. About twenty feet from my car, I can hear Charlene snoring, like fucking loud, surprised she isn't scaring the wildlife around here. I just stood over her. She looks done right in, swollen bright red face, hair is a mess. Fucking disgusts me. I call her name a couple times, nothing. Move her with my leg and nothing, I would piss on her just like the guy I punched, but she would ruin the interior of my car, so I give her a pretty good kick in the ass, this brings her around. She now sits up and looks at me. Spinning, the girl is spinning. She goes to lay back down but I tell her time to go home. No concept of what I am saying. I have to pick her up, and no way am I very gentle. I put her in the front seat. As she sits, she says her ass is sore.

Too be honest, not sure if it is from my kick, or her getting ass fucked all night. I don't say shit, I fire up the beast, put it in first gear, next stop, her apartment. Want no part of her anymore. By the time I get on the highway, she is out cold, snoring once again. I also had more time to rethink about what went down last night. And when she came to, I asked how she felt. "Rough, how are you feeling?"

"I am hurting but not as bad as you. Will be glad to get home and get some sleep." Then there was just silence until I asked if she wanted to talk about last night. She took a deep breath and asked if I plan on breaking up with her now with a little anger in her voice. She said was so ashamed of herself.

"No, I don't plan on breaking up with you. As much as it was a turn on seeing you in action, I never want to see that again. It was a voyeur fantasy fulfilled. You told me the stories about your swinging parties from the past. And it totally tuned me on. Now, I want to be the only cock in you."

"And that makes me so happy to hear that, Mitch. When I do coke mixed with lots of booze, I lose all my inhibitions, makes me wonder if there was some Spanish Fly in my drink. When Dave and I were doing the swinging party scene there was always coke there. Last night was the first time I have done it since I was with him. I am sorry that I upset you so bad last night." She then started to cry.

"It's all right, baby. Yeah, something about coke makes you lose perspective. I was just as guilty fucking Lynn in the ass. And I gave you permission to have fun. I just lost it when that goof who I knocked out calling you a whore and pissing on you, who the fuck does that? I ever see him again, he will get a bullet in the head." She put her head on my shoulder and called me her hero. The drive back was pretty good. Charlene slept most of the way. Once we got back to my place, she said she really needs a long shower and asked if I would like to join her. I said thanks but no thanks. I fought sleep the whole way home. I am going to smoke a joint then sleep. She jumped in the shower to cleanse herself of all lustful sins committed from last night. I will say if she all of a sudden gets pregnant, a coat hanger will be coming her way. I did find myself getting hard again replaying her in action, so hot. But the battle between lust and jealousy is never a good one. Especially if she is out with her girlfriends, and I get a weird vibe. But rest assured, everything that took place is fresh in my memory spank bank. Later that afternoon I received a call from Connor. He said he is tied up with the bar and could I pick up Joseph from the airport. I asked what time his flight came in at. He said midnight, that is not a problem I told him. Charlene left shortly after dinner. I was hoping for a quickie but she said she is way too sore. She did ask before she drove off if we are good. I assured her we are good. And I was telling the truth, for now.

Normally I would go and workout, but I am still feeling a bit rough from last night's madness. So, I went inside, rolled up a joint. Had a beer and put on Hawkwind "In search of Space", very trippy album. So trippy I went deep into thought and passed out. I woke up drenched and looked at the alarm clock, it was eleven thirty. I better change my shirt and haul ass to the airport, or I won't hear the end of this. I showed up right at midnight. Thank God good parking was plenty. I walked in and checked the flight board. Of course, it is at the other end of the terminal. I do a light jog and I see Joseph waiting for his luggage. I also see Anita also looking for her luggage. I look at Joseph and ask how the flight was. He looks at me, and then looks at Anita who has now spotted me. He doesn't even answer me as Anita is giving me this big hug and asking am I here to pick her up. "No, I am picking up Joseph, but I will give you a ride home. You don't mind Joseph, do you?"

I can tell he is not pleased as he said, "Not at all. But drop me off first please, stud." I almost burst out laughing at him, but I know better. I did tell Anita to jump in the back, no fucking way am I pushing my luck by putting Joseph in the back and her in front. It was a bit of a quiet ride to say the least. But every time I looked in the rear-view mirror Anita would make funny faces or just to tease me had her tongue rolling around and pushing out the side of her cheek to simulate oral sex. I don't think Joseph saw any of this, but he was a little more crusty then normal. He said I was driving like an old lady. So, I picked up the pace a bit. How do I know if the guy has anything on him that if we get pulled over would bust him? Eventually we pulled up to his locked gated driveway. Joseph handed me the key and told me to be snappy about it. Once again, I knew he was in a mood, so I got out of the car, opened up the gate and then drove us up to his front doors.

I asked him if he wanted me to bring his luggage inside for him. "I can handle that myself, lad. Drop by the bar around noon. We have to talk." I told him it sounds good, see him then. Anita then jumped in the front seat, and we drove away. My gut was now a little nervous as Joseph didn't seem happy at all. Fuck is he pissed I took last night off to attend Herschel's wedding? Yeah, he never did ask if there were any issues at the bar. I then asked Anita where she lives. She said in this shit hole apartment in Oakland.

"So should I go home first and grab a 9MM?"

"It's not that bad, just a little rough. Now if you have some weed at home that would be far out."

"I do actually/"

"You wouldn't want to sell me some would you?"

"How much are you looking for?"

"A pound if you could?" Then she started to laugh.

"I don't have a pound, but I am pretty sure I can get you a pound if you are really interested."

"Yes, I am interested. It helps make up for the shit pay I earn at the bank. Every sense Hank got popped funds are a little tight."

"Too late tonight to call anyone, but tomorrow for sure. I can spot you half an ounce if you just want to get high."

"That works too, thanks Mitch." Anita then came in and gave me a long kiss. I have to say I had a little bit of guilt going on. I am just going to kiss and that is it. Get the weed, take her home, maybe smoke a joint and then say I have a busy day tomorrow. I pulled up out front and she asked about the name Pamdora's Box.

"It is named after my sister actually." She was shocked and asked if I owned the shop. I said yeah. Very cool was her response. We both went upstairs, and I went into my bedroom and brought an ounce out along with my scales and another sandwich bag. I weighed it up right in front of her and said good? Very good was her answer. She then looked at me and said she had a question. I told her to go ahead.

"I am pretty sure you are not married. But you do have a steady girlfriend, right?" Fuck, am I that obvious?

"I do have a girlfriend, steady is still debatable, why and how did you come to that conclusion?"

"There is a purse on the living room couch. I am pretty sure you are not a guy who cross dresses," she said with a laugh.

"Good observation. You wanna get going now?" She could tell I felt kind of uncomfortable now.

"Mitch, I will be honest with you. I am not looking for a boyfriend. I am looking for someone solid to play with from time to time. I really liked sucking your cock in Boston. I am done my period and was kind of hoping we could fuck, no strings attached, what do you say?"

I have to say it kind of turned me on a female being so sexually honest. "That works for me, but not here, your place?" Her eyes lit up, she smiled and said that works for her. On the drive over she was all over me. She was like a cat in heat. And as soon as we got inside her apartment, we ripped each other's clothes off and then I carried her to her queen size waterbed. Never fucked on one of these before. I was biting her necks and breasts while she steered my cock right into her soaked pussy. It took me a couple minutes to get used to the motion of the waterbed. Anita was a moaner who liked to talk dirty while being fucked. Such a turn on. Now that I have the rhythm, I really started to put my hips into it. I was slamming her really hard and talking dirty back to her. She was so into this; it was like we have fucked a million times in the past. Eventually I could feel my orgasm start to build. I said were to you want me to cum?" She said on her stomach as she isn't on anything. I pulled out and realized I pulled out too soon. I threw it back in with all my might. Anita now jumped up and was screaming in pain. I am now blowing my load from the excitement as she now runs into the bathroom crying. I of course lose all muscle control and collapse on the bed still cumming. I am now in a state of shock as to what just happened. I am truly at a loss for words. I now roll onto my back and call for Anita.

She comes out of the bathroom crying and walking real funny. "What the hell happened and why are you crying?" She stares at me in disbelief and says I really don't know. I just shake my head no.

"You nailed my ass full force. You moved your hips, and I caught a wave and you nailed my fucking ass. Fuck am I sore, damn Mitch have better aim next time."

"This is my first time on a waterbed. I am sorry, honest." Yeah, she was not happy at all.

"I am fucking bleeding Mitch, God damn it."

"What the fuck, I already said sorry, keeps the weed, and don't worry about paying me back."

"Strongbow, you will owe me more than a half bag, damn that hurts. I will let you know right now; I am not into anal at all."

"Fair enough, I promise it won't happen again." Still not sure if she believes me or not, fuck it. We smoked the whole half bag before passing out. Her alarm clock went off at eight A.M. I still had the buzz happening as I didn't have a clue where I was. After a couple minutes my eyes and senses came to, and I saw a fully naked Anita walking around. She had a big smile on her face; she leaned in and gave me a good morning kiss.

"Did you sleep well, big guy?"

"I don't even remember falling asleep to be honest, yourself?"

"Well, my ass is still pretty sore, and yes you will be compensating me for that. You wanna join me in the shower?" My morning hard-on answered for me before I had the words out of my mouth. Speaking of mouths Anita gave me another earth-shattering blowjob. Fuck, this girl can suck cock like no other. She made me a fried egg sandwich and a coffee. She brought up the pound of weed and I told her I will find out by the end of the day. I asked if she was paying cash. She jokingly said can she have it on her credit.

"In God we trust, all others pay cash," was my response. She said that was not an issue. I told her not to talk over the phone and I will only do business with her and no one else. She agreed to all terms, see how this goes. Anita went to work, and I went to see Donnie about the weed. I just hope I didn't run into Charlene, or she sees me and wonders what I am doing in Oakland this early in the morning. I made it to Donnie's shop without any girlfriend visuals. I asked Donnie if he had any weed.

He smiled and said, "In fact I do, I want you to try this new weed my guy just brought up from Columbia. Mitch, it is twice as strong as the Mexican crap. I can guarantee you that you will never smoke Mexican again." I was totally intrigued and told him to spark one up. So, we went out back of his shop and smoked a joint. Four tokes later

I was really buzzing, by the time we finished the joint I was pretty baked. "God damn that is killer shit, Donnie. Fuck, I am impressed. How much for an elbow?"

"For you, four hundred clams." Now I normally pay one hundred and sixty bucks for a pound of Mexican.

"So how much does an ounce of this go for?"

"I am hearing forty to fifty for an ounce."

"I am slamming this chick on the side from the bank. She wants a pound. Can you give me a couple joints for her to try?" Donnie went and gave me a dimes worth. I thanked him and told him Joseph was miserable when I picked him up last night. I also said the bank chick was also at the airport so I gave her a ride also; maybe that is why Joseph was so cranky. Donnie said he has noticed Joseph has been a little grumpier then normal also. But he did suggest keeping my chicks away when I am on his clock.

I told him about what Anita and I did on the plane. Donnie laughed and told me to be careful as Joseph already thinks I am a whore master. I told him I have to meet Joseph at noon at the restaurant; I would give him a heads up if it is anything serious. I looked at my watch and it was now eleven. I better haul ass home and change clothes, you know Joseph will remember what I was wearing last night and if he thinks I am a whore master, the same clothes will give me away. As I was driving to my place and I was still super stoned, man this is good shit. Seeing how Joseph had been so gnarly as soon as I got home, I ate a bunch of vitamin C pills and drank a liter of water, changed my clothes and off to meet the angry Irishman. Man, even driving to the bar I was still buzzing really good. Dry tongue, I am sure still bloodshot eyes and all. So, I pull up in front, get out of the car and it feels like everything is in slow motion. I keep my sunglasses on. Walk inside the bar and much to my chagrin I see Joseph with a glass of whiskey on the go. I give him a nod and order a draught beer. I down the draught straight back and order another before heading over and sitting with Joseph.

"Thirsty, lad?"

"Yeah, just finished a killer workout," my mom raised no dummies.

"Good stuff, Mitchell. Let's go in the back and talk." So, I grabbed my beer and joined him in his office. He asked what I thought of the whole Boston run and coming back, did I have any issues or concerns. Fuck is he pissed that I flirted with and picked up Anita? I did my job well unlike Frank.

"Yes, I do actually. When we flew back in from Boston, Rene met us not Frank. I had no idea if Rene knew what we were doing, I couldn't ask her if she had any weapons in the car in case anyone wanted our cargo. Now she told me Frank is pulling a *woe is me* pity trip shit with her moving to New York. The guy is not solid. He put Connor, me and his daughter in danger."

"So, she is moving for sure, she told you this?"

"Heard it from her own lips, in fact she should be gone by now."

"Well, lad; Frank has said he can't work with you. He told me to make a decision and make the right one."

"What the fuck, man? I save his daughter's life from her ex, and that other fucking goof, and this is the thanks I get?"

"I have reminded him of that. He says you had sex with her under his roof. Says he can't get that out of his head."

"Did he think she was a virgin, and I took her cherry? Is he really that fucking stupid or naive?"

"Says she is a good Catholic girl. Personally, I think he never pictured his Irish Catholic daughter with a half kraut, half Indian heathen. God forbid you got her knocked up." That statement actually made me laugh. Even Joseph did a little snicker

"So now what, Joseph?"

"I am going to have another sit down with him. I am the boss of this crew. And you are right, he let his emotions and personal life interfere with our business affairs."

"Thanks, Joseph, for believing in me. And Rene has moved away. And if she comes home and wants to hook up. I promise you we will keep it dead quiet."

"How about you just don't fuck her at all, Mitchell. You seem to have an endless supply of pussy as it is now. You fuck that girl from the plane?"

"Yes, I did actually."

"And are you still seeing that red head?"

"Yeah, still seeing her. I know you seem to get your back up over the way I am. But I was locked up for almost two years. I will never get that time back."

"Then be smart; bag your beast, lad." I just nodded my head. Yeah, I had VD once and it hurt like a bastard. Never mind that cotton swab that goes down your pee hole. That thought caused me to have a couple more beers. I thanked Joseph and then headed to Anita's bank. I stood in line like a customer. Made sure to have her serve me. I withdrew a double sawbuck and told her I have something that will blow her mind. She said she gets off at three, can she come over to my place. I said yeah that is cool. After all this is a business deal if Charlene does show up. Shortly after three my doorbell went off, it was Anita. I told her to come on up. As she was coming up the stairs I got hard, the chick is so damn hot. I gave her a hug and asked if she would like a beer. Of course she said. I then showed her the bag of weed that Donnie gave me. Told her all about it and how it is so fucking much stronger then Mexican. She looked at it and said no seeds but there was stalk. I said the stalk you can use to make tea out of, she smiled and said she liked that idea.

So, she asked if I minded if she rolled one up, I told her to help herself. She lit it up and took a couple tokes before passing it over. About half way through the joint you could tell she was pretty buzzed. I didn't say anything, I just smiled at her. By the time we finished off the joint she commented how wicked and strong the buzz was. "Fuck, Mitch; I am wasted off one joint," she then started to laugh.

"It is like being high for the first time."

"Told you this stuff was awesome."

"So, mister Strongbow, how much for a pound is how much is an ounce going for?" Now there is no way I am going to give her the same price as I get it for. Jake would roll over in his grave.

"I am hearing fifty bucks an ounce. I can get you a pound for five hundred and fifty. So, you sell it as ounces you will make two hundred and fifty bucks, hell of a lot more profit then Mexican and better quality weed."

"Fuck, Mitch; I am so stoned I have to think about this. Now, can I give some to the people I normally deal with?" I rolled three joints and gave her the rest of the bag. I think she was a little shocked by this. I asked how her ass was today and once again apologized for slamming it.

"You know what, come to think about it, if I take a pound, I want it for five and a quarter, compensation Mitch. It has been sore all day."

"I think that is fair. Yeah, deal" Anita had one more beer and said she will let me know in the next couple days. I reiterated once again no talking over the phone. Cash only and the key word will be meet her for lunch, her treat. She laughed and said as long as she remembers the code word. Anita finished her beer then she split for home. I really liked this weed; I am thinking about getting back into dealing. Donnie does, so I think I should talk to him and see about Joseph's views on this. Charlene called and asked where I was last night as she called up to midnight and no answer. I just said I had to pick up Joseph from the airport and had to do some running around for him. Sometimes just the way someone answers you they don't trust you.

"I really need a date night. I was thinking tomorrow seeing how you are working this weekend we go out for dinner and then see that movie, Jaws. Everyone at work said you will never swim in the ocean again. I really need this, Mitch."

"I can see it, yeah, we need a date night. Do you want to come here or am I going to Oakland?" I know what her answer is going to be already.

"Your place, I like the restaurants better near you. I will stay over and leave for work the next morning if that is alright with you?"

"Of course it is, baby."

"Hey, did I leave my purse at your place? Please say I did, or I left it at Herschel's."

"Yes, you left it here. I am looking at it right now on the coffee table." So, she said she would be here right after work, yeah that is cool. So, I stayed in that night, cleaned up the place. Called Rachel to see how she is doing. Said she was fine, her and Mike are still going strong. She said Tash went back home quite distraught. She also said she has been filling out applications at different law firms in the Sacramento area. I told her I was surprised Uncle Karl couldn't get her a job. She said she wanted this on her own accord, right now no favours. I fully respected that, a Strongbow never asks for help, but then again, legal help is always welcomed. That night as I was laying in bed, I kept replaying everything that went down at Herschel's wedding. My brain was like a VCR, I was replaying everything. All I could think about, and saw was Charlene in action. Taking every new hard cock on, being double penetrated, that look in her face. Before I knew it, I was beating off. Tiz truly a wicked game, but I can't share her like that again, the jealousy post sex is much stronger then the lust during sex.

I truly believe I can't trust myself being with only one partner, so why should I trust Charlene, especially seeing her in action. The next morning, I called Donnie and asked him if he wanted to workout. We met up and had a killer workout. I told him what Joseph said about Frank. Donnie said he never really cared for the guy much. He said all the guy does is deal with death like it is nothing. Funny coming from a guy with lots of kills under his belt. I also told him I will let him know about the weed. The odds are I will grab a couple pounds.

All in all, it was a really good day. I crashed out for a bit after lunch and before I knew it Charlene was pushing the door button. Good thing I crashed on the couch and not the bedroom. I gave my head a shake to wake up and let her in. I was totally shocked as she brought me a bouquet of flowers. So glad to see my girl, she seems so happy and makes me so happy. I got cleaned up and then we went to Chinatown for some authentic Chinese food. Dinner was good, we spent a lot of time just staring at each other and smiling. Neither one of us brought up what happened at Herschel's. No reason too, or at least not right now. We held hands and munched on popcorn while watching Jaws. What a great movie. After the show I asked if she wanted to go for a drink. "No thanks, Mitch. I would rather go back to your place and suck your cock and get fucked."

That works for me just fine.

We necked from the time we got in to the time we got to my bedroom. I undressed Charlene and was taken back a bit. She still had hickeys on her breasts and bruises on her ass cheeks. Charlene seemed ashamed by this, and she said sorry. "Please don't be sorry, baby. We both agreed to what took place that night. It's all good. I actually beat off last night replaying what took place. You filled that kinky fantasy of mine. I just don't wanna do it again."

"We won't do it again, I promise, unless you want to." I gave her a kiss and started to play with her. The whole sexual act was amazing to be honest. The phone rang and Charlene asked if she could answer it seeing how I was shitting. I said yeah that is cool. I was expecting Joseph to call and was wondering how he made out talking to Frank. I could tell right away when Charlene's voice changed a bit and asked the caller who it is once again, she told them to hang on. She came to the bathroom door and said it was Anita with a scowl on her face. I got off the crapper and headed to the phone all the while trying to stay calm and cool.

"Hey Anita, how are you? Oh, you wanna meet for lunch tomorrow.

Yeah, that works. Yep, okay, see you tomorrow." The fiery redhead came out in Charlene.

"Who the fuck is Anita and why are you meeting another woman for lunch?"

"Anita is a girl who works at the bank. I am actually not meeting her for lunch. It is code for she wants to buy a pound of weed."

"Do you expect me to believe that?" she was pissed.

"Lunch is the key word, can't say yeah you want a pound of weed, not a problem. If I had something to hide, I wouldn't tell you to answer the phone now, would I?"

She thought about what I was saying. "And is she pretty?"

"Yes, she is pretty, but not as pretty as you baby"

"What does she look like Mitchell?"

"She is Apache, about five foot seven, maybe a hundred and twenty pounds. I would say a small B size cup"

"Great she makes me look like a whale"

I got pissed at that. "You are fucking beautiful, don't do that to yourself. I love your curves baby, and your double D monsters." She was still a little off by this. I leaned in and gave her a long kiss and told her I loved her and only her. And that really was the truth.

"And how did you manage to talk to her about buying a pound of weed?"

"Actually, this weed is fairly new, it is called Columbian."

"Columbian weed, really Mitch?"

"It is ten times stronger than Mexican. You wanna try a couple tokes seeing at how you don't believe me?"

"Yes, I do actually." So, I went to my stash and pulled out a joint. I said here I am going to get a beer, you want one also. She said yes. As I walked in the kitchen, I smelt the weed burning and Charlene coughing. I came back in the living room and Charlene passed me the joint. I would say she was starting to catch a nice buzz. We finished off the joint together and Charlene just stared straight ahead. I put on Pink Floyd "Ummagumma" and let the music do its magic. Within two minutes of "Set the controls for the heart of Sun" I too just stared ahead. I would take sips of beer and just vegged. Fucking good shit. I eventually opened Charlene's beer and handed it to her. Those stones eyes don't lie, and she eventually said I was telling the truth, good shit she said. By the time the beer was finished and both sides of the album were over she said she had to go to bed. I looked at the clock and it was almost midnight. Asked her what time she needed the alarm set for. She was too stoned to respond so I set it for seven.

I gave her a kiss goodnight, then hugged her nice and tight and fell asleep really quick. The next morning brought groans and bewilderment from Charlene. "Mitch, I don't really remember going to bed. I still feel kind of stoned."

"I told you it was great weed. And honest I am just selling her a pound of weed and that is it."

"I can totally trust you with her?"

"Yeah, you can, strictly business, you keep me so happy in bed. I don't need anyone else."

"Mitch, before I leave, I am going to make sure you have no jam left in your cupboard. Get on top and fuck me hard." I can't have a jealous girlfriend, what kind of a decent boyfriend does that? So, I jumped on top and totally did as she requested. Charlene grabbed a shower afterwards while I made her a kick ass cheese omelet for breakfast. After she ate and was dressed, I gave her a kiss goodbye, told her I loved her and then I crashed out for an hour or so. I woke up and called Donnie and told him I would slide by after the gym. Jerry and I had a pretty good workout. He asked if Rachel was still with Mike. I said yes. I asked if he tried any of the Columbian weed yet?

"Yeah, primo shit, I am not even going to grow anymore, not worth the risk. I don't make enough profit. This will be the future of weed Mitch, you should jump in on the ground floor." I do have a loyalty to Donnie, but Jerry is family, hmm decisions.

"How much can you get me a pound for?"

"Four hundred unless you want, say ten pounds. Then three and a quarter."

"I promised Donnie I would take a pound off his hands. But I will keep this in mind. Thanks, Jerry." I then stopped by Donnie's shop with four hundred bucks. For now, I am going to grab just one pound till I know others that want weed. No way am I sitting on ten pounds of weed. But I did ask if I wanted ten pounds how much.

"How much did your cousin tell you?" that actually made me laugh. Donnie, like Jerry, is a smart businessman.

"Three and a quarter, how much would you charge me?"

"Stick with your cousin, he can give you a better deal then me. I can give it to you, but I wouldn't be making any profit." I thanked Donnie for his honesty. I also told him about the whole sit down with Joseph and wondered if he heard anything. Not a word said Donnie. He laughed when I told him that Joseph said I get enough pussy. Before I left, I asked him if Joseph would bust my balls if he knew I was dealing.

"Joseph knows I do other business on the side. He also knows I am solid and if I get caught, he will distance himself from me. Now if I was popped doing something for him, he would go to the wall for me. Something to keep in mind. So, for now, don't let him know anything else." I thanked Donnie for his advice and then I took the pound and went back to my place. I also realized that I have a safe for cash and guns but no real place to store say ten pounds of weed. Where is a place that the Scooby Doo kids couldn't even find hidden weed? The safest and most secure place would be in my bedroom. But better downstairs maybe? Will have a look later on after Janine has left the store. Now for the biggest question, who would want some weed that wouldn't get it from Donnie or Jerry? I think after Anita leaves time to hook up with some old school friends, vets who I served with and prison pals. I weighed up her pound, it came in around a half ounce over. So, I took out that extra weed as I will now have to give samples to future buyers. Anita came by shortly after three. I brought out the weed and a scale and she weighed it up. You can tell she was a shrewd businesswoman. A part of me wanted her to stick around and see if we fuck but a part of me knows right now Charlene is really sensitive and I can't preach about her keeping her pants on and me banging Anita. So, I let fate decide what happens. I asked if she wanted a beer. She said normally she would, but she has people waiting for the weed.

She gave me a long kiss goodbye and said she will be in touch. Well too early to go out and start tracking future clients down. Most people I know who are dealers don't leave their houses until the sun goes down. Vampire syndrome. Janine was just getting ready to lock up shop soon. I told her to leave early, and I will do it. She seemed a bit confused about this and asked if everything was good. I said great, just feel like spending some time here and check out what we have in stock. Now, I did ask her if she wanted to smoke a joint of this new killer weed She laughed and said no thanks as she has to make dinner. So, I said maybe tomorrow. After Janine left, I started to look around the back and wondered just where would be the best spot to hide weed. I checked all the cabinets, closet space and nothing stood out. Time to go down into the spooky basement. A shiver runs up my spine and I am ready for the battle as off to the right I see three figures. I bring up my fists and let out a growl, fucking mannequins, all three of them. My heart is still racing as I start to laugh. Moe, Curly and Larry, I call them. Yeah, tons of places down here to store weed. This will not be an issue. As I am looking at the mannequins, I have a brilliant idea. One of the easiest ways to get popped dealing is by the cops listening in.

So, I think I am going to have one mannequin in the window, if he is wearing a shirt with a dead musician, it means I have no weed. If he is wearing a shirt with a live musician, it means I have weed. Yeah, that works. Now, how do I move the weed from the basement to leaving the shop? I really don't want Janine knowing anything about me dealing. All deals will have to take place before or after shop hours. I bring up Curly and leave Moe and Larry downstairs, Curly was always my favourite stooge. Over the next week or so I hit every pool hall and bar where I know either friends or associates from school, army or prison would hangout at. I didn't want to do business with guys or chicks who wanted a nickel bag. Minimal purchase would be a half pound. And the biggest factor in determining who I would do busy with is who is a solid person with criminal values aka the only good rat is a dead rat. Cash only and don't ever show up with a stranger or even another person I might know.

Every person who tried the Columbian weed loved it. And when all was said and done, I had enough interest to buy ten pounds from Jerry. Jerry of course never has hands on. He had Scotty Katonescu drop off the weed. We had a beer, toke and laughed about the shit we got away with in school. I felt like it was 1967 without the madness and sadness. I moved all my weed that day without any issues. I explained to each one of them the Moe Howard rock t-shirt display. I laid in bed that night twenty-five hundred dollars richer, life was good. Or so I thought, perhaps I cursed myself thinking of 1967 as the phone rang just after midnight. It was Rachel, she said they found Natasha's stepdad, Barry, and two other guys in a swamp dead. She said Tash just called her and she is flying here first thing in the morning. I asked if Katrina is coming. She said yes and that is why she is calling me. She said Natasha was very happy I listened to her, and have been looking for answers, and that she wants the four of us to meet. However, and of course, there is always a however, she still doesn't want Katrina to know I am her dad. Tash promised soon though. Rachel asked what I thought. Better than nothing was my response.

If it wasn't so late, I would drop by and see Donnie and Joseph, too late, Barry will still be dead in the morning. Unfortunately, I would be joining the dead as I didn't sleep a wink at all. Katrina was all I could think about. Do I buy her a gift? Will she get creeped out with me just staring at her? Yeah, coffee will be my best friend today. I scarfed down my breakfast with a gallon of black juice from hell aka coffee. I headed right to Donnie's motorcycle shop and told him the news. He thanked me and asked if I could drive over to Joseph's house and let him know. I said that was not a problem, fired up my bike and off I headed to see the boss. Joseph appeared to be in a good mood when he invited me in until I told him about Barry. He mumbled something but I didn't ask what. After all, if he wanted me to know he would come right out and tell me. Joseph is anything but shy. Joseph had this very serious look on his face when he asked me did I like the bar business. He knows I am always asking questions about running a bar, over head, handling patrons and staff. He could tell it just wasn't conversation to pass the time. "Mitchell, are you truly interested in more of a hands-on job at the bar?"

"Yeah, for sure I am. One day I can see owning my own bar, why what's up. You have another person who owes you cash, and I am going to take over their bar?" I laughed until Joseph said, "I am making a few organization changes. Frank wants to move closer to his daughter. Connor said he will take over the funeral parlour and I want to know if you want to manage the Drunken Leprechaun on the weekends?"

"Absolutely, Joseph. When do I start training?"

"I will let you know right now that as much as I like your enthusiasm you have been known to take time off on weekends, that will have to stop unless Sandra will work for you, as she will remain my weeknight manager. You missed the Saturday when I was away, correct?" Joseph then raised his right eyebrow.

"Yes, I did. It was to attend the wedding of a friend."

"Well, you know what my concerns are. Don't let me down, lad and make sure that girlfriend of yours never gets that fucked up in the bar when you are working."

"I won't let you down Joseph, and I will make sure she doesn't show up that wasted, I promise" I wonder how Rene feels with her dad moving to be close to her? Fuck, Frank won't be enjoying retirement long when she decides to kill him. I left Joseph's feeling really good. I can see myself one day owning my own bar and what better tutelage to run a bar, launder money and look like a legit businessman than to be taken under the wing of Joseph. On the way home there was a major league accident, so I had to take the back roads home and through my old stomping grounds.

I found myself stopped at a red light right outside Natasha's parents' place. I looked over and saw a taxi pull up. Sure as fuck, it was Tash, Katrina and Stan. To be honest, when I saw Natasha get out, I had a few butterflies start to flutter, but when I saw just how big Katrina is now, my heart skipped a beat. The light must have turned green as the car behind me honked its horn. Nat must have sensed to look over and was in shock. I was coming from a complete opposite direction so not like I am following them. The car honked once again and normally I would have gotten off my bike and beat the idiot within a breath of their life. But I just did a slight wave and head nod then raced away. Two stop lights later, with no Hotz family looking on, I got off my bike and walked up to the driver of the car.

It was this fat ugly cunt. I pointed at her and said, "Looks like someone already hit you with the ugly stick. You honk at me again I will knock your teeth down your throat, you cunt." She was a tough broad, she just stared at me. No fear at all.

I jumped back on my back and went home and grabbed my gym gear. Seeing Stan really makes me feel like hitting the heavy bag. After my workout I went home and checked the answering machine. Once again, the flutters happened when I received a voicemail from Tash. She reiterated what Rachel told me. She thanked me for everything I did for her. She also said they are in town all week and would I like to meet her and Katrina at the Red Baron Ice Cream Dairy for cones, Friday afternoon. If interested just let Rachel know. She also told me they hope tomorrow they can bury Stan as soon as the police release his body to her family. A part of me felt kind of bad hearing her voice tremble as she talked, just a small part though. So, I called Rachel and left a message for her to call me back. Anita gave me a shout later in the afternoon and asked if she could drop by. I said sure. Anita came by right after work and asked if I could score her two more pounds. I said that shouldn't be a problem. She then asked where I hide my profits. I said in a safe place, why? "Well, you need to hide your cash legally. I know a couple ways to do it if you are interested. I just don't want the cops to question why you have all this cash if they search your place."

"I am listening, go ahead."

"I really think you should launder the money two separate ways. First one is to start having phoney receipts for t-shirts sold at Pamdora's. Second way is to set up a phoney account at my bank. You will want access to quick cash if for whatever reason you need to leave town right away. My boyfriend did the same."

"So, I can set up an account under Willie Hertz and you will make sure it is all good to go, no questions from your bank manager or other staff, correct? And will I be the only one allowed to deposit or withdraw?"

"I will make sure you look as legit as Gerald R Ford."

"And I assume there will be a modest fee for this?" She smiled, then laughed and said, "Yes, a small fee. I am risking my job. I would like five percent of everything you deposit. Nothing for withdrawal." I would ask Joseph about this, but I know Donnie said to keep things on the hush. So, I stuck out my hand and said deal. She shook it and then I pulled her in and started to bite her neck. She giggled and then put her hand on my groin area and started to squeeze my cock. With my idle and evil hands, I started to rub her breasts. Within seconds she had my hard cock out and was stroking me. It felt so good and then when she got on her knees and started to blow me, I just closed my eyes and felt every single action. The girl is so talented, fuck. I actually tell her to stop as I really wanna fuck her, and yes, no accidental anal slamming. So, I pick her up and throw her over my shoulder and start to talk to the bedroom when the buzzer goes off. I have this flash that it is Tash, so I tell Anita I have to see who it is. I answer it and it is Charlene. I try to deflate my hard-on go and tell Anita it is my girlfriend and just have a seat on the couch. She says really, and then smiles and snickers. Fuck, not good. I pull up my pants and tuck my still hard cock in. Do up the zipper and run down the stairs and let her in. Charlene is eye to eye with my cock as I am up a step, and she gives it a little feel.

"I like that you are ready for me Mitch, so sexy." Then Anita sneezed and Charlene's brows went up and she asked who was upstairs.

"Just Anita picking up some stuff."

Oh she was pissed. "What stuff?"

"Remember how I said I do certain business and it is best you don't know about it?"

"Well, I think there is monkey business happening." Charlene walked right past me and upstairs to see Anita on the couch. A smiling Anita stood up and stuck her hand out and introduced herself. And then said I speak highly of her all the time. Charlene didn't know how to react. She shook her hand out and said nice to meet you, her voice was shaking the whole time. Then Anita said she has people to meet and does he have goods. I said yes so, she started counting out eleven one-hundred-dollar bills. I went into the bedroom and got out the final two pounds I had. Will have to order maybe twenty-five pounds tomorrow. I brought up the scale; she weighed them up and was happy. She thanked me and shook my hand; told Charlene it was nice to meet her. I walked her to the bottom of the stairs and was totally blown away the way she handled herself. As I came up Charlene had this smile on her face, I asked why.

"I do like my bad boys Mitchell, fuck me right now." What kind of a boyfriend would I be to deny her request? We fucked three times that night, and yes part of the time I would be thinking of Anita. Charlene spent the night and left for work the next morning. I hit the gym and had a pretty solid and intense workout. Got showered and changed and then headed to Anita's bank with all my phoney Willie Hertz identification. As soon as Anita saw me in line her smile lit up the whole bank, and those eyes, I just wanna jump over the counter and make a special deposit in her. Just like a pro, Anita took down all my information and I set up a new bank account. I deposited five thousand dollars cash which in turn would profit Anita two hundred and fifty bucks. Five grand should be able to get me out of the country if shit hits the fan. I did say for that amount of cash I am hoping for some action. Anita smiled; looked at one of the old hag tellers and said Martha will give me a gum job. Martha must have sensed we were talking about her as she looked over.

I looked at two-hundred-year-old grey haired Martha and gave her a wink. Anita covered her mouth as she could stop laughing. Martha just scowled at me. She did say maybe she can drop by for a noon quickie on her lunch break on Thursday. My turn to smile and do something I never thought I would do. I had to turn her down as I am meeting Tash and Katrina. Anita was cool with my reason why. I thanked her for the banking and said I can give her cash, or I can deduct the money I owe her off her next purchase of dope. She smiled, raised her eyebrows, and said, "I will always take the cash." So, I handed her an envelope as I figured that is what she would say. She knew better than to open it at work, she just said thanks and she would be in touch.

That night I had a lot of little demons running through my head. Tash called and said the police didn't release the body right away so she can't meet with Rachel and me on Thursday. She said Wednesday was a visitation, and the funeral would be on Thursday. I had a lump in my throat and my stomach flipped. I felt my ears and face getting hot. I felt really alone and let down. She could tell I was disappointed, but she reassured me that we can meet Friday at two

in the afternoon at the ice cream parlour. So, Tuesday night before I
slept, I wrestled with showing up for the visitation as quite frankly
I really wanted to spend as much time with Katrina as I could.
And Natasha looked pretty damn hot, yeah hot enough that night I
pleasured myself to her. I guess getting rid of that sexual frustration
last night cleared my brain. Joseph and Donnie would put a bullet in
my head. But that doesn't mean I can hit the coffee shop right across
the street and watch Katrina and Natasha. Visitations started at one,
so I went and had a killer workout. Trying to get rid of that nervous
energy and all. As I drove over to the coffee shop, I was praying I
wasn't seen by Tash or Joseph, he senses when I am up to no good
and would find some stupid fucking chore. I parked my truck at
the back of the coffee shop, wore a Raiders ball cap and a pair of
sunglasses. I took my seat looking right out the window. Ordered
a coffee and a slice of apple pie and let the viewing game begin. I
sort of had a calm feeling looking over and waiting for the joy that
kept me alive in Nam to appear, and yes seeing that cunt mom of
Natasha's to show up weeping like a fool. Two cars showed up in the
empty parking lot of the funeral home. The first car closest to me was
Natasha's brother Glen and his wife Evelyn. The second car driver
didn't even have to get fully out of the car, and I sensed great evil.
Sure as fuck it was the bitch herself. I then saw Stan, I clenched my
jaws and started to make a fist. Ready for the fight, then I saw Katrina
in a dress. The anger now left me as I had this warm rush come over
me. I feel high just seeing her. So young, so innocent. Not a care in
the world, her whole life ahead of her. And of course, Tash was the
final mourner. I was totally drawn into. I eyed her up and down and.
Man, she looks so elegant. My little flower child hippie girlfriend is
now all grown up. A firefight could have started in the coffee shop,
and I wouldn't have noticed, I was so transfixed on Tash and Katrina.
Stan and Katrina went inside the parlour as Tash and Glen stood
outside with their Mom as she had a cigarette, fuck Glen just lit up as
well. Hmm…when did he start smoking? I hope and pray Tash hasn't
also started.

   She didn't, thank God. After the smokes were butted out, they all
went inside. I was now up to three coffees when people started to pull
up and go inside. With Tash not smoking no reason for her or Katrina
to go back outside. I might as well make my exit. I put my head down
with one eye straining left to see if my girls go outside. Tomorrow is
the funeral; I wonder if there is another coffee shop for me to hang
out at? When I arrived home, I checked the mail and had a letter from

Oscar. He is being released next Friday and could I come and pick him up. So, I wrote back and said yes. I better also let Joseph and Donnie know our newest team member will be joining us. I will also read Oscar the riot act about pissing off or not respecting Donnie or Joseph, will result in him looking for other work or possibly a bullet to the back of the brain. That night I headed to see Charlene. I have been pretty horny and now that I am working weekends at the bar in a good job, a job I will take more serious I am not sure how this will affect our relationship. I really hope she is understanding. I decided we should go out for dinner and talk. Wine and dine and hopefully everything will be fine. Charlene said that is a nice surprise and was very receptive to my dinner date. We just ordered our drinks and going over the food menu when she put down her menu and she said, "Mitch, I have this strange vibe. Are we good as a couple?"

I felt my eyes roll back in my head. "Of course, we are good baby, never been better." She wasn't sure about my response, and she decided to dig a little deeper.

"Is Natasha back in town? I have this really strong vibe that I can't shake or reason with." Fucking witch, I swear to God. My face now went red as I could feel my blood pressure rise.

"Yes, she is in town, the cops found the lifeless body of her stepdad. But I have not saw her."

"Is her husband and your daughter also here with her?"

"Yes, they are." I then took a deep breath as I know what question is coming sooner than later.

"Are you going to visitations, or the funeral?"

"Fuck no, if her Mom see's me they might as well do a double funeral as she will have a massive heart attack."

She just stared at me, a little smile, a little grin.

"And do you have plans on hooking up with her at all?"

Fuck it, be honest, not doing anything wrong.

"I am meeting with her, Katrina and Rachel at this ice cream parlour on Friday afternoon." She closed her menu and said she has now lost her appetite. I took a deep breath, drank the remaining fluids in my drink and slammed my glass down on the table. Looked at her rather seriously and asked what her problem was.

"My problem is that you had no intentions of telling me about this little rendezvous if I didn't have this vibe Mitch, that is my problem."

"We are meeting in an ice cream parlour; I wouldn't call that a rendezvous. I love you Charlene and I have zero interests in any other chick, but I will not give up a chance to spend time with Katrina, fuck, Rachel will be there."

"You don't get it, Mitch; you keep me in the dark with so many things. You say it is for my own good and safety, can't say I agree."

"So, do you want to blow a shift and sit with us and eat ice cream and listen to what we are talking about?" She opened up her menu once again and didn't answer me. The waiter came over and took our order and the menus away. She can't hide behind it now. After about five minutes of silence, I decided to change the subject. And seeing at how she is already pissed about me having so many secrets why not get almost everything out in the open.

"Joseph has asked me to be the new weekend manager at the bar. What do you think?"

"So, I guess this means you will be spending less time with me then what you already do now?"

"I am really trying to live the straight and narrow life; have an honest tax paying job and you are busting my balls about this. I could go back to a life of crime and take a chance of not seeing you for twenty years unless you come and visit me back in prison. Is that what you want?"

"Why can't you get a normal Monday to Friday job like the rest of the world?"

"Because I am not a normal person. I never want to be a Monday to Friday guy. Just put a fucking bullet in me if I ever become that guy. And you know what? Why not put a bullet in us as a couple. I take you out to celebrate my new job and all you have done is fucking bitch to me, fuck you. I just lost my appetite." I threw some cash on the table for the meal and for her to take a taxi home. I got up and stormed out of there. Fuck, am I pissed. Headed back to San Fran but the last thing I wanted to do was to go home to an empty apartment. I knew booze was going to be poured into my belly tonight, so I better get something to eat. I pulled up to this Mexican joint that had a liquor license. I also didn't feel like being alone and needed a good solid anger fuck. So, before I ordered my food I called Anita to see if she wanted to get drunk and laid. No answer, fuck. I scarfed down about a half dozen tacos and then washed them back with several shots of tequila and about a dozen beers. By the time I left I had a really nice buzz happening, I was also horny, so I needed to see some titties and have a few more beers. Electric Ladyland is the perfect spot. And yep, every time I pull into the parking lot I can see where I killed General and Gifford. And every time I snicker, fucking losers. I headed straight to the bar and asked to see Mike.

The topless bartender signalled the one bouncer over who went into Mike's office to tell him I wanted to see him. After about ten minutes Mike appeared out of the back with the bouncer. He smiled but he seemed a bit off. He told the bartender to give me whatever I wanted to drink; it was on the house. So, I ordered a shot of Jack and a Miller beer. Mike asked me to sit in the one booth with him. The bouncer also tagged along which I found a bit weird. Mike sheepishly asked how Rachel is doing. Just the way he said it I knew something was up. "She is good, but my gut tells me things aren't so good between you two?"

"So, she hasn't told you we broke up last week?"

"Can't say she has, sorry to hear that, Mike."

"Mitch, your sister is a great girl. Things just didn't work out." Mike then sent his bouncer over to get us a pitcher of beer and a bottle of Jack. Guess I am getting drunk tonight. I never did ask why they split. If Rachel wants me to know she would have told me already. And as long as I don't see any marks on her face, all good. I told Mike that I believe me and Charlene are also done. I can't take the mood swings, jealousy, yeah, Herschel's wedding, can't shake that trust, and yet I tried, I certainly tried my best. She should take a page from me. So just like being back in Nam we drank and drank while having naked chicks dance for us. And just like being back in Nam I found this one Asian stripper totally did it for me. But unlike being in Saigon I didn't have to pay a mama-San for her pussy. Mike told her to take care of me. On the house of course. I was so drunk when I took her into Mike's storage area, she had to work hard to get me hard. But once I was hard, I fucked the living shit out of her. The last cum drop was not even out when the room started to spin. I know what I had to do. I raced to the washroom and stuck two fingers down my throat and threw up all that free whiskey and beer.

At one point I saw two shadows come up from behind me. I broke out in a cold sweat when I saw both of them reach into their midsection and pull out what looked like handguns. I struggled to turn around and no one was there. I am totally fucked up and definitely freaked out. I staggered to the sink and threw tons of water in my face and whetted a paper towel and cooled off the back of my neck. Once the room had stopped spinning and my guts settled down, I did my best to walk back to Mike and say I am out of here. Mike had that glazed look over her face. Yeah, he is about a drink away from hurling himself. I went outside and the fresh air seemed to help. That was until I looked over to where the killings had taken place.

This time I didn't snicker. I had a cold rush of air go right through me. Freaked me right out. I got in my car and fired it up as quickly as I could, did not like the vibe I was feeling. I barely managed to make it home. It was a battle to not only fit my key in the door, but to tackle the stairs. After about fifteen minutes I found myself in the living room. I sat on the couch and stared at the picture of Katrina. That was the last thing I remembered that night. The phone brought me out of my drunken stupor, but I was still too drunk and exhausted to answer it. I also don't know why I passed out on the couch and not my bed. The phone rings again but this time I am pissed, and I answer it to tell whoever it is to fuck off.

"What!" with a gruff voice I bark into the phone.

"Hey celly, it is Oscar. The screws say I am out this Friday not next Friday. You can still get me, right?" Friday, fuck I am meeting Tash, Rachel and Katrina. I won't miss that for anyone or anything.

"What time are they cutting you lose at?"

"09:00 brother. Is that a problem?"

"Give me a minute I have to clear my head."

"Strongbow hurry up, the screws are signalling me to wrap up this call."

"Yeah, that is not a problem, see you on the outside." I hung up the phone and looked at the clock. Fuck me it was two in the afternoon. I smoked a joint to try and stop the pounding that took place in my head. As much as I tried to recall what happened the night before, the weed that was helping my headache also affected my memory. Total blank other than recalling Mike and Rachel breaking up. I called her but no answer, so I jumped in the shower and the water performed its magic. It did help, I made some dry toast and a pot of tea. Things were starting to come around and I was feeling alive. I tried Rachel again and still no answer. So, I decided to call Joseph and let him know that Oscar is a free man and when would he like to meet him. Joseph said drop by for breakfast at the bar the morning he is released. He also said to drop by the bar tonight around seven as Connor wants to show me some stuff on a slow night. I looked at the clock and said no problems. But I wasn't about to learn anything while my head is hurting and stoned could be a problem, a big problem. I think I need a good sweat. Didn't have the strength and ambition for the gym. So, I did a home workout just like I would when I was locked up in the "Hole" at San Quentin. And with all the booze from last night it didn't take long before I started to sweat. I could smell the beer and Jack coming out of my pores.

After about an hour I went for a long run in the hot sun. I came home drenched and feeling amazing. Time for another shower and try once again to track down Rachel. Still not able to get a hold of her. I got changed and went out for some Chinese food and believe it or not, I had chocolate milk with my meal rather than beer. Peter the owner asked me if everything was all right. I think I totally freaked out Sandra when I walked into the bar, and she asked what was my poison tonight. I said coffee. She had the whole deer in the headlights look. "Seriously Mitch, you are pretty funny. Jack or draught beer?"

I said I was here to learn stuff from Connor and Joseph. Sandra then told me to stay still as she went into the back and brought me out this huge mug full of coffee. "Trust me Mitch, you will need this much caffeine. You know Joseph doesn't want everything in print." I stayed at the bar drinking my coffee until Joseph and Connor showed up. They too were shocked to see me drinking coffee. In fact, Joseph even smelt it to see if I put any booze in it. He smiled as he gave me the mug back. He patted me on the shoulder and told me to follow him and Connor into his office. Joseph said he runs two businesses.

Semi legit, they are the bar and the jewellery store for an income. But having said that Joseph still indirectly will use proceeds of crime for the bar. Such as stolen booze. What he does as all booze served in bars will have a government stamp on it so he will pour the stolen booze into a stamped legit bottle. He said he never waters down his booze as an inspector will come in and do a cork test to make sure if it says eighty proof, it *is* eighty proof. To make the books legit he will continue to get his normal booze order and sell the bottles to bootleggers or underground gambling houses. He made it clear that anyone looking under twenty-five better have some form of legit identification on them. He says the cops know he is up to no good, they just haven't had a chance to nail his Irish ass yet. He asked me if I knew a way for the bar to bring in more income. Now this is something I have thought about seeing how I have hit so many bars across the world. "Sunday nights are dead in here. I would have an open mic where local acts can showcase themselves. You would be surprised how many up-and-coming acts have a decent following but just haven't had their break to get on the bar tour." Joseph went deep in thought and then smiled. He said he really liked this idea.

"The one girl Beth who works for me on the weekends is a college kid who is a very talented musician, you were impressed by her. She also has access to her school's newspaper; I can see her being the M.C. Say best act for the night wins a twenty-five-dollar gift certificate for the bar. You know they will go through the winnings quickly and continue to party even more."

Connor turned to Joseph and said, "I told you he is smarter than he looks." Joseph said to talk to Beth and see what she can do for us. We went over a few more things and all and all I was ready to start my training with Joseph, Connor, and Sandra. Joseph then asked about what Oscar can bring to our team.

"A pilot with his own plane. He was special ops, so he has been deep in the shit. He is solid."

"He better be solid as I had to pull in some favours to keep him alive. He fucks up he is your problem, and I will expect you to keep him in line, or kill him."

"I will take responsibility for him. He will prove his worth." The three of us then went out front and had a couple beers. Before I left, Joseph reiterated to me once again about no playing with that staff. I said that is not a problem. He said he will see us for breakfast in the morning. That night I decided to keep a low profile. I still had no luck getting a hold of Rachel and was starting to worry now to be honest. Around nine I did get a call from Anita. She asked if I wanted to go out for a drink with her as she wanted to discuss something with me. I was horny and intrigued, and yes, I know to make sure tonight is not a repeat of last night. So, I jumped on the bike and headed over to her place. When she answered the door, I was in complete awe. Her jeans were skin-tight and she was wearing a striped tube top sporting a sexy sinister smile. I wanted to throw her over my shoulder and carry her back inside and fuck the living shit right out of her.

"You look amazing baby, God damn." Just the way she smiled and said thanks I can tell she was up to something. She suggested we hit this bar a couple blocks from her place. She said it is nice and quiet, a spot where people can talk. We took a seat in the corner, there wasn't even a waitress, just a bartender so I ordered a pitcher of draught.

I poured us each a glass, Anita raised her glass and said to future work. I clanged with her and was intrigued as to what she meant. So, after the first glass that went down really well, I asked that exact statement. "I don't know exactly what you do for a living. I have heard stories about your boss and have seen the way you fight. I need someone dealt with Mitch. I have cash if you are interested."

"Define dealt with, and how much cash?"

Anita looked down at the table, then looked up at me and with the most serious face said, "I want my ex killed, and I am willing to pay you five thousand cash."

"He is still in prison, correct?"

"Yes, he is, you think that will be a huge problem as I would like the job done as soon as possible?" I broke one of Donnie's commandments and asked what the hurry was. Anita now looked up to the ceiling for a couple seconds. When she finally made eye contact, she said,

"My sister in Boston, the one who just had the baby. She caught her husband fooling around with a girl from his work. She is totally devastated. My branch manager has set it up that I can transfer to Boston. In the past Hank has said if I move away on him, he will kill me and my family. I honestly believe him. So, I would rather be proactive and kill him first. He is a shit boyfriend to be honest and deserves to die. He is a rat, and I am sure the cops or prison officials will see it as his partners in crime just getting even with him."

"So does Hank know you plan on moving away?"

"Not at all. Another reason I would like it done as soon as you can."

"I will see what I can do. Tomorrow morning it will be my second priority."

"And what is your first priority, Mitch?"

"To give you a good morning fuck."

"I think that is a great priority. Your place or mine, Mister Strongbow?"

"Doesn't matter to me. I do have to pick up a celly who is being released from San Quentin tomorrow at nine."

"And you aren't worried about your girlfriend showing up at your place?"

"We are taking a break from each other. More than likely permanent."

"Well, I am sure if she sees me riding you, it will definitely be permanent." We both laughed at her statement. Deep down I do wish Charlene would accept my past as much as I have accepted her past. We finished our drinks and Anita said my place would be better and she can head to work in the morning. I drove her back to her place to get a change of clothes for work. As soon as we got in, I grabbed us each a bowl and put a bag of weed on the table. I told Anita to help herself as I checked the phone messages in front of her. Rachel finally got back to me. She said not to call as she is out for the night and will slide by here around eleven and we can do lunch before meeting Tash and Katrina. I was glad to finally hear from her. Was a little tense to be honest. I felt bad she didn't tell me about her and Mike splitting. Anita and I smoked a couple bowels, had a couple beers before heading to the bedroom and fucking our brains out. In between rounds one and two I set the alarm just in case and good thing I did as the last cum drop was not out of me before falling asleep. As soon as the alarm went off the next morning Anita said I owed her something. I totally forgot and asked her what. "A good morning fuck." Who am I to reneg? I can use a good cock draining today. Then we grabbed a shower, and I would have ripped off another piece of tail but I know when I was released and if Donnie was a no show I would be pissed.

So, I turned down Anita and said I would make it up for her. I promised I would inquire about getting her ex murdered. Gave her a couple bucks for breakfast and then a kiss goodbye before heading to San Quentin. I grabbed a coffee and muffin before heading out. My asshole started to tighten, and my guts started to roll the closer I got to San Quentin. Fuck I hate this place. I pulled into the visitors parking with fifteen minutes to spare. I got out of my car and just stared at the evil palace of pain. Two minutes later a two-person prison patrol unit pulled up. The older screw knew me and asked what I was doing in the lot. "Just waiting for Oscar to be released. I am his ride."

"Strongbow you have always been a decent guy for a con. Oscar is nothing but bad news. Do yourself a favour, distance yourself from him or else you will find yourself back in here. And don't think for one moment he would sell you out."

This screw was a decent, so I just nodded at him and said, "I will take this under advisement." I could tell the way the screws' face changed; Oscar has now cleared the front gates. They then drove off as soon as Oscar yelled out my name. He came over and gave me a big hug. Looked at Emma and said nice ride. I said a great ride and told him to get in.

As soon as he jumped in he said, "I hope you have a couple whores back at your place for me Strongbow and a joint for me to smoke right now."

"Sorry man, Joseph wants to see you at his place. Now I have stuck my neck on the line for you and Joseph kept the Russians from seeking revenge on you while inside. So, make sure to thank him and show him respect. He is not a man to piss off and yes, he will be able to pick up on us being high."

"I dig where you are coming from. Then we get the whores and weed right?"

"No, then I have to meet my ex and my daughter. But I will give you weed to get high."

Oscar did a sigh; I could tell he was getting a bit pissy when he asked then tonight we get the whores. "I am actually working for Joseph tonight at the bar. I have a friend who owns a strip joint. Mike Battaglia you hear of him?"

"Of course, I have heard of him. Albert and Sammy work for his Dad correct?"

"Yes, they do, Mike runs the bay area of the business."

"Okay, Strongbow. I can stay at your place until I get on my feet and find a place, right?"

"Yeah, I promised you that."

We talked about what has happened in the joint since I left. I asked him if anyone was charged for George's murder or did, he have any ideas who might have killed him.

"Not a clue Strongbow, you know George, he always opened his big mouth without fear. I am sure he pissed off the wrong people, more than likely the north Mexican's. Yeah, that would be my guess." There was a little bit of silence after that. Oscar went deep into thought for a bit. He finally asked me if I had a steady girlfriend.

"I did for a bit, and you know her. Charlene that used to be the librarian."

Oscar just nodded and said, "Not anymore?"

"No, we seem to fight too much. I have been banging this hot chick from the bank, yeah fucked her all night and just before I left to pick you up."

As we pulled up, I reiterated to Oscar about the respect thing for Joseph. "Don't worry Strongbow I won't let you down." Oscar can be a bit off the wall, so I did worry. As we walked in Donnie and Joseph were sitting in a booth drinking coffee. I did the introductions; they shook hands with him and asked if he wanted anything to eat.

"I have been craving steak and eggs and an ice-cold beer. Your cook is good here?" Joseph just nodded his head and called Lauren over to take Oscar and my order. She asked Oscar how he wanted his steak cooked.

"I want it blue, thirty seconds each side and that is it." Joseph told her to pour a beer in a coffee mug. As soon as Lauren walked away, Joseph said to Oscar, "I run a tight crew, I don't like people who showboat or become heat scores. No talking to anyone outside of the four of us sitting at the table. You fuck up on your time I might be able to help you, no promises. You go down for the count on my time, you will have my backing one hundred percent.

I like my men to be ghosts, do you know what I mean, Oscar?"

"Of course I do, I was special Ops."

"If I have a job for you, I expect you to be there on time and fit for duty just like when you were in Special ops. I understand you have your pilots license and your own plane, correct?"

"Yes sir, a legit license and plane. I also know how to get in and out of the country without being detected by the feds. I also know of all kinds of abandoned airfields in pretty much every state. Hawaii is a problem if we are doing anything illegal though." The conversation stopped when Lauren brought out his meal. Oscar still eats like a pig, slops his food back and talks with his mouth full of food.

"And you will be staying with Mitch until you get your own place, correct?"

"Yeah, I will be there for a couple weeks I would say."

"I own some apartment buildings in and around the bay area. I have one come open in San Jose in the middle of July if you are interested."

"If it is clean, I will take it"

"I would never let my men stay in a dump. I will write down the address, you and Mitch can check it out tomorrow." Joseph looked at Donnie who really didn't say too much.

"So Oscar, a couple rules for all my men. No playing with needles, only legitimate conversations over the phone and I have no interest in meeting anyone else wanting to join the crew. If you think anyone can help us, you deal with them and you only. If they are starting to prove their worth Mitchell and Donnie will talk to them. Nothing personal, just business."

Oscar nodded his head and said, "That only stands to reason." Joseph then stuck out his hand and said welcome to the crew. I was thankful that Oscar showed Joseph respect. Donnie shook his hand and then said he had to go to work. Something is up with him. Very standoffish. Joseph said he would see me later tonight. So, we drove back to my place. Oscar brought up all his belongings and put them in the spare room. I threw an ounce on the coffee table and said I would be right back. I went downstairs and asked Janine to get a hold of Beth for me. Once I told her what it was for, she was pretty excited for her.

She said, "Beth starts at four today if I am around as she is in school till then." I said yeah that works, call me once she shows up. By the time I got upstairs Oscar was staring straight ahead in outer space. I walked right past him, and he didn't even blink or flinch.

"Hey Oscar, you like that weed?"

He turned to me and said, "This shit is fucking me up. What is it?"

"Columbian man, good shit hey?" Oscar didn't answer me at first, man he was totally zoned. In San Quentin the weed is normally a combo of Mexican, parsley and bird seeds as stupid as it sound. Someone smuggles you in an ounce, it gets diluted to almost a quarter pound and you are paying five times the street cost. I went and grabbed him a beer and said cheers. Now as much as I wanted to kick er down with him, meeting Tash, Katrina and Rachel are my first priority. And also, my first night training on the job. I had one more joint with Oscar, I kept feeding him shots of Jack and beers and by the time Rachel rang the doorbell Oscar was passed out on the couch. I gave her a hug and said come on up. She looked over to Oscar drooling and snorting on the couch.

"A buddy from Nam and prison, he will be staying here for about a month then Joseph has a pad lined up for him. So how are you, Rach? I had beers with Mike, and he told me you guys split, sorry sis."

"Thanks Mitch, yeah it was fun while it lasted."

"Feel like talking about it? You have always been there for me." She pointed to Oscar, and I said he is truly dead to the world.

"I am contemplating working for this law firm out of Sacramento that actually is used to do subcontracting work for the district attorney's office. If they found out who my boyfriend was I would more than likely be let go. And word would get around and I would be blackballed working for any decent law firm. To Mike's credit he was very understanding. It wasn't a knock down fight break up. All good, Mitch." I went in and gave her a hug and told her I was so proud of her.

She thanked me and asked if I was feeling up for today. "You know I am. I have found peace to a certain degree. I have accepted in time she will know who I am, and we will have that father daughter bond." Rachel came back in and said how proud she was of me. I asked what she was craving for lunch. Fish and chips on the Wharf was her response. I asked if she wanted to smoke a joint first. She smiled and said maybe after we leave the ice cream shop. "I don't want Tash to pick up that we are both stoned."

So, we both took our bikes and drove down to Wharf and scarfed back some fresh fish and chips. Washed it down with an ice-cold soda even though I could use a beer or ten as by now my nerves were starting to kick in. I kept looking at my watch, Rachel said, "We have lots of time, but if you would like to get their early that is fine." I told her I would really like that. So, we fired up our bikes and headed over. We were about three blocks from the ice cream parlour when we were both cut off by this taxi driver. We both had to lock our bikes up and Rachel ended up dumping her bike. She went for quite the tumble. My heart stopped as I went racing over to her.

I totally concentrated all my energies on her. She had blood coming from her nose and ear. By now a crowd of passersby were gathered. I frantically told one of them to call an ambulance. Rachel's eyes were rolling in her head. I was telling her to stay with me until I heard it. The voice of the taxi driver yelling at us in some foreign accent. Fucking yelling at Rachel lying on the ground. Calling her a stunned cunt. The love and fear I had for my sister were cast aside as I had rage come over my body that I haven't felt since San Quentin. I jumped up off the ground and charged right at the mouthy heartless driver throwing nothing but punches and kicks. I fucking lost it. I had him knocked out cold within seconds but that didn't stop my onslaught. I didn't even notice the cops show up. Next thing I knew I had four cops on my back trying with all their brawn to pull me off him. The only way they halted me was to break a Billy club over my head. Major league head spin and as I lost the ability to fight, they tackled me and were able to cuff my hands and feet. I was coming out of the fog when I saw Rachel being put in the back of the ambulance. I was completely covered in not only the taxi drivers' blood, but my own. The four cops now picked me up and were carrying me to the back of a cruiser when I was drawn to this mother and daughter across the street. Natasha with her hand over her mouth crying and now a visibly shaken up Katrina also crying. I just put my head down in shame as the cops threw me in the back of the cruiser.

The sergeant came over and looked in and told the patrol cop to take me to the hospital. I had now also broken out in a sweat. This has now become my worst nightmare. I don't know if Rachel is going to live, and whatever inroads I have made with Tash in seeing Katrina have been washed away. And I really don't care at this point if I even killed the taxi driver or not. As we pulled up out front, the passenger cop said he will take off the leg shackles as long as I promise not to fight. "You will have my word as long as you can find out how my sister is doing."

"That was your sister who was the other cyclist?"

"Yeah, that's her man."

"I will see what I can do for you." I thanked him and as they took the shackles off, and I went to stand up my legs gave out on me. I closed my eyes and told the cops you better get me a stretcher as my legs are gone. The blood was still flowing down from the back of my skull and starting to soak my jeans and underwear. I flashed back to Clark Air force base in the Philippines and the base hospital where I had to learn to walk all over again after surgery. The cops must have fucked up one of the nerves in my back when they jumped on me. The one cop stayed with me while his partner went inside for help.

The cop outside was nervous to be alone with me.

"Listen man I ain't pull the wool over your eyes. I ain't going to be trouble."

He didn't say anything, but he was scared.

Within a minute the other cop who I promised I would be good too was back with a couple orderlies, a nurse and a stretcher.

The nurse looked at the back of my skull and asked if I was shot. Fuck that reassured me that all was good.

She ordered the cop to take the cuffs off me and for them to help me on the stretcher as she held the pillowcase and started to apply pressure to the back of my skull.

As soon as they got me on the stretcher the nurse asked if I could move my feet and legs which I could.

The nurse said for the orderlies to put me on a bed and then roll me into room five.

The cops stopped the orderlies and cuffed my right wrist to the bed. Then they said I can be moved into room five, with of course one of them, by my side at all times.

The nurse then continued the assessment of my head wound and said I will need a whack of stitches.

I asked if she knew anything about my sister who was also brought in with injuries.

I told the nurse the whole story even with the cop standing by us. I blame my stupidity on the concussion.

She said she will check with the trauma doctor as soon as she is done with me.

As soon as she left the room the cop took out his notebook and started to take down all my information.

And when he asked for prior criminal convictions.

That is when my head really started to pound.

I asked if he could get the nurse. He looked at me, saw that I was handcuffed and covered in blood. I already have done time for an involuntary manslaughter charge.

"Stay in bed, you try to escape I will shoot you; I will not tell you to halt, it will be me emptying my weapon, understood?"

He popped his head outside and within a second his partner came in. Now this is the guy I made the promise to about not acting up.

"Your sister is being examined right now. She is fine, a broken collar bone, lots of bruises and they are making sure she didn't break any ribs." I took a big breath and an even bigger sigh of relief.

"Thanks man, she is all I have left, our parents and one brother and sister are dead." I just closed my eyes and all I could see was a flashback of Rachel tumbling and of course the look on Tash's and Katrina's face. I was starting to drift off when the doctor came in and put that little flashlight in my face. How can something so small seem as if it was brighter then the searchlight looking for planes. It killed my eyes. He then looked at the gash in my head. Checked around my neck and asked to try and do neck rolls. I struggled but was able. He said I have a severe concussion but everything else seemed good. He said he would be back in a couple minutes to stitch me up. My head was major league spinning. Fuck, just put a syringe into me and end it right here and now. The doc did come back in with a syringe, but it was for freezing my skull.

He asked the cop to uncuff me so I could get cleaned up before he sews me up. He then told me to follow him if I could. I was able to get up slowly with the help of him and a nurse he summoned for. They walked me down to this one room that had a shower. The doctor told the nurse once I am showered up and clean to send me back to room five and he will stitch me. The two cops and the nurse watched me shower, fuck this reminded me of being back in San Quentin. The nurse handed me this hospital gown and then I was walked back to my room. I sit on the edge of the bed as the nurse and two cops watch the doc first try and freeze my head then sew my scalp back together like a Rawlings baseball. And of course, my jet-black long hair had to be shaved away near the open wound. In my lifetime I think it would be safe to say I have had at least a thousand stitches; fuck, I would make Frankenstein monster look like a pussy. I looked at the clock on the wall and I had the good doctor tied up for almost an hour. Eighty-two stitches later I was done. The cops asked if they could now take me down to the station to be charged. Doc said no, he said with it being a severe concussion I have to be watched closely and this would be the safest place for me. So, once again. I had my right wrist handcuffed to the bed. The young cop stayed with me while the other cop left the room. Within minutes two detectives came in and showed me their tin and asked for a statement as to what transpired today.

"This is not my first rodeo; I have a grade five severe concussion. I am truly not of sound mind; in fact, my head is pounding because of your guys. I ain't saying shit without my lawyer present."

They looked at each other and the one said, "You are an ex-con, if he dies you will be going in the electric chair Strongbow."

"Not likely, I have a really good lawyer, I wanna talk to him."

Once again, they look at each other and say fine. "Mitchell Strongbow you are charged with attempted murder." I sort of blanked out while they read me the rest of my Miranda rights.

Once again, they asked if I had anything to say. I shook my head no, and once again said I want to see my lawyer. They asked what my lawyer's name was, and for the life of me I couldn't remember. I even looked at the clock on the wall and I had no clue if it was AM or PM. They looked at the nurse and asked if I was just playing a game or not. She told them I lost a lot of blood and had blunt force trauma to the skull and brain. The one detective asked if he was a lawyer in the Bay Area or not. "I think so, I am drawing a total blank." The other detective got out his notebook and asked if it was the same lawyer that defended me and helped me take the cops to court.

"Yes, he's Jewish, David Levy I think." He just nodded his head and said yes, he would call him for me. I had one last look around the room before closing my eyes. How the fuck did I end up back in the hospital waiting for my lawyer to deal with a damn serious charge? You would think I would know by now. I closed my eyes and all I could see was Rachel going ass over tea kettle and me not being able to stop her fall and tumble. Deep down this bothers me more than the pending charges. No, I lie, equally bothersome is the fact that Tash and Katrina saw me beat the taxi driver to within a breath of his life. That I really don't recall, fucker. I was startled when the uniformed cop woke me to tell me my lawyer was present. He asked the nurse and all cops to leave the room. The cops knew better. Once all parties left Levy asked me what happened. I told him what I remembered. I then asked what he thought.

"Mitch, I believe you and your sister's lives were in danger from the taxi driver. He tried to purposely run you down because you and your sister are native Americans. Sounds like to me you tried to defend your sister whose life he almost took. Do you understand what I am saying?" A huge smile came to my face, and I said yes.

"Now, will you be able to get the story to Rachel as she is a lawyer and I have a feeling she will tell the truth."

"Not to alarm you, but most head traumas you lose a lot of memory. I think it will be safe to say your sister won't recall much of what happened this morning." I also asked if he could let Joseph know what happened.

"I already called Joseph and he will have bail money set aside for you come Monday morning. He sends his best to you and your sister."

"Any chance they will let me see my sister?"

"They will ask for something from us and we will counter with you seeing her. I doubt they will ask it, but why not try?"

He asked how my head is. "It is killing me, over eighty stitches."

"I am going to read the police report. We might go after them for excessive force. Did you hit any of the officers?"

"Not that I can recall. And they never mentioned resisting arrest."

"No, they didn't, there must have been lots of witnesses. So, at any point your head hurts too much you let me know and I will stop the interrogation. They can come back once you are more of a sound mind. Did they give you anything for pain?"

"Just freezing when they were stitching me up."

Levy then went out and came back with the two detectives and a nurse. I went with the story that Levy talked about. I said about four blocks before that the taxi driver pulled up beside us and started mocking us, asking if we planned on scalping him. I told him to fuck off and get a life. It angered him and he was chasing us. We tried our best to get away from him. He purposely knocked Rachel off her bike. He got out of his taxi and to me it looked like he was ready to finish us off. He was ranting like some lunatic. I know witnesses heard it. I went at him as I was worried he had a weapon. Levy turned to the detectives and reminded them that my mom and older sister were killed by a drunk driver. The one detective said he is well aware of my history, but Abdul Salaam is laying upstairs with a broken jaw, nose and over ten teeth knocked out of his head.

"Rachel Strongbow is also upstairs and damn lucky to be alive. If it wasn't for the actions of her brother, Salaam would have killed her. I hope he is also going to be charged with attempted murder. He used his car as a weapon."

"We will be interviewing him and different witnesses as soon as we can. But for now, we are charging your client with aggravated assault causing bodily harm." They said the district attorney's office will be asking for me to be remanded in custody until a bail hearing can be set. Levy told them he has talked to the doctor, and I will be under observation for the next forty eight hours. And they will have a room on the eighth floor for me.

The detectives said that is fine. A uniformed cop will be outside my door all weekend and come Monday morning I will go before a judge at ten AM. Levy said that is fine. He told me he will meet me at the courthouse. The detectives left as well as Levy. The uniformed cop came back inside as a porter came in to take me up to the eighth floor. The cop made sure it was just the four of us going up in the elevator. Room eight eleven will be my home for this weekend, not quite the swanky hotel I was hoping for, but I will get peace and quiet, something my pounding head needs right now seeing how they won't give me any sort of pain killer. Before the nurse left the room I asked if she could find out how Rachel is doing and please tell her I love her. She said she will see what she can do. The nurse also shut off the overhead lights and said if I needed anything just to buzz her. At least she wasn't treating me like a criminal. The freezing was wearing off big time. With them not giving me anything for pain, I tried to go back and control my breathing as a way to release natural endorphins for pain management, learnt this trick in Special Ops. For the most part it worked, I managed to drift off, but the nurses and a cop would come in every two hours to wake me up. I am sure the cop was told don't let me slip into a coma and die, yeah with me suing and getting cash from the cops for harassment already, Rachel and Katrina would be rich, and heads would roll.

By the time the sun rose in the morning I felt like I was a hundred years old. I was mentally and physically drained. The doc came by and checked out my stitches and asked how I felt. I said I would be better with something to help kill the pain.

"If you can eat breakfast and keep everything down. I will have the nurse come by just after ten with something for the pain." He checked my eyes and the stitches. Once again, they asked me to move all my limbs. I moved all but the right arm which was still cuffed to the bed. I did ask the cop if I could use the washroom.

"My orders are only if you are going to shit. You have to piss, use the jug." Before the doc left, I asked if he had seen my sister yet today?

"In fact, I did. She is being discharged at noon. She has a broken left collarbone and right wrist. She has a concussion, but a mild one. She is very lucky to be alive." I just stared at the cop, looked back at the doc, and said thank you very much. They all left, and I breathed a huge sigh of relief. I was so worried about Rachel. I hope she understands why I did what I did. Maybe one day I will tell her how I tortured and killed Getz in the name of a Strongbow revenge.

I have had better and worse breakfast, but I was able to keep it down. At ten, I buzzed the nurse and when she walked in with the cop I smiled and said, "Hit me with the good stuff, baby." She blushed and then laughed. The cop, stoned face and that is exactly what I was hoping for. The nurse left and came back with her the shadow aka the cop in tow and handed me some pain pills. I asked what they are. Codeine was her answer. I am happy. Within twenty minutes of taking the meds I was in the zone, that warm fuzzy feeling. I guess the heroin addict in me will always have this craving and for now, codeine will suffice. I felt myself peacefully drifting off. It only cost me only eighty-two stitches and an assault charge. I might as well enjoy the trip. I closed my eyes and had visions of canoeing with my grandfather on the reserve.

My nurse came in a couple hours later and asked a still very buzzed me how I feel. "Can you get me a syringe of some of your finest white China?" I was startled when I saw the cop now walk in front of her and asked me to repeat what I just said. I did a quick shake and then I closed my eyes and drifted off again. When I finally woke up, I had no clue what time it was. The drapes were closed in my room. Felt a little anxious and lots of nauseous to be honest. Like any opiate I love the high but hate coming down. My head felt brutal again. Even worse than when I first came in. So, I pushed the button for the nurse. Within a couple minutes that felt like a lifetime she and the cop came back in. I told her how I felt. She checked my stitches and said she will get me something for both. Well, she came back in with two syringes. One went into my left butt cheek and one for my right butt cheek. Right away I felt the rush come over me. With the pills it is slow and gradual. Once again, I closed my eyes and went into a comatose zone.

I woke up a couple times and I was fucked right up. It was not fully alert, almost a fine line between a dream state and a hallucinogenic trip. At one point I saw puppies playing ice hockey on the floor. Another time I saw Oscar dressed in a ninja suit telling me all will be good. Then death my old friend decided to fuck with my head. Barry Getz was standing at the foot of my bed in uniform. "Once a cop, always a cop, Strongbow. I will be looking forward to seeing you fry in the electric chair." I was finally awoken from my slumber by this big ugly bitch nurse. Never saw her or the new uniformed cop in my room before. She didn't say shit, just started to move my head which was killing again.

"What the fuck are you doing?"

"I am doing my job. Now stay still and cooperate, damn you." I made sure to make eye contact and told her.

"Fucking manners go a long way." She went to grab my head again and I smacked her hand away.

"I am already up on an attempted murder, why not make it two counts?" The cop came in and jabbed me in the ribs really hard. The sudden jolt ripped the shit out of my right wrist.

"You fucking cocksuckers!" The cop now drew back the club and told me to shut it or I will get more stitches courtesy of the San Francisco police department. The nurse didn't show any fear and now that I am becoming more sober, the more she looks familiar.

"You were a nurse in San Quentin, weren't you?" She didn't answer me as she left the room. She came back in a couple minutes later with her supervisor. The supervisor told me if I didn't cooperate, she would make sure to sign my release papers and have me sent to county lock up. I am in no condition to survive that. So, you suck it up and let the vile sloth of a woman examine your stitches. But you also make sure to make eye contact with her and no matter how much it hurts, you don't let her see it.

I did ask for some more pain killers, fucking cunt looked at me and said I seem fine. I swear I am going to get even with this bitch once I am free. As she was examining my stitches the doc came in. He asked the cunt how everything looked, she said fine. He then asked me how I felt and as I went to answer she butted in and said I was fine.

"I am not fine; I am in a lot of pain. I have asked her for some pain killers, and she refused." The doc looked at her and shot her the same dirty look I did and told her to get me ten milligrams of codeine. She was not happy, fuck her. I took the pills and smiled at the nurse. Before I knew it, I was drifting off into another nice buzz. I crashed solid and when I woke up, I had that nice nurse back in my room asking how I was feeling.

Now I am not sure if it was the effect of the meds and her actually being decent but she looked really good today. "I am feeling better now that you are here" She smiled and said I was a flirt.

"That doesn't make me a bad person, does it?"

"No, it doesn't. But the fact you are handcuffed to a bed and have a cop outside your door does," she said laughing. I just smiled and said sometimes it is what it is. I told her about my run in with the twat nurse. She didn't say much other then, "You are not the first patient to complain" She re-examined my stitches and said everything looks good. She asked how my appetite was. I told her I was hungry which she said was a good sign. Just like yesterday I ate my meal. She gave me more pain killers and said she would come and check on me before her shift was done and if I needed anything to just buzz.

I smiled and looked down at my cock, she went red and said, "I don't think so," and then left the room smiling. I thought of Amy, thought of Liz and I think I do have a thing for nurses. I closed my eyes and tried to picture a threesome with Amy and Liz. Next thing you know I am jerking off. I was so tempted to push the buzzer and see if she would finish me off, but that moral side of me said no, and I can see the cop walking in ahead of her. So, I made it a foursome thought and before I knew it my left hand accomplished my vision. As I was trying to clean up, I passed right out. I was awoken by the nice nurse. She was done her shift and knew in the morning I was to be discharged and to appear before a judge in the morning. She wished me luck. I thanked her and said if I get off these charges, I owe her drinks at the Drunken Leprechaun. She did this intriguing sort of smile and said thanks. She passed me two more codeine pills and a sleeping pill. I popped them and just gave her a smile as she left. The next morning came and two orderlies, a nurse and two cops walked into my room. The brightness of the lights killed my Aryan eyes. It reminded me of when the screws would do a surprise raid on your house in San Quentin. I looked at all of them and asked what the fuck is going on. They could tell I was freaked right out. The cops of course pull out their clubs once again and tell me to get fucking mellow right now. The one orderly, this big black dude tells the cops to chill.

He says they are here to clean me up before I am discharged. "You mean a shower?"

"Yes, a shower, we are here to help you not to fight with you." I gave him the peace sign and said thanks. The cops still have this sucked on a lemon look on their faces as they come over and unlock my right wrist. I move my wrist around and my shoulder which fucking hurts like a bastard now. The two orderlies help me up out of my bed. My legs are like jelly, nice and shaky, they actually have to hang onto me and walk me to the shower. The one starts to run the shower and I said I should be fine. I have to say it felt good getting cleaned up, everything except when the water hit my stitches. That hurt like a mother fucker. Knowing I was on my way to court I really didn't feel like getting out. Nice and warm feeling inside the shower. But I had to. When I came out, I saw my pants and motorcycle jacket on the bed.

My t-shirt that I was wearing when the fight happened was there also but covered in blood. I asked if they could grab me a clean t-shirt, it didn't matter what it was. They came back with a 49er shirt, the dreaded rival of my Raiders. Beggars can't be choosers but that doesn't mean I won't have my jacket all the way up. After I got dressed, I was handcuffed in the back and had shackles placed on my ankles. Placed in a wheelchair and rolled out to an awaiting police car. It was rush hour traffic, but the cops used their siren and lights to get me to court in time. I would hate a bench warrant out for me and a failing to appear charge all because of no fault of my own. We pulled up out front and several other cops and bailiffs came and helped to escort me in the courthouse. I was taken right to the holding cells. Was let out of my handcuffs and shackles.

I was joining ten other not so lucky souls. All of them will profess their innocence of course. I eyed and figured out which one would be a threat. Now I was hurting, my head was still kind of loopy from the cops beating and the meds. But I did have a couple things going for me; I am a Strongbow. I was in for an attempted murder charge and once they found out I already did a deuce in San Quentin. I was given space. Shortly after eleven my name was called. The bailiff had my pic which I don't remember them taking. I was taking up through the rear elevators and before you knew it, I was walking down a corridor and then ushered into the back of the court and led into the prisoner's box.

I looked around the gallery and saw Rachel wearing a cast and, in a sling, sitting beside Joseph and Donnie. I may have more smarts in the jungle than in a courthouse, but my gut tells me something is up as the D.A. and Levy seem to be having a pretty in-depth conversation. And I also believe it would be fair to say that Levy was winning the battle as he seemed calm while the D.A. was red in the face and looked totally flustered. The judge came in and asked the bailiff to announce the charges. "The state of California versus Mitchell Strongbow. The charges are aggravated assault."

The judge asked Levy how I was prepared to plead, "Not guilty your honour." He then turned to the D.A. and asked about bail.

"Mister Strongbow is a convicted felon with a long history of violence. We would like to see him remanded in custody until trial, your honour."

The judge then looked at Levy who smiled first and said, "Your honour the man who my client supposedly assaulted is missing. It appears he was in this country illegally. For my client to sit in jail until the D.A. can find him would be a travesty. My client has a full-time job and a business that employees three people." The judge was not impressed as he looked at the D.A.

"Bail will be set at ten thousand dollars. Mr. Murphy do you have any idea where the assault victim is at all?"

"He left the hospital in the middle of the night. We are actively looking, your honor."

"Mr. Murphy, I am giving you till Friday at seventeen hundred hours to find him or all charges will be dropped against Mr. Strongbow. Do I make myself clear?"

"Yes, sir." The judge banged down his gavel and said next. I was taken back downstairs to the holding cells and within twenty minutes I heard my name called again. Joseph put the cash up for my bail bond. I was let out the back and walked around to the front. As soon as I saw all the marks on her face and her wearing a cast, I knew I did the right thing. I gave her a side hug, gave Donnie a full hug and shook Joseph's hand and said thanks a lot.

"I would have done the same, lad." Joseph asked me to turn around and looked at the mess the cops did to me.

"We should go after the cops for this. I am going to talk to Levy," said a pissed off Joseph. "I want you seeing this one doctor this aft'. He will send in a full legal report for the right amount of cash." I could use more meds, so I fully agreed with him. We all went for lunch together, the beaten and busted up Strongbow's turned more heads than Donnie who was wearing his Hell Hound colours. As much as I wanted a drink, I knew my head would spin with taking all the meds. Rachel went to the washroom, and I asked the boys if Oscar has been coming around at all. I said I was a little annoyed he wasn't in court. Donnie and Joseph both looked at each other. Then Joseph said.

"I told Oscar to stay away. He is in Los Angeles for the next week or so."

"Doing business?" I asked.

"No, he did business here. He proved himself to Donnie and me. That guy you punched out didn't take off because he was an illegal immigrant. Oscar kidnapped him from the hospital and put two rounds in his head. Now I know he has a set of balls, a smart set of balls to be precise, and now I know I can trust him." That made me feel good, what didn't make me feel good was when I asked Rachel if Tash and Katrina had left yet.

Rachel looked at her watch and said, "They are halfway there I assume. Natasha saw the whole incident unfold in front of her and Katrina. She also read the newspaper the next day and your charges. Whatever in roads you made were thrown out the window, Mitch, sorry."

"So now what, sis?"

"I don't know what to say, I wish I did. I am so sorry, Mitch. I feel this is all my fault." Rachel started to cry which made me even more angry on everything that went down.

Donnie set her straight and told her, "This is not your fault. If the asshole would have been paying attention none of this would have happened. Do you know how many guys in the club have been killed or badly injured because of fuckheads like him? Rachel, I love you like a sister, please don't do this to yourself, you have done nothing wrong."

He kissed the top of her forehead. Joseph tapped the top of her good hand and said, "The saints kept you with us. He deserved what happened to him."

"I am done riding, for now on it is four wheels or nothing. Mitchell, sell the bike and get whatever you can and keep the money." She just looked at me and now it was a full stream of tears as she shook her head no.

"I love you Rach, if you don't want to ride again then don't. We won't think anything less of you, honest." She nodded her head yes but kept crying. I swear if anyone in the place mocks her, they will have three of the meanest sons of a bitches on the planet ready to beat them to death. Once Rachel stopped crying and composed herself, she asked Joseph if he could take her back to get her vehicle back at his place. Once there, Joseph said he would get this doctor's office to call me with an appointment. I thanked him and Donnie and asked Rachel if she wanted to go back to my place for a bit. She said yes. On the drive over she was so deep in thought it scared me to be honest.

Once upstairs I asked if she wanted a coffee or tea. She said tea and as I was making it, she just stared at the pic I have of Katrina on my coffee table. When I came back in with the tea, she was tearing up again. I put her tea down and said, "It is all good, Rach."

"It is not good, Mitchell. This is my first time dealing with death. I truly thought I was going to die. I didn't want to leave you on this shitty planet all alone. I want to be an amazing aunt to Katrina.' Full water works now. I have learned over the years to let them get everything off their chest.

"And I'm pissed off that taxi driver left the country. He doesn't care what happens to you or me. We could be dead, and he wouldn't waste a second thought on us. Just like Getz, he got away with murdering Mom and Pam and where is he now? Living off a cop pension and enjoying life to fullest. Every time I drop flowers off at the grave, I wished so badly to see a grave with his name on it."

I am not sure if it is the concussion, meds or just seeing Rachel so upset and doubting life I broke a cardinal sin that Donnie instilled into me.

"Getz is dead, Rachel." She stopped her crying, and her hand went over her mouth.

"How do you know this? I thought he went into this police protection program."

"I know this because I am the one who took his life." Rachel's colour in her face went bone white. Her stomach started to do these like contractions as her eyes got really big. She staggered to get up then and raced for the washroom. I am sure eight years of Getz frustration and anxiety was just released via vomit. I came in and started to rub her back. I didn't say anything else. I believe I have said enough. Rachel finally stood up and hugged me, she was trembling and drenched in sweat. I walked her back to the couch and told her to lay down and just relax. She just stared at me and rolled up into a ball, not sure if this was a good thing or a bad thing. After a couple minutes of watching her shake I went and got her a blanket off my bed. She thanked me and then she went back deep into thought.

I got up and went to the one chair. Rolled a joint and sparked it up and just stared at my sis. I asked if she wanted some and she just shook her head no. By the time I was done my joint, Rachel was starting to get some colour back in her face. She then did a little bit of a smile and said in a quivering voice, "I hope you made that bastard suffer."

"His last couple of hours alive he truly suffered, no doubts about that. His death was quick, but a total mind fuck leading up to it for him."

"Mom and Pam would want justice, but that didn't happen, did it Mitch? Dad and Jake would be proud, and you know what, so am I."

"Remember what Dad always said, there is a revenge, then there is a Strongbow revenge. I have to implore that you can never tell anyone what I told you today, Rach. Word gets out, my ass will be fried in an electric chair." Rachel got up and said she loves me, and she also knows if word did get out and I am executed for his death, then Getz took another Strongbow life, even from his grave.

"So, I guess Natasha will crawl back into a bunker with regards to me seeing Katrina."

"I believe you are right, she also had to bury her stepdad who was murdered. I will see what I can do for you. I have no doubts that Katrina means the world to you. Let's see what happens with the charges. I hope and pray you get off all of them and then I will talk to Tash. I promise, Mitch." Rachel had one more tea and then she had to take off. Tomorrow was her first day as a lawyer at this law firm in Sacramento. I walked her to her car. She gave me this long hug goodbye and said she was proud of me.

"Rach, I am proud of you. A career woman, an honest career at that although not sure if being a lawyer is so honest."

She laughed and said, "Thanks. I am proud of you for doing what had to be done, there is a revenge then there is a Strongbow revenge. Right, big brother?"

"Bang on, little sister." I watched her drive away when Janine came out and gave me this big hug.

"Nice to see you, Mitch. I read what happened in the papers. How are you and your sister feeling?"

"Thanks, much appreciated. You should have come out and asked Rach herself."

"You two seemed to be in a really deep place. I didn't want to disturb you." I thanked her and then she asked me inside Pamdora's.

We went in and she said she talked to Beth and explained what happened. "Now she is definitely interested in the Sunday night jamming and yes she will talk to the school newspaper editor." I thanked her and she came in and gave me a hug, a long hug.

"I was really worried about you. I have nothing but respect for you as a boss and you really are an all-around good guy. I don't pay attention to what they wrote about you in the paper." I asked if she still had the paper. She actually cut the article out. The heading was "*X-Con goes berserk*" it made me laugh and of course it was all about me being just released from San Quentin and having *"ties"* to the Hell Hounds. Nothing about the injuries that Rachel had sustained.

I thanked Janine and gave her back the paper. I also noticed she undid one of the buttons on her blouse. She was also all smiles and had this almost cat in heat coming off her. Concussion or not I can tell if a chick digs me or not. I can still hear what Joseph told me, but fuck she is looking good, and I would never force her to do anything she wouldn't want to do. So, I looked at her now exposed cleavage and smiled. She blushed big time and her smile got even bigger as she looked at the bigger than life bulge in my pants. Fuck it, I have had this thing for her since she hung with Pam, I am going for it. I ran my index finger along her cheek and then pulled her in for a kiss. She didn't fight it at all, in fact she put her hands on my ass cheeks to grind me right into her. I was not even a second into a kiss when the phone rang. She jumped back and her eyes got big, I actually saw fear in her face. She even stuttered as she answered the phone. And then when I heard her say, "Yes Joseph he is right here, just a minute," she handed the phone to me, shrugged her shoulders and went *oops*.

"This doc will see you at five. Make sure you are not late as this is the last appointment of the day. Speaking of which, your bail bond had you home by eleven Mitchell. Don't break it." I assured Joseph that I wouldn't let him down. Speaking of down my cock went south hearing Joseph's voice. I swear he has a crystal ball. Janine must have gone into the backroom and when she came back in, the button was once again done up. I looked at my watch. It was four, yeah, I better head over to the doc or I will never hear the end of this from my boss. I gave Janine a wink goodbye, told her to have a good night and will talk tomorrow.

She smiled and gave me a wink back. I will be beating off tonight thinking of her, I can still see her teaching her girlfriends back in the day how to deepthroat a Popsicle. Watching it drip all over her chin and breasts. I arrived at an overcrowded waiting room at Joseph's doctors' office. The receptionist also seemed dingy which didn't help me. I felt myself getting pissed as sick kids and old people were coughing and sneezing all around. Snot running down their noses, holy Aqualung.

I looked at my watch and an hour had passed by. I will find my own doctor as this waiting is insane.

6

I was the second to last person to be called. I was taken into a room and the nurse asked what I was there for. "Just to make sure my stitches are good." She asked where the stitches are and as I turned around to show her, she went eww, not what I wanted to hear. She said the doctor would be in shortly, fuck they said my appointment would be shortly also. The doc was in the next room talking to this chick, or at least I thought it was a chick, the voice was deeper and harsher sounding then mine. I heard her complaining about some ooze coming from her cunt. As God is my witness, I could smell her stinky fishy cunt seeping right through the walls. I started to gag; I am out of here. I come out of the room and there is the doc looking at me with a cigarette hanging out of his mouth. I just shook my head no and left. What a fucking joke. I got in my car and was hungry, horny, and needed some pain killers. In the distance I saw this redhead who looked just like Charlene. My heart skipped a beat and the butterflies started to flutter in my gut. I shut the car off and got out and headed to her. I called her name but the closer I got I sadly realized it was not her. I really fucking miss her. I guess she won't have to worry about Tash being around in the near distant future. Screw it, I called her to see if she wanted to talk. No answer. So, I left a message. "It's Mitch; miss you, baby. Hope all is well, call me, lets talk." Now what, maybe try Anita and see if she wants to go out for a double bite, first the food then she can chomp down on my cock. Just like Charlene just voice mail. As I hung up the phone, I remembered her asking me to have her ex whacked. This blow to the head has really affected some memory. So, my next call was to Donnie. Figures a guy would be home.

"You wanna go out for a beer and a burg?"

"I just ate but I can see a beer, meet you at the Leprechaun in fifteen." I said that works. I was really craving a burg and they are one of the best menu items. When I showed up, Nyah was working, she had this huge smile come to her face and she came right over and gave me this big hug.

"Mitch, I was so worried about you." I thanked her and I was looking around to make sure her dad was not in the bar as he worries me. She asked if I wanted a draft and a shot of Jack. I totally shocked her when I said just a coke.

"Is part of your bail conditions that you can't drink?"

"Not that I am aware of. My head is still pounding from the cops."

I turned around and showed her the coppers work and she said it was brutal. "What did they give you for painkillers?"

"Nothing, Joseph sent me to this quack this aft', but I wouldn't trust him to go near my head."

"Listen, I get migraines really bad at times and I have a prescription for painkillers, would you like a few?"

"I would love some. I will pay you, hon."

"Mitchell Strongbow your money's no good. We are all family here." She took my order for the burg and then went into the back and put a couple painkillers in a tissue for me. I told her I would give her some weed for this. She said that would be awesome just don't tell her dad. That goes without saying. I washed down one of the pills with my soda. Donnie just sat down as Nyah brought my burg and fries. She gave me a wink as she put it down. As Nyah walked away, I was drawn to her ass. Donnie said I better watch myself as Sean wouldn't even ask Joseph's permission to put a slug in my brain. He then asked what was up.

"I have been seeing this chick Anita, on the side. She offered me five grand to kill her ex-boyfriend."

Donnie raised an eyebrow and said that is a lot of money. "Well, he is in Folsom prison. You have anyone in your brotherhood that is solid enough to take the contract? I will give you five hundred cash for arranging the hit, and him two grand for the kill."

"That's a fair offer, can't say I know anyone in there or any of the brothers out that way. You really have to be careful as guys in puppet clubs are not as solid." I thanked Donnie for his honesty and advice before he left. I was sitting in the booth thinking about what Donnie said and I knew in prison the mob would hire me to have someone whacked. I wonder if I talk to Mike Battaglia would he know of anyone to take up the contract for me. Nyah came over with the cheque and asked if I needed anything else. Like Janine I could tell she was flirting with me, but with her comes one hell of a death wish.

"No, I am good, hon. Thanks anyways." She just smiled at me, twirled her hair, and asked if she could drop by later and get that weed off me.

"Next week is study week and I am all out. I will be stressed to the max." I owe her and I will give her a nickel bag then she can be on her way.

"Sure, what time are you off work at?"

"We close at eleven, I can be by your place like fifteen minutes later if that is not to late for you."

"Not too late at all. I am a nighthawk." She thanked me once again and gave me this long hug. By the time I left, the painkiller was really starting to kick in. But the survivalist in me still had my smarts. As soon as I got home, I took a long hot shower, thought about the sex Charlene and I used to have with other couples. Jerked off and shot a load to get rid of this sexual tension that has been dogging me all day. Then I stayed in the shower and turned the water ice cold for a solid five minutes. I looked in the mirror when I got out, I had a turtle head cock and blue lips. All good, no lust left in me at all. I checked the answering machine and no messages from anyone. I looked at my watch and it was just after nine. I also started to feel tired, must be the meds so I put on some Bowie, got deep in thought about why Charlene has been AWOL. Next thing you know I hear my door buzzer going off. It startles the hell right out of me. It goes again and as I look at the clock on the wall it is almost twenty after eleven, it has to be Nyah. So, I stand up, catch a little head rush and slowly make my way down the stairs, yeah wiping out would not be cool. Joseph will call that quack to take care of me. I look through the peephole and it is Nyah looking super fucking sexy. I open up the door and she once again gives me this long hug. This time I get hard as a rock. I tell her to come on up. I ask if she wants a beer, and she says hell yeah. I have a dime bag on the coffee table, and I tell her to roll us one and I will get her beer. I fetched her a beer and when I came back in the room Nyah was sitting on the couch topless. Her skin was mulatto but her nipples were jet black. And Nyah was a full-figured woman, doubles d cup for sure and they were solid. You could dunk me in a frozen lake, and I would still be able to get hard. She looked almost angelic as her hair was down. I just stood there in awe of her beauty and what she just did. "I am thirsty, Mitch…and not just for the beer."

Fuck her old man, fuck what Donnie and Joseph have said to me. I put the beer on the coffee table and sat down beside her and started to suck on those big dark nipples of hers. She moaned ever so gently. She put her head back and just closed her eyes. After about five minutes of doing this, I stood up. Held out my hand and said come with me. Her smile became huge as she put her hand in my hand and then stood up. I led the way to my bedroom. I lit a few candles once inside there and then I pulled the sheets back and started to take my shirt and pants off. By the time I was naked, Nyah was already under the sheets wearing nothing but a smile. Now, I have heard stories from the boys that black chicks taste different than white chicks and not in a good way. But Nyah was also half Irish, so I thought I have to find this out for myself. One thing was for sure, she was pretty hairy down below and I mean very tight coarse hairs. After some fingering I gave a little sniff, and all seemed good, so I decided to do the taste test for myself. She tasted fine if you ask me, such liars are those redneck boys. After at least two orgasms I decided to switch positions and have her gobble on my cock. I had to watch for a bit as Nyah has such sexy thick lips. After about ten minutes it was time to penetrate her. Missionary seemed to be the best position as I certainly wanted back on her boobs, and I also love seeing a good sized rack move around when I start to fuck hard. And fuck hard I did, slow and easy at first and then I pounded her super hard. That jerk off in the shower gave me stamina as I should have shot within five minutes. Instead, I lasted almost a half hour. And when I shot it was truly like a volcano erupting. My head as I was shooting my load also felt like it was about to erupt and as soon as I was done, I laid on my back with my hand over my left eye. I fell back to the bed and was moaning. I truly thought I was having an aneurysm. Nyah was now starting to freak and was asking if I was all right. "No, I am good." But I wasn't. The room was spinning, I broke out in a sweat and then felt my stomach flip. I rolled over and faced the wall and started to puke. That delicious burger and the taste of Nyah's pussy were repeating on me. Fuck, maybe the guys didn't lie after all. Nyah asked if I needed an ambulance. "No ambulance. I have a bail curfew and the pigs would charge me and Joseph would be out ten grand. Get me a cold wet cloth, Nyah."

7

My breathing was still a bit erratic when Nyah came back with the cloth. I put it over my eyes and just tried to slow everything down. I truly don't remember passing out but at some point, I must have as I took the cloth off my eyes and saw a very concerned Nyah asking me how I felt. "I am feeling better." I looked at my alarm clock and it was just after one in the morning.

"You should have gone home, baby. I don't want your Dad killing the two of us." She smiled and phoned her parents and said she was sleeping over at her friend Judy's. My head was still pounding so I asked Nyah if she could get me a glass of water and one of her painkillers. She jumped right up and did as asked. I washed back the painkiller, kissed her hand and thanked her.

I took a deep breath and then said, "What we did tonight was amazing. But there are certain people who wouldn't find it amazing; your Dad and Joseph who has threatened to fire me if he found out I was sleeping with any of his staff. And your Dad is a hardcore tough guy who still isn't too sure of me. Donnie picked up the chemistry between the two of us earlier on. I can never be your boyfriend, but I have no issues if you ever want to hook up. But you have to be very careful, hon." She smiled which I was glad to see.

"My Dad scares most of the guys I try to date. I know you are pretty fearless and to be honest, I have never been with an Indian and I always thought you were hot."

I laughed and said, "I have never been with anyone with negro in them. And you were pretty amazing and yes right from the first time I saw you I fantasized about you, Nyah."

She actually blushed, yes, I could see it. "So, you would like to do this again?"

"Absolutely I would. Other than me thinking I was going to die afterwards, I really enjoyed it." I moved the sheets to show that I was rock hard again.

She burst out laughing and said "Let's wait until you are all healed up before doing it again. You kind of freaked me out to be honest."

We both went into the living room, smoked another joint then came back to the bedroom, did some kissing and as much as I wanted to go again she said no. She even got up and put on her underwear to make sure no silliness happened while sleeping. The next morning Nyah made me breakfast, then we both took a shower together. It was a great morning. Before she left, Nyah asked if I could get her those couple pounds of weed. I said I am due for a delivery. As soon as it comes in, I will drop by the bar or call me later tonight. Just ask if she can drop by for a visit, if I say yes, you know I have the weed. One last long kiss then the lovely Nyah was on her way to school. Well normally I would hit the gym, but not with the way my head is feeling. I think I will give Mike Battaglia a call and see if he wants to do lunch. We can talk business. I will slide by Donnie's and see about Rachel's bike and then see Jerry and get some more weed. So, I did end up at the gym but just to order the dope. I walked into the weight room and regs came over and asked how I was doing. I turned around and showed them. Nice seeing all their faces grimace. Jerry and I went into his office. He was pretty concerned about Rachel and the charges against me. I said Rachel was pretty shook up, she says she is done driving on two wheels. I said he should call her. Let her know it is okay to stick to four wheels. I also told him she is now working as an official lawyer. This made him laugh. He asked if she was still going out with the Italian, Battaglia. I said no, different directions in life. He also said he would send Scotty Kantonescu over later with the weed. Next stop was Donnie's bike shop. I walked over to Rachel's bike and felt a shiver go up my spine. I asked Donnie what he thought. "Gas tank is cracked; front tire is shot. Everything else is not that bad. Has she put a claim into the insurance people yet?"

"I think so and they are going after the taxi driver and the company. So, after all is done how much do you think you can get for it?"

"I can see getting twenty-five hundred for it." I thanked him, and a part of me wanted to tell him that Nyah and I hooked up. But I can't give her a warning about loose lips and be flapping my own gums. Next stop was meeting Mike for lunch. He said he felt like German, so we hit this place I have never been to. I was the first to arrive and the smells reminded me of my mom's cooking. A nice warm feeling came over me; God, I miss her and Pam so much. And after Rach's near miss with death. Yeah, feeling humble. Mike showed up with his one driver aka bodyguard Rocco. He was a monster with no feelings. As cold blooded as they come. They both came in and after Rocco looked around the room, he went back out to the car to sit and wait. I am glad Joseph doesn't treat us like that. First thing out of Mike's mouth was how Rachel is. I said she was pretty shook up, broken arm and collarbone. "I will kill that cabby with my own two hands."

He then asked how I was doing. "You know how solid my coconut skull is, eighty two stitches courtesy of San Fran's finest."

"Fucking bastards. You think the charges will be stayed? I heard the cabby is missing." I looked around and said he will never be found. Mike looked at me and started to laugh.

"I need to talk to you about some business."

Mike smiled and told me to go ahead. "I need someone killed."

"Mitch, you can't kill him yourself?"

"Getting to him is a problem. He is in Folsom prison. If there is anyone who might know anyone in there it would be you. I have cash; just let me know how much."

Mike went deep in thought, took a drink of his beer and then his eyes lit up and he said yes. "Mitch, I can take care of this matter for you. And it won't cost you anything financially. Now because your guy is going to be hard to get at. I actually need you to take out two people for me. And both will be together."

"Sure, that works. Right now, I have an eleven-p.m. curfew. I would have to do it in the daytime hours which can be more than risky; do you think that would be a problem?"

"Yes, I do. When do you figure charges will be dropped?"

"My lawyer says by Thursday it should be dropped."

"Hopefully Thursday night you can't take care of business for me. Now you know both of these guys from San Quentin." Now this intrigued me. Frankie and Albert aren't due to be released to the end of December. Hopefully it is not Oscar either. So, I asked Mike who they were exactly.

"Jimmy "Beans" Palermo and Billy "Swift Feet" Thompson."

"Fuck, they were both pretty tight in prison. Can I ask what they did to deserve their fate? I have been taught don't ask. But I know these guys."

Mike nodded his head and said, "I will tell you but now you have to go on with the kills, correct?" I just nodded my head yes

"We are looking to expand our gambling empire onto the Santa Ynez reservation. Jimmy took a lot of our cash and has decided the money would be better fit helping out the redskins, nothing personal, Mitch. And that is why this would be better you taking them out as my guys going onto a reservation they would stand out." I never liked Jimmy; he was a fucking know it all and would hustle people for bets inside San Quentin. I do like Billy, but now that I have asked why. I have agreed to kill them both.

"That's cool. I will do the job. You have an idea where they are staying at as the reserve has a lot of places John Q Law can't even find." Mike promised me he would get me as much information as he can. He asked for Anita's ex's name.

"Hank Gibson, I was told he rolled on his partner in crime, so it won't come as a surprise to the general population and prison officials when he gets taken out. They will view it as just another dead rat." Mike said he will get someone on this right away. He jokingly said anything else I need.

"Yeah, there is, I need a doctor. Do you know anyone taking patients?"

"Like just a family doctor?"

"Yeah, just a family doctor, I wanna make sure none of these stitches get infected and they will have to come out and I need some painkillers, head's pounding."

"You remember my cousin Tony?"

"Aren't all your cousins called Tony?"

"Smart ass; know my cousin Tony Mattina the 49ers team doctor." I nodded my head yes.

"Well, his daughter Gabriela just opened up her own practice like two weeks ago. I have her number at home. I will call her, warn her about you"

He said jokingly, I think. "And I will get you in right away to see her"

I thanked Mike and assured him as soon as I find out about my legal situation, I will let him know. Within five minutes of getting home I received a call from Mike who told me his cousin Gabriela will see me at five. I will be her last patient of the day. I took a deep breath and flashed back to yesterday's cluster fuck and a half.

I told him five works great. He gave me the address and told me to have a good day. My day will be good if I walk in and only twenty people are ahead of me. I went home smoked a joint and then crashed out, yeah until I get something for my head, sleep and weed are my only painkillers. Woke up with the same headache I had before I laid down. I took a long shower and was pretty horny thinking about what happened between Nyah and me. But was nervous to shoot a load in case that wicked migraine comes back, ugh. On the drive over I said I am having a 30-minute time limit of waiting for doctor Mattina. Next stop will be getting meds from someone on the street. She was up on the third floor, so I decided to take the stairs and get rid of any angst that I had going on. Saw door 307, walked inside and there was only one other person sitting there. I walked over and checked in with the receptionist. She had me this form to fill out with my medical history; this alone may take most of the night. I was maybe one quarter through it when the nurse came out and asked me to follow her. I was put into this room, and she asked if I had completed my medical history. I laughed and said too much history. She then asked why I was there today.

"I need a new doctor and right now I am having lots of really bad headaches from a trauma that happened last Friday." I turned around and showed her the back of my head. She had a look and said that must have hurt. She said the doc would be in shortly. I am still writing out my medical history when the door opens and in walks this little fireball wearing a white lab coat, a short leather mini skirt and four inch platform heels. Big black rimmed glasses and long blonde hair. She stuck out her hand and introduced herself as Doctor Ella Mattina.

I shook her very small hands and said, "Nice to meet you doc, Mike speaks very highly of you."

"Nice to finally meet you. I have heard all about you back in the day." My head was now starting to spin; fuck, how much bad shit did she hear about me? I guess not that bad to still see me.

"How far back in the day and what all did you hear?"

"Your Mom was my teacher at Polk High. She was a great teacher and even better person. Sorry for your loss." I thanked her as she now started to go over my medical history.

"You have been through a lot of traumas for a young man. Can you turn around so I can exam your stitches and wound." I took a seat as I had to half at least almost a foot on her even with her wearing her heels. She put on the gloves and started to feel around the wound. She then asked me to roll my neck, felt around my jaw and asked how bad the headaches are. I was actually getting goosebumps while she was feeling around.

"They are brutal to be honest."

"And what are you taking for pain relief?"

"Just aspirin and it is not even touching it."

"No street drugs at all?" I just stared at her and wasn't sure how I should respond.

"Mitch, I really need an honest relationship with my patients. I will never call the police on you."

"Some weed, no pills at all. I would rather do things legit as you never know what you are buying on the street." She thanked me for trusting her and then wrote on her prescription pad a week's supply of painkillers for me.

"Before you leave when was the last time you had a complete physical?"

"I think when I was discharged from the army, so three years now."

"Tell Laura to book you sometime next week for a physical and stitch removal." I gave her the thumbs up, finished off my medical history, paid for today's appointment and then booked for next Friday at one. I went to the drugstore downstairs, got the meds filled and then headed to the Drunken Leprechaun and to see Nyah. I was greeted with a warm smile and a hug. As soon as I broke away, out of the corner of my eye was Joseph staring at us.

"Drop by when you get off work, I will have your weed for you, hon." Her smile got even bigger. She asked how I was feeling and did I need any more pain pills. I said the new doc gave me a prescription for pain meds. I then walked over to see Joseph was having a drink.

"How did you make out at the docs?"

"That fucking idiot; I left after sitting there for almost ninety minutes. I have a new doctor. A good young doctor who knows her shit. Curious Joseph, I am willing to bet a hundred bucks that quack you sent me too is not your doctor, is he?"

"No, he is not, but for the right amount of cash he will put in print whatever I want or need"

"Sorry, Joseph. But this time I needed a real doctor, I am already a bit fucked up, infection gets into my brain, hell I may start to talk with an Irish accent." I know when Joseph squints his eyes I touched a nerve with him. So, I blew him a kiss and asked if he still loved me

"You are a sick bastard, Mitchell Strongbow." If only he knew, then again, I am sure he does.

"Its okay boss, I think all of us in our group are a little sick and twisted, if we weren't, life would be boring as fuck"

"You are right there, lad, now tell me why did you hug Nyah with a little more oomph then normal?"

"She gave me some painkillers until I got in to see Doctor Mattina. She asked how I made out and I told her. All good, Joseph." He just did a slight nod and once again, Joseph knows me. I told him I had to head home as I have company coming over. He said as soon as the charges are dropped let him know. I said I would. Once back home I called Charlene, left a message, just calling to say how she is. I did get a hold of Anita and I asked her to drop by. Sat back on the couch and popped one of those painkillers. Put on some Pink Floyd and once the meds started to kick in, I went deep in thought, really deep in thought. This whole killing of Billy Thompson kind of bothers me. I know my grandfather does so much for his people. He is helping bring hope and spirit to the community with this extra and unexpected cash flow. How ironic that this tax-free windfall is blood money from the mob. It will now have more blood spilled because of it. I felt the urge to call my grandpa when my door buzzer went off. I went downstairs and it was Anita. As soon as I opened the door she came in and started necking with me.

"Oh, Mitch, I was so worried about you. How are you feeling?" I turned around and showed her the stitches, I can never hear enough of someone slamming the cops. We went upstairs and I asked if she wanted a beer or drink. Vodka on the rocks is what she asked for. As she was sipping her drink I told her about me taking care of Hank. She did this almost Disney cartoon villain smile and said she loved me. I can always tell when a chick is either going to ask me something naughty or devious and I wasn't wrong the way Anita was looking at me.

"How would you like to make another five grand, Mitch?"

"I am all ears baby, talk to me."

"I was wondering if you can get some phoney identification made up and withdraw all the cash from Hank's account. You think you can pull it off?"

"So, five for taking care of Charlie, and five for getting all of his cash? From a bank I assume?"

"Yes at a bank in San Jose. As soon as Charlie is dead, come in and withdraw the cash. I will be giving my two weeks' notice and then heading to Boston."

"And a blowjob. I would fuck you, but anything to strenuous makes my head pound…the one on my shoulders."

Anita smiled, little giggle, finished off her drink and then told me to get my pants off. I did as instructed and my beautiful and amazing cock sucker went to town on me. It felt so good with the buzz from the painkiller making it more sensual. Once she finally leaves, I am really going to miss this. When I was just getting ready to blow, I just stared at her face and watched the perfect coordination of her hand, mouth and tongue. Like the champ she is, Anita took my complete load and swallowed me whole. So, we had a game plan in place, I would contact Donnie about getting me the phoney identification. I will tell Mike to let me know as soon as the job is done. I will call the bank and tell them I need this money ready in twenty-four hours time. Anita said the more identification I have the better it will be. She knows exactly what the manager will ask for and yes it will be a manager I will be dealing with. Now seeing how she is willing to kill her ex. I think I will have Donnie in the shadows in case she has made a deal with someone else to take me out. The only people I trust with my life are Donnie and Joseph, at times still not one hundred percent positive about Joseph. I told Anita I will be in touch with her and for her to be ready also. As she was about to leave Scott showed up with a gym bag full of weed for me. I did the intros and Scott just gave me this big smile. Without even thinking I gave her a kiss goodbye, Anita whispered in my ear, "How do you taste?" It took like ten seconds before I clued in. I wiped my mouth as she burst out laughing. Scotty asked what was so funny, I told him I would let him later. A now pardon the pun, cocky, Anita said, "Of course you will."

As soon as she left, I headed right to the washroom, gargled and then brushed my teeth. I came out and told Scott what happened. "That is a fine-looking piece of tail. Good job, Strongbow." Scotty had a couple beers, and we were talking about the shit we used to get into in high school when the buzzer rang. I looked at my watch and knew it would be Nyah.

"That buzzer is another good friend of mine. I want you to play nice around her. She is a great person."

"Hey man, I am always nice to your female friends, is she cute?"

"I think she is hot."

"Fuck, Strongbow, if she is hot then why would I have to play nice, you know I am going to anyways."

"She is half black."

He just shook his head no, "I accepted you with the Jew, but that's as far as I go."

"I mean it, play nice. Her dad is one badass mother fucker who is also muscle for the Leprechaun, and she also works there, her name is Nyah." I went downstairs with still no affirmation from Scotty. Once again, I was met with a hug and kiss. I told her to come up and I had company. Yes, always better to forewarn then have her say something that might embarrass herself. Nyah was her usual bubbly self. I asked if she wanted a beer and she said yes. Scotty got up and said he had to get going and did I have something for him. Nyah could sense something was up. She said she was sorry for interrupting, and she can get what she came for and leave. Scotty said no he has to go. So, I went and grabbed him the cash for the weed. Before he left, he said the club is doing a run this weekend to Los Angeles if I wanted in. I thanked him and said my head is way too sore but thanks anyways. He left without saying goodbye to Nyah, kind of pissed me off as she asked if it was because she is black.

"Don't take it personal. He is a Hell Hound. It is part of their culture, hon. You could save his life, and he would still not thank you." The mother to my daughter is Jewish. My older brother Jake was a Hell Hound, and it took a bit for him to see past her religion. But I love hanging with you, hon. You are a great person." This made her smile, she asked for a kiss to prove I am not like Scotty. This made me laugh inside, good thing I gargled and brushed my teeth. We messed around a bit and as much as I wanted to fuck her. I know with me blowing my load a little while ago I will last longer, and it will be more of an effort, and I really don't wanna freak her out again by passing out. So, I had to back off and told her to give me a couple days and I will bang her silly. Nyah said she will take a rain check for sure and fully understood why. I gave her two pounds of weed. She had one more beer and then she headed home. I took another painkiller and was in bed by midnight. Before I closed my eyes I realized all and all I have a pretty good life. And part of that is being a good businessman. I don't discriminate about race, creed, or gender. This too also makes me a good lover. I woke up the next morning fully hard and wished Nyah was here right now. I looked at the clock and it was eight twenty, I think Charlene doesn't leave for work till eight thirty. This time a telephone company recording came on and said the number you have reached is no longer in service. I felt my gut flip. I am going to eat, grab a shower, and head over to her apartment. Nervous energy, all kinds of it was flowing through me as I drove over to Charlene's apartment. As I pulled up, I took a really deep breath and got out of the car. I knocked on her door and got no answer. At the end of the hall this lady was mopping the floors, so I went over and said I am a friend of Charlene Borden and I haven't heard from her in a bit and I was concerned. This older lady said with this European accent said, "Miss Borden move away."

Another gut flip, "Where did she move to?"

She just raised her arms up and said, "I don't know. Now, are you going to mop these floors as they won't get done by themselves." I clenched my jaws and stormed out of there. For the life of me I couldn't remember the name of the private school she was at. So, I drove around and was hoping it would come to me. It didn't. So, after many miles put on I headed to see Donnie about getting the phony identification. I also told him I would pay him to watch my back. He asked what the whole plan was, I told him and said I was smart asking for backup. When I asked how much, Donnie said five hundred bucks. Money well spent, just in case. I paid Donnie for the identification. He said it takes about a day. He will call me once it is in. I then drove over to see Mike Battaglia and said as soon as this goes down with Hank to let me know. He asked if I heard anything from my lawyer. I said not yet but as soon as I do, I will fulfill my contract with him. Over the next couple days, I called in all kinds of favours from people I knew in Oakland and tried to track Charlene down. I know there is a huge part of me that still loves her. And there is the ego in me pissed she it seems has started a whole new life without even saying goodbye. Fuck, I was the strong one in our relationship, not her. Then it hit me. Why would she want to disappear on me? She is either shacked up with one of her ex-prison guard lovers from San Quentin or a cop. Fuck, she always had a thing for cops. And if he ran my priors, he would dump her ass. On Friday afternoon, I got a call from Levy that all charges against me were dropped as the cab driver is no where to be found. I was on my way over to see Mike when my buzzer went off. I went downstairs and it was Mike and Rocco.

"I was just on my way down to see you. Levy just called and said all charges are dropped against me."

"And I am here to tell you that Charlie Gibson is laying on a slab in the morgue wearing only a toe tag." Mike also handed me the info I asked for earlier this week about where Jimmy Palermo and Billy Thompson are staying. I told Mike I will head there tonight and do some recon. I also promised him that both will be dead by Monday morning.

8

After they left, I called the bank in San Jose and said I am Charlie Gibson and I wish to close my account. I gave them all the information and they said they will have everything ready tomorrow and to ask for Joe Walmsley, the branch manager that is. They asked, all large bills? I said yes. Then I hauled ass to Anita's branch and made sure to get in her line. "Charlie is dead. I have the withdraw set up for tomorrow."

"Good stuff, Mitch. I will drop by after work, actually I will spend the night and we can do a nice breakfast and then head over." I said that works for me. Time for another mad dash. Off to Donnie's shop I headed. His workers said he left with the club about an hour ago. Fuck, the run to Los Angeles. Now what? I looked at them, but I really don't know them. I can't go to Joseph as Donnie said to keep him out of my private life as much as I can, and it is one fuck of a long story to tell and you know Joseph will want to know everything. I called every member of the Hell Hounds I trusted, and everyone was gone for the club run. I trust Mike but I don't trust any of his men and no way would Mike get involved, plus he is a heat score. So, I will have to rely on my own street smarts to keep me alive, and a 9MM and a snub nose 38 in my boot. Anita dropped by after work with an overnight bag. She said she is craving steak and lobster, her treat. That works for me. So, we went to this high end surf and turf restaurant. All through dinner I am trying to get any read off her. But it is hard as she is so happy. I can always tell it is genuine as people tend to talk more, almost like a manic high. Even on the drive back to my place she was non-stop talking and lots of hand holding in between shifting gears. My heart did get that shot of adrenaline as when we pulled up to my place it was all lit up and I know I shot off all the lights. Anita did pick up something that was not right. I asked her if I shut off all the lights when we left. She said yeah, good with my brain still hurting I had to make sure. I told her to stay in the car as I got out and pulled out my 9MM. I examined the lock on the door, and it didn't appear to have been jimmied. The door itself was still locked. So, I slowly opened the door and once inside stood at the landing and listened to any movement. And yes, there was movement. I heard the fridge open; someone was moving around the bottles of beer. Fridge closed and whomever it is has moved back to the living room. Deep breath took and I slowly made my way up the stairs. I made it to the final stair, and I could see a pair of legs wearing socks no footwear. Pretty ballsy making themselves at home. I then heard them make an inhaling noise followed by some coughing. Fuck, they are smoking my dope. They are coughing so they won't be ready for me So, like a tiger in the jungle, I jumped up and raced in with my gun pointed at the perp. It was Oscar for fuck sakes. "Strongbow, it's me! Chill, man!"

"Fuck, Oscar! I thought it was a thief. Good to see you, brother."
He gave me this hug and asked how I was feeling.

"My nerves are shot right now, but all good. I heard you took out the garbage for me."

"Yes, I did, he will never be found."

I then heard the door open and realized I had forgotten all about Anita. "Come on up, baby; all is good."

Anita came up and I did the intros. Oscar certainly liked the look of her and asked if she had any friends that could drop by and party with us. Let me see what I can do. Anita got on the phone and started to call her friends. I took Oscar in the kitchen and said I have a job for him tomorrow. He asked what and I told him to keep me alive. I told him part of the story; I didn't tell him how much cash was involved. Oscar said for sure he would watch my back. Within twenty minutes, two of Anita's girlfriends showed up. I had a couple beers, yeah with still taking the painkillers and smoking dope it didn't take me too long before Anita and I headed to my room. Oscar stayed up to party with both girls. I know he will end up fucking them both by the morning, just the horny pig he is. I was pretty fucked up, so Anita decided to do all the work as she jumped on top of me and went for a ride. After about ten minutes or so she stopped, she had this confused look on her face. I asked if all was all right. She said listen, at first all I heard was giggling but then I started to hear moans from both girls. Fucking Oscar has both in the bedroom with him. Anita looked down at me and smiled, gave me a wink and started to ride once again, this time she was a little more vocal. Maybe to prove to her friends she can't be out done. The whole and groaning show brought back memories of the orgy with me and Charlene at Herschel's wedding. Needless to say, I blew a load and a half. Anita rolled off me and just giggled, gave me a kiss and then I passed right out. I woke up the next morning with Anita sprawled across me. My bladder told me it had to be drained, so I rolled her off me. Made my way to the washroom, but first I had to look in on Oscar. Hey, my house, and the door was wide open. Both girls were on each side of him, lucky bastard. I did my business and looked at the clock in the kitchen, it was ten after eight. Anita and I have some banking to do, time to wake everyone up. I walked buck naked into Oscar's room and turned the light on. "Mitch you are as evil as the screws in San Quentin. Me and the girls need more sleep."

"No more sleep, we have business to do, remember?"

Oscar said I was right, he spanked both their asses and said let's all jump in the shower. "Please don't use up all the hot water, Anita and I need to get in there."

"Come join us, the more the merrier right girls?" The one actually grabbed my cock and said for me to join them. Maybe next time was my answer.

My turn to be the ass smacker. "Hey baby, we have business to take care of." Anita smiled at me and said yes, we do.

"I would like to shower but Oscar and both girls are in the shower right now.

"Give them ten minutes Mitch then I will go in and flush the toilet, oops!" She started to laugh as did I.

"You know, Anita... I am really going to miss you when you move away."

"There is nothing stopping you from coming to visit me there?"

"No, nothing at all. I would really like that." She gave me a kiss before heading to the washroom. I went deep in thought once again until I heard two females and a male scream, I guess Anita flushed the toilet, oops. I heard Anita say five more minutes the toilet gets flushed again, wrap it up. They were all out and drying off within the five minutes. When we jumped in the shower we locked the door, mama raised no dummies. Before we left for the bank, I told Anita that Oscar is going to tag along just in case anyone gets silly. She also saw both of us pack our weapons. She got quiet and her face changed, yeah, she was now nervous I could tell.

"All good baby, just in case." I double checked to make sure I had all my Hank Gibson identification on me. Then the three of us jumped in the mustang and headed to San Jose. Anita didn't say two words the whole way there. Oscar kept falling asleep in the back seat, those girls must have worn him right out. We pulled up about a block from the bank. I woke up Oscar and said look alive, game time. We all got out. I told Oscar to have a seat on a bench directly across from the bank. Anita put on a very fashionable hat and big sunglasses, perfect disguise, and me, just my sunglasses and a gym bag. We walked in the bank together. Two armed guards made sure to make eye contact with us. I walked over to the help desk and said I am here to see Mr. Walmsley. She asked my name, and without missing a beat, I said Hank Gibson. She told Anita and I too have a seat and he would be right out. I looked at Anita and smiled, fuck she was nervous. I hope she doesn't think we plan on robbing and killing her. An older very rigid guy came out and said he was Mr. Walmsley and to please come with him. We went into his office with the one senior teller. He asked to see my identification. I pulled it out and he and the teller both checked it out. He then asked did the bank do something wrong for me to withdraw all my cash.

"No sir, not at all. My girl and I are moving to her hometown in Canada." Now they both looked at her and asked where in Canada she was from.

"Montreal, born there and went to school here at SFU. Done my schooling, will be coming back with a degree and a fiancé."

"Good for you two, so nice to see a young couple have their heads on straight. I have all the money in a money bag. I assume you would like it put in the gym bag." I said yes please. They asked if I would like one of the guards to escort us to our car.

"No thanks, that will draw too much attention." He said I was right. He made me sign off on the account. He showed me all the final transactions and bank charges. Fuck me, Charlie had over a hundred grand in this account. One hundred and twelve thousand to be exact. I carried the gym bag, and my eyes were roaming like a hawk. Once outside, I nodded to Oscar who now looked at anything coming our way as he got up.

We headed to the car, and I went to put the gym bag in the trunk and Anita said, "I need you to drive two blocks south as I am depositing the cash in another bank and having it wired to a Boston bank." Yeah, she has thought this out and made sure if we were going to rob her it would be difficult. She said she wanted to hold the bag while we drove to the bank. She said she would count out my cash. We were there in a matter of minutes. She handed me my cash and said she wanted to go in herself.

"I think you carrying all that cash by yourself is silly, hon."

"It is my cash; I can afford to be silly." I wasn't going to argue with her. I did watch her the whole way in case someone did try and grab the bag and run off with all the cash. She came out of the bank a hell of a lot happier than when she was in the car. On the drive back I asked her if she thought we were going to rob her.

Her face went beat red and she reluctantly said, "The thought had crossed her mind." Once back in town I went to my bank and deposited my loot from the sting. When the teller handed me my balance I smiled, it is really starting to grow. Oscar asked Anita if she could call her friends and see if they wanna kick it down again tonight. I said as much as I would like that I am going out of town in five. I didn't tell Oscar what I was up to. With this being my first kills for Mike outside prison. I will only ask for help if I really need it. I gave Anita a long kiss goodbye and thanked her. She smiled and said I was the one to be thanked. I went upstairs and changed my clothes, got the info on where to find Billy and Jimmy, jumped on my bike and headed there. I did keep my 9MM and my 32 snub in my boot. But I know this kill will not come easy and will have to be planned. Not like I am going to see them broke down on the side of the highway hitchhiking. It was a bit longer on the bike that I had planned, but my Mustang would stand out on a reservation. And my bike I can find off road paths. Weather wise it was a great ride. My head hurt a bit but the fresh air helped not only my brain, but I also got deep into thought on the bike. And my thought is to get in, out and off the reservation before, during and after the kill.

It took me about five hours before I was on the actual reservation. Santa Ynez is a hell of a lot smaller than Pine Ridge and they seem to be farmers here. The land is flat or at least the first bit of it.

9

Billy lives on Refugio Road which seemed to go on forever. I did find one spot where these two cement pillars and a solid steel cast iron gate were meant to keep everyone out. The house had to be at least a thousand yards in the distance. But about fifty yards from the gate was a small lake which had a dock.

Other than a creek this was the only decent body of water I could find. I remember Billy telling me how he stocked this small lake on his property, and he would fish it and eat what he caught. Just like his elders did. Funny, I don't ever recall my grandfather telling me about them stocking any personal lakes on our property. No way could I get close enough without being detected. And with it being a Saturday night you know they will be at the casino. I do have a good game plan, but not tonight, tomorrow as I don't have the proper tools. I got back into San Fran around midnight. I headed straight to the Drunken Leprechaun.

Sean Quinn was working the door. My balls shrunk a little bit I must say. "Strongbow, how are you feeling?" Fuck, actual concern from the big man.

"I am feeling good, Sean. Yeah, the headaches are finally starting to let up. Thanks, man." I went inside and hugged all the girls working, not just Nyah although I did whisper that she looked hot. And guess who was at the bar chatting it up with a couple chicks, yep Oscar. So, I grabbed a beer and told him and the girls he was with, let's grab a booth.

The band was really tight and also really loud. They also had a decent light show. Within thirty seconds of a strobe light being on for the drum solo I felt that migraine starting to creep back. The one chick that was sitting beside me was cute, but the last thing on my hurting brain was sex. I also knew if I didn't get home right away, I would have to leave my bike here and that wasn't going to happen, it would be stolen for sure. Oscar commented that I didn't look good all of a sudden. "Head is pounding again; I am heading home, man."

As I got up to leave, Nyah came over and asked if I was all right. "Migraine, babe. Sorry I have to leave." Sean stopped me and asked if everything was good. I couldn't even talk by now. I just pointed to my head. He patted me on the shoulder and said feel better. It took everything in me to try and fire over my bike. I had no coordination and I know it will be a death trap for me even if I had someone start it for me. I can't even think straight, it is really starting to pound. I could feel the whole heartbeat in my left eye. My stomach now flips, and I start to hurl. I am hanging onto my bike for dear life to hold me up. I have tuned out the whole outside world. A hand is now on my back asking if I am all right.

I look through my bleary eyes and I think it is the nurse from the hospital, the good one. Then I hear a familiar voice standing beside her and they know my name. I wipe my eyes and it is Beth who works for me at the t-shirt place. The nurses name it turns out is Nancy, she says I really shouldn't be drinking with a post concussion. I explain I had two sips of beer and the loudness of the band, and the strobe light brought this on. Nancy then asked if there was any trauma today or just from the music.

"Just the music, honest."

"No, that is good, Mitch. Listen, Liz and I will drive you home."

"I can't leave my bike here. Go inside and ask for Sean the bouncer, tell him I need him outside." Liz went in while Nancy stayed with me. I thanked her for taking care of me back in the hospital. She said it was her pleasure. She said she could tell I was a decent guy deep down. Sean came out and saw me really hurting. "I can't drive my bike home, too fucked up. Can you make sure it ends up in the back fenced area?"

"Sure thing, Mitch." I thanked him then both girls drove me to my place. I was so fucked up I was telling them how to get there. Beth laughed and reminded me she works right under my apartment. My eyes were closed the whole trip home, all I could do though was smell gas. So strong.

They both helped me upstairs. On the living room table, I had my painkillers. I popped two and then sat down. I also had a dime bag and told them to take it. At first, they said no. I reminded Beth that I am her boss and that is a direct order or I will fire her ass. She said fine. Both of them helped me to my room and helped me get undressed.

Nancy was a little freaked out when she first found the 9MM and then the 38 snub in her boot. I think Beth knew I was not your average businessman. They then helped me into my bed before they left. It is a good thing that Nancy put both pistols far away from me as I swear my head hurt so bad, I would have blown my brains out.

10

I woke up completely drenched in sweat. I was parched as if I was on a two-day bender. The clock showed four twenty and I really needed something to drink. My head was still sore but not pounding, so I went out to make a glass of Tang and in the living, room was this naked chick on the couch watching television. If that didn't freak me out enough it was also bright as hell for this early in the morning. No, my alarm clock must have died. I said good morning to the chick, she laughed and said good afternoon. I was still kind of groggy from the pain meds. I don't think she was here with me last night. "Humour me; you are here with Oscar, where is he?"

She laughed once again and said yes, "He is in the washroom. You were sitting at a booth with me last night then you got really sick and went home. How are you feeling?"

"Not sure yet, and I really don't remember everything, sorry." I went into the kitchen and made some Tang. Drank it back along with it seemed like a gallon of water. I came out and Oscar was now beside the naked chick on the couch.

He too was naked and the stench coming from the bathroom was brutal. "Oscar, get on some fucking clothes, I don't want your smelly naked ass on my couch." He went yeah yeah, the chick also got up,

"Honey you can stay naked."

"You are sweet, but I have to get going, would you like me to make you something to eat before I leave?" I didn't have the greatest appetite, but I knew I had to eat something.

"Well how about a couple fried egg sandwiches?" She said sure after she got dressed. She said grease splatter hurts like a bitch. As she was cooking, I asked Oscar if he had plans today. He said no so I said I need a spotter for a job, and I would pay him.

"What kind of job, Strongbow?"

"Do you remember Jimmy Palermo and Billy Thompson?"

"Yeah, I remember them."

"I plan on shooting them both dead. Problem is that they are held up on an Indian reservation about five hours from here and it will be a bit of a challenge to get to them. I just need you to warn me if anyone else spots me and there could be an intense firefight getting off the reservation if shit goes south. And make no mistakes about it every man, woman, and child have firearms on every reservation." Oscar said he is in, but can I give him weapons until he can head to Catalina and get all his weapons. I said that is not a problem. The chick, aka Louise, brought me out my breakfast, she gave Oscar a kiss goodbye and told him not to be a stranger. I thanked her and then she left.

"You know Oscar, if she shows up here after you move out, I will try and fuck her; she was pretty hot and cool." I also told Oscar we will leave here around seven and should be there just after midnight. I figure by seven I will know whether I am able to kill Jim and Bill. The last thing I want is to get close enough and I go down with the same migraine as last night. I would be an easy target and I would also be putting Oscar life on the line. After I ate, I made a coffee and popped a couple aspirins. My head was definitely becoming more clear. The shakes and dehydration issue had stopped. Let the killing begin. Oscar was quite impressed with my weapons I decided to bring along. For him a FN-C1 with three fifteen round clips. His own 9MM and a 12-gauge shotgun. My game plan was to kill them from a distance. So, I brought my M-21 sniper rifle. My 9MM and 38 snub nose in one boot and of course my Fairburn Sykes knife down my other boot. Oscar asked if we were taking the Mustang and I said no.

"We are taking the pickup truck and will stop off at Donnie's and get my canoe."

At first Oscar was a little shocked. "No, this house is really awkward to get at by car or truck. We would be spotted, I plan on rowing over and getting as close as I can, and if I have to, we will break into the place and kill them while they sleep in their beds." Both 9MM and the M-21 have silencers on them and also a muzzle flash for the rifle. The FN-C1, it is loud. When we pulled up to Donnie's he was just getting home from the club run.

"Kind of late for fishing would you say, Mitch?"

"I have a paid job on the side. You wanna come along?"

No doubts Donnie would be my first choice.

"As much as I would, my ass is tired from the ride. I don't think I could handle another five plus hours on the road and hours waiting to execute your plan."

Donnie looked at Oscar and said, "No games here, just like in Nam, in and out right, Oscar?" Oscar said of course. Donnie wished us both good luck and said to drop by and let him know all is good. I thanked him, we threw the canoe in the back of the truck and off we went to the Sana Ynez reservation. My head was still a bit off. I didn't feel like a whole in-depth conversation with Oscar, just the layout of the land, and some back up plans if all hell breaks loose. Now, I have killed others with Oscar while in Special Forces. This will be our first kills as civilians. Well...maybe civilians are the wrong word. Contract killers? Assassins? Nah, I like taker of souls. Sounds way cooler. Now, the only thing that made me nervous was the fact it was a full moon. If we were in Nam, the mission would be scrubbed. But I promised Mike they would both be dead by Monday morning, and he already delivered for me. The butterflies started to flutter as soon as we turned off the main highway and onto the reservation. I looked at my watch and it was twenty after twelve. I killed the lights on the truck and prayed my memory of these roads were good. Really hoping the meds and migraine from last night don't leave me in the fog. I pulled off into this field where there is a lot of tree cover about a mile from the gated area.

I asked Oscar if he still remembered his hand signals from Special Ops and he gave me the thumbs up. So, we gathered up all our weapons. Made sure no one was coming and picked up the canoe and carried it to the launch site. The whole time it brought back painful memories on my Innipi trek with my grandfather. The Sioux in me still has a bit of guilt about killing Thompson. It was a really humid night. By the time we got to the fenced area I was starting to sweat really good. I also had this weak pulse starting in the back of my head. I have a feeling I know where this is going to go. I have to get these two killed as soon as possible. Oscar scaled the fence first and I passed him all the weapons and then the canoe. As I scaled the fence that slight pulse in my left eye got a little bit stronger. As I landed on the other side, I had a dizzy spell. I actually had to hang onto the fence for a second. My face was just dripping sweat like crazy; it was stinging my eyes and my shirt was soaked.

Oscar said let's finish this job in a couple days. I said no I gave my word it would be done tonight. He just nodded yes; he knows my work ethic is only bested by my word. We carried the canoe to the water, put it in and then I took off my shirt and soaked it in the water and then rang it out over my head. It certainly helped, that was for sure. As we were rowing over, I saw what appeared to be two torches burning in the distance. Oscar asked if that is where we are headed. I nodded yes.

"You think it is a welcoming committee, Strongbow?"

"Well, we did come bearing gifts." As I held up my rifle. Once we hit shore, we dragged the canoe onto land and hid it. We were about three hundred away. With the flames flickering I had to get even closer to make a confirmation visual as there were three bodies walking around. Not sure how many inside the house either. The wild grass was quite high which made it perfect for us doing a front crawl. Eventually, we were about fifty yards away and I had a confirmation it was Jimmy Palermo and Billy Thompson through my rifle scope. The third member was a female, she looked native. It has to be Billy's wife. My headache that went away was starting to come back as I had no intentions of killing her.

If this was Nam and it was mama San, I wouldn't even think twice. So, I told Oscar that it is Jimmy and Billy. "And who is the third person?" he asked.

"Not sure, a female. I am hoping she hits the dirt and is too distraught to react." Oscar just gave me that look and firmly asked if I was serious.

"She is a civilian. Not part of the deal man. Not taking an innocent life."

"This is your gig not mine, if it was, all three would be dead. Can you at least shoot her, so she doesn't race inside and call for help?" I thought about what he said, and yeah, it did make sense. So, the game plan is this. I told Oscar that Jimmy is the bigger threat. I will shoot him first. I told Oscar to keep his rifle focused on Billy and only shoot if he thinks he will get away. Once Jimmy is down, I will go to Billy and then he will focus on the female. I will then put one in her shoulder. I reminded Oscar that I have a silencer on my rifle, and they won't know what hit them. And the lack of noise will keep anyone in the house from being alerted. As soon as all of them drop and seeing how I am using "Mushroom Bullets" they will all drop, and we head back to the canoe. Oscar will paddle and I will keep my rifle pointed at anyone trying to follow.

"Strongbow, you don't think we should check to see if the guys are dead first before leaving? After all, it is a contract kill not wound or maim. Not busting your balls, man… but I have been doing this for a couple years now. Donnie I am sure would have you confirm they are dead?"

"You're right, Oscar. I am a rookie and I appreciate your advice."

"Look man, seeing at how you are still having headaches I think it is best for me to check on them. I can run faster than you right now. Are you sure you can take the shots?"

"Yeah, my vision is clear. Good advice. You have to be quick; I want off this reservation as quick as we can, or Billy's tribe will skin us alive, they will show no mercy and will make sure we don't have a very slow, but very painful death."

"You do your job Strongbow, and I will do mine." So, I pulled the breach back and put a bullet in the chamber. I aimed my rifle towards Jimmy. Lined up the scope with the target and started to control my breathing. All three of them were sitting down within ten feet of each other. And everything is about timing. And for Jimmy, this was going to be his last sip of beer. As soon as the beer can touched his lips, I fired a shot right in the middle of his chest. You don't admire your shot; you move on to Billy who was now leaning over a fallen Jim. I nailed him right in the head. That I did see spray everywhere. The female stood up and started to bolt towards the house.

"Take the shot, Strongbow! For fucks sakes," said Oscar. I don't answer him; I realign my sights and nail her in full flight. She hits the ground hard. I tap Oscar on the shoulder and tell him to go. I now stand up in a firing position and am totally focused on the back door of the house. Oscar stands over Jimmy and Billy and puts a round into each of them from his 9MM. He now heads to the female and puts two rounds in her, fucker killed her. I can't let my rage get in the way. I am still focused on anyone coming out of the house. Oscar then races back to me with this big smile, an evil fucking smile at that. We both head to the canoe. I don't say shit as I want no noises at all. The canoe goes in smoothly, he paddles, and I have my rifle still pointed towards the house. We pull the canoe out of the water and carry it to the other side of the fence. My head is starting to pound again so I tell Oscar to haul ass and get the truck, I remind him no headlights on at all. I look down at my watch and he is back within eight minutes, not bad. We put the canoe in the back, and I ask for the keys. He is a little bit hesitant until I am firm and tell him to give me the keys.

We both get in and I head out of here as quick as I can considering I am driving without headlights. Not even two minutes into our mad dash escape, Oscar says, "She was ready to yell for help. I did what had to be done, Strongbow."

"Please don't talk; it is more important I get us out of here." He said something in Syrian and then looked out the window. As soon as we got back on the highway, I turned my headlights back on. I also made sure to only do the speed limit. With all the firepower we have on us and being two recently released federal prisoners, yeah, not cool at all. We just passed the outskirts of Santa Maria when I pulled the truck over. Oscar asked if everything was all right. I shook my head no and pulled out my bottle of painkillers. I popped two and told Oscar he was driving.

"Don't do anything stupid to get us pulled over by the cops." Oscar gave me the fucking really look and then put the truck in gear.

Within a matter of minutes, I was dead to the world. You know when you wake up from a dream and it takes you a while to determine if the dream you just had was real or not. Well, I had this dream I was on a beach with Frankie and Annette. I can hear the waves crashing and the sound of those shit hawks. I can smell the ocean breeze and feel the sun beating down on me.

Then I hear this tapping sound, an annoying tapping sound. Then a stern voice, "Hey buddy wake up". Too real so I open up my eyes and all I can see is this blurred silhouette of a human. The sun is so bright, blinding. I pulled the hair on my knuckles, and it hurt, no longer a dream.

I then recognize Oscar's voice saying, "All is good, officer." Officer? What the fuck? My dream has now become a bit of a waking nightmare. I look out the front window of the truck and I don't have a clue where we are. The cop now asks if I am all right, I reach down to grab my 9MM as the cop turns around to talk to Oscar.

"Sorry, officer. We drove all night; my friend here fell asleep." He looked at both of us. Asked what we were doing here.

Oscar pointed to the canoe and said, "Fishing, what do you think?" He looked at the canoe, then Oscar, and then me and told us to have a good day. As soon as the cop was far enough away, I asked Oscar where the fuck are we as this doesn't look like any part of San Francisco I recognize.

"I had to divert our route home as I spotted cops about a half mile away from us. Not sure if there was an accident or a roadblock. Either way Mitch all I saw was flashing blue lights. I took your direction and avoided the cops."

"So, where the fuck are we exactly?"

"Huntington Beach."

"Are you fucking serious? We are what eight hours away from home now?"

"Yeah, eight hours sounds about right. But we are about an hour boat ride from me getting you the five gallons of hash oil I promised you from prison" He then handed me a couple breakfast burritos and a coffee.

"How are you feeling, man?"

"My head isn't pounding, all good now."

"Good, eat up. Chill on the beach, get some rays and I will be back before you know it with the oil." Yeah, the last thing I want to do is to go on the ocean and get sea sick.

"You don't think dragging all this oil ashore will make us a heat score?"

"No, they are in five-gallon jerry cans." I ate the food he gave me; I was also dressed all in black and it gets really hot in late June. So, I asked Oscar if there was a place around here I could buy a pair of shorts. He pulled a bag out of the box and in it was a pair of shorts for me.

"See, Strongbow? I am always looking out for you." I told him to stand guard as I took off my pants and slid on the shorts. Maybe this is what I need, total down time. No rushing around or tension. I saw Oscar wave to this boat that pulled up to the pier. He said he would be back in a couple hours, three max. I looked at my watch and it was almost ten. I wished him luck and then pulled up a piece of sand. Not too far away from the truck as we still had all our weapons in the cabin and tucked inside the canoe. So, I got out of the truck, saw these late teens playing beach volleyball about twenty yards away and they had something I needed. Two things actually. So, I took my shirt off to show off my muscles and scars. This way they will be less likely to say no. The closer I got the more attention I was getting. I waited till there was a break and said, "I was wondering if you guys would rent me one of your chairs and can I also buy a couple of those beers I know you have on ice in the cooler" They didn't know what to really think of me. I have over eighty stitches in the back of my head. I am as big as any guy on that muscle beach in Venice Beach. I have a Wolf wearing an SS Helmet on my chest and my 75th LRRP insignia. Bullet and knife wounds scars. The one guy said pull up a chair or play with us, that is free. The beer is fifty cents.

I gave him a buck and said thanks. Yeah, the truck is close enough. They asked once again if I wanted to play. I said nah, I have all these stitches to keep my skull and brain together. They were all good kids. Going to college and decided to extend their weekend an extra day.

Eventually everyone took a break and they asked me about Vietnam. They wanted to know how fucked up it was and whether or not it was a just war.

"All you guys are lucky the draft ended three years ago. It was a living nightmare what man can do against man. Fucked me up. Left for dead a couple times. Came home a heroin addict. Cost me my relationship with my daughter's Mom. I still wake up from time to time and think I am back there; I hear a noise and I am ready to kill. Some mornings you get up and have to hang your sheets on the line to dry. It not only took four years of my life, but it also took my soul." I have no idea why I bared my soul to these kids. It just felt like the right thing to do. Eventually they broke out some weed after asking if I was a cop.

"I just did two years in San Quentin, not a cop." Fuck, they even fed me. Good kids. By the time Oscar came ashore, I had lots of color in my face, a nice buzz happening and a full belly. I thanked all the kids and told them that if they are even in San Fran, they have to visit my t-shirt store and the Drunken Leprechaun. Oscar shook his head and asked me to help him. He actually had four five-gallon Jerry cans full of oil. We put the drugs in the cab of the truck. He said he would drive us home as I was a little more buzzed then normal. I guess the pain killers were still buzzing in my bloodstream. Yeah, must have been buzzed as I told him I totally respected him killing that chick.

"Brother, the last thing we needed was some split tail ratting us out and you and I on twin electric chairs. Fuck her." I told him to crank up the Frank Zappa Apostrophe that was in the eight-track player. I sang Yellow Snow like a rock star. It was a long drive home and about a quarter way home the rain started. My good happy buzz went away, and I went deep in thought once again. Fuck, I was so close to get back on Tash's good side and possibly into Katrina's life. I certainly have a problem keeping the woman in my life close to me. We pulled into San Fran just as the sun was setting. Yeah, seven hours of rain, get home and the sun is out for like five minutes. Story of my life. I told Oscar to pull up to the Drunken Leprechaun as I wanna drive my bike home. I told Oscar I would meet him back home. As I went inside, Joseph was having a pint at the bar. He called me over and asked how I was feeling.

"Headaches still get bad. No reason why I can't be back at work hopefully by this weekend, stitches come out Friday."

"You have some color in your face, I tried to call you, where were you?"

"I went with Oscar to pick up some stuff in Catalina."

"Do you feel fit enough to go and take out some garbage for me?"

I am thinking, does he know I killed for Battaglia yesterday?

"It depends on whether or not I have to make up and close contact. Why, what is going on?"

"This set of three brothers out of Texas tried to rip off my cousin Seamus. Now normally Seamus would like nothing more than to track them down and take their lives. But he is getting married this coming weekend and his crew will also be attending the wedding. So, I have the twins looking for the rip off artists."

"Who are the twins?"

"Candice and Chuck Redmond from Beaumont Texas. If Noah's Ark was in the south, these two bounty hunters would find it."

"Candice is a chick, right?"

"Yes, but tough as nails and almost as lethal as you are, not too shabby on the eyes either, lad. But heed my warning Mitchell, she is all business."

"So would it be just me and the twins then?"

"No, once they are found, they will contact me with the info. If I am away, they will contact Donnie. I want Oscar to fly you down. I want you to come in under the cloak of darkness. This crew we are after, play rough and are from Texas. They will have more people on their payroll to keep them from us."

"I will call the doc tomorrow and get the stitches out as soon as I can. I will see Oscar and tell him we have work and not to disappear."

"Thanks lad, Seamus will pay you well."

"When are you heading to Boston for the wedding?"

"Cathy, Connor, Meg and I are leaving Thursday morning."

"Well, if I am still here you want a ride to the airport?"

"Thanks, Mitch, I would appreciate that." I had a beer with Joseph before jumping on my bike and heading home. Once home I went upstairs to see Oscar cutting some of the oil up on the stove.

"Hey man, where exactly is your plane stored?"

"At Bonny Doon in Santa Cruz, why?"

"Joseph has a job for us. He said it pays well. Once we get the info he is waiting for, we head out."

"And who is *we* exactly and what kind of job?"

"You, me, and Terek. Pretty sure it will be a search and destroy mission. He has these bounty hunters in Texas looking for these bandits, and once they are found, we will see what our orders are."

"You know me, Strongbow; have planes and guns, will travel. Listen, you know anyone with a baby?" I was kind of taken back and asked why.

"I need as many empty baby food jars to put the cut oil into."

"I can't think of anyone off hand."

"No worries, tomorrow I will get us a bunch at the market. I hope you like baby food as we will be eating lots." He is dead serious, fucking whacked if you ask me. The next morning, Oscar went baby food shopping. I called Doctor Mattina and asked if I could get my stitches taken out today as I am going out of town for a bit. The receptionist asked the good Doctor and she said that was fine. I had a one o'clock appointment. So I jumped in my truck and headed to see Donnie at his shop and drop off the canoe. He asked how everything went. I told him everything including Oscar killing the chick. I asked what he would have done. The exact same thing Oscar did. I was also curious about the twins and whether or not he has worked with them.

"I actually served with Chuck in Special Forces, solid guy, Mitch."

"I heard his sister is nice on the eyes and that is from Joseph of all people."

"She is that typical tall, solid looking Texas chick. But she would smile at you while slicing your dick off. She is tough as nails like her brother, but good people." My gut told me that Candice and I are going to get along just fine. I left Donnie's work and headed to see Mike Battaglia at his bar. It just opened for the day; in fact, I was the first customer but all I wanted was to see Mike. The bartender called him in the office and Mike told her to send me back. Mike asked how everything went.

"Everything was taken care of." He smiled and said let's go for lunch. Man, these Italians like to eat. I looked at my watch and told him I had to meet with his cousin at one. So, he and Rocco went and found some street meat.

It was killer sausage fully loaded, sure as fuck beats Oscar's baby food. But all I could think of was I better buy a pack of Juicy Fruit gum. Yeah onions, hot peppers and sauerkraut might not go over so well.

11

I thanked Mike for lunch, picked up a pack of gum, and then headed to see his cousin. I walked into an empty lobby, checked in and they took me into a room right away. As I was sitting there, I had this quick vision of me fucking the shit out of little doctor Ella Mattina right here. She looked smoking hot in her short skirt and white coat last time. Doc came in a couple minutes later, I still had the hard-on from the lustful vision. And in my tight jeans I had quite the bulge. She looked right at my crotch and did this little snicker and smile as she pushed her glasses back. I wanted to ask if she could do something about the swelling there, but her nurse came in with this silver tray. Its contents killed my hard on. Scissors, a needle, a small vile of liquid and these little tweezers. Doc stuck the syringe in the small bottle and drew back some fluids.

"I know you are a tough guy Mitch, so this will hurt only a bit, just some freezing." She then stuck the needle into several parts of my scalp where the stitches are. I don't care if I felt any pain. No way would she hear a peep from me. She must have hit about six spots on each side of my zipper. The needle was put back on the tray and she said that was the worst part.

Then it was time for her to go to work, her touch was fairly gentle, she kept talking to me telling me each step of the way. It only took her I would say fifteen minutes till I was stitch free. She then dampened a cloth with iodine and gently padded the back of my head. The damp cloth was now put on the tray, I looked at it and she assured me it was not blood just the color of iodine.

"I believe you doc, thanks." She smiled and I mean smiled, God she is so cute with those dimples.

"You are welcome, Mitch. Once the freezing comes out you will have some pain, do you still have some pain killers left?"

"Yeah, I am good" She then just stared at me as the nurse left the room with the tray. She laughed as she knew what I was up to and asked when was the last time I had a physical again.

Fuck it, nothing ventured, nothing gained. "If you wanna see me naked, let's do dinner and drinks first. Then I can also do a full body exam." Her face went beet red, she took a deep breath and grabbed her prescription pad and wrote something on it.

She handed me it and said, "I need you to be more discreet, as I can lose my license for this." I read the paper and it was her home phone number.

"I am as solid as they come. You have my word. What day works for you?"

"Tomorrow night I am free. Call me tonight and we can talk." I thanked her for trusting me and for giving me her number. I said I would call around seven. She smiled and then left the room. I paid the receptionist at the front and then left with quite the bounce in my step. Came home, took a painkiller, and then jerked off. Test number one, as when I woke up, I grabbed a shower and washed my hair. I got dressed and asked Oscar what he wanted to do for dinner.

"Strongbow, you have this happiness about you, what's her name?"

"No one man, just happy my stitches are out. Doc said I can start hitting the gym by the end of the week."

"I think you are bullshitting me, but what do I know?"

"Let's grab some steaks and BBQ them." After dinner I kept looking at my watch and the clock.

"You expecting someone, Strongbow?"

"Yes I am, do me a favor, here is twenty bucks, go out for beers man." Oscar took the twenty and off he went. I called right at seven and no answer, now what? Not going to chase anyone or play games right off the bat. So, I left my number, and she can call me. Went to the fridge and grabbed a beer. Thought about smoking a joint but I still had a little buzz from the painkiller I took early. Yeah, don't need to sound totally fucked up when or if she calls. By twenty after the phone rang. You get those little butterflies just like when you were a teen. It was Ella and she sounded nervous, that has to be a good sign. She apologized right off the bat saying she went to her parents for dinner. And you can't tell Italian parents you are expecting an important call as three hundred questions will come right after that and the guilt of not spending enough time with them. I said no need to apologize, all good. She asked how my head felt, I wanted to say which one, but not yet.

The more we talked the more relaxed she seemed to get. "I remember you driving up to school on your motorcycle to meet Natasha. We all thought you were dangerous, and she was nuts after the brawl at the football game. Everyone in school hated you except your Mom, me and Natasha I guess."

"You didn't hate me? Well, that is good, thanks," I said laughing.

"I will be honest with you; I had a little crush on you back then. You seemed so much more grown up then any of the other kids in school."

"I think not having a Dad around I had to grow up even faster, not much choice to be honest."

"I guess you had to. Horrible way to grow up. Is your daughter in your life?"

"No, she is not. Tash's choice, not mine." Then there was that awkward moment of silence.

"Listen Ella, I would like to take you out for dinner, maybe a movie if you are interested?"

"I am very interested. When were you thinking? I am off Wednesday so tomorrow night would work."

That kind of shocked me, I thought for sure she would say in a couple weeks and then say sorry no real free time.

"Yeah, tomorrow works. What are you craving and what movie are you interested in seeing?"

"Oddly enough, I have heard some people talk about this surf and turf restaurant in San Jose that serves shark. I have always wanted to try it. I am not worried about seeing a movie right now. I think dinner, drinks and conversation is what this doctor needs." Ella said she would make reservations for us at eight and I would pick her up shortly before seven. I asked bike, car or canoe? She laughed and said car please. She gave me her address, we talked for a little bit longer and then we called it a night. Oscar came home and looked around and asked if I was stood up. Not at all, just talked on the phone tonight, tomorrow is date night, first date with her. Oscar was all curious about her and whether or not she had any hot, fuckable friends or sisters. I said I have no idea. As I laid in bed that night, I sort of had this horrifying thought; I have never been on a date with a professional person. I don't have a clue about all these different forks you have to eat with.

I have no doubts she doesn't date people like me, recovering heroin addicts just out of prison who shot and killed two people not even forty-eight hours ago. I got up in a bit of a cold sweat, smoked a bowl and went back to bed with my overactive brain shut off.

12

The next day I was still a little nervous, so I went and sought the advice of my boss, Joseph O'Reilly He was at home and was actually shocked I came to him for dating advice. I explained she was a doctor, in typical Joseph dry Irish humor he said, "Are you sure she is not a psychiatrist, and she is doing a case study on Neanderthals, lad?"

"You are so funny you should be touring with Bob Hope, both about the same age, right?" So, after all was said and done, Joseph gave me this advice: Get dressed up including a suit jacket, a tight black t-shirt and tighter jeans won't work. Don't burp and fart at the table and it is not necessary to try and get into her pants on the first date. He said be a gentleman, open the door for her, bring her flowers and no matter how good-looking other females may be in the restaurant, don't give them the eye or time. I thanked him and hit a flower shop on the way home. Not to sound like a chick but I made sure I had an outfit to wear tonight. The scoring part will always be open for debate. I made sure Emma was clean, shiny and smelt good. I got dressed, I fucking looked sharp but I was still uptight, so I smoked a joint and it did help. I left feeling relaxed and ready for this challenge. I showed up at ten to seven. I pushed her apartment buzzer and she said she would be right down. I stood in the lobby entrance and when she got off the elevator I was totally taken back. I knew she had legs, but that white coat hid everything else. She had one killer figure and she wore her makeup and hair like Miss America herself.

"God damn, you look fucking smoking hot!" Pretty sure Joseph would want me to say it more classier then that, but fuck she look more hotter then what I even imagined. She blushed, snickered, and said thank you and said I looked very nice also.

As we walked towards Emma she said, "Sweet ride. I would expect nothing less of you, Mitch." I opened the door for her. And then when I got in, I reached into the back seat and handed her the bouquet of flowers. She was shocked but also very grateful. And she also shocked me by leaning in to kiss me and said thanks. Now, the only thing so far that threw me off was I passed her my eight-track case and told her to pick out something for us to listen to for the drive.

She asked if I had any Abba, Olivia Newton John, or the Carpenters. I was thinking if I *did* have any of them Emma would drive herself off a cliff. So, I suggested some Pink Floyd. She laughed and said she only listens to Floyd when she is high. Well, that raised both eyebrows and a huge smile. "Would you like to get high?"

"Yes, I would Mitch, I would really like that, but just some grass. Nothing heavy, okay?"

"I just do weed or oils, have you ever tried hash, weed or cherry oil?"

She just smiled and said of course. "You don't have any weed on you, do you?" Wow she sounded like she really needed a fix. And who am I to ever let my doctor down, never mind on a first date. So, I told her to take out the Ziggy Stardust eight track and open it up. She did as instructed and inside were a couple joints. I told her to help herself. She took a couple tokes, exhaled and then this huge laid-back smile came to her face and she said, "Yeah" in a funky voice and then she started to giggle. I had to ask her if she was going to Bogart the whole joint, or was she going to share it? She started laughing even harder and said sorry and then passed the doobie over to me. Now this made me finally relax. Yeah, the most relaxed I have been all night. I threw in Jethro Tull's "Thick as a Brick" and told her to enjoy it. Every time I looked over at her she was smiling like a kid waiting to see Santa. It was a goofy smile, but it made me happy. Once we got in San Jose, I asked her for directions. She sort of came out her buzz enough for us to find the restaurant. It was valet parking. I looked at the kid and said, "Don't take her for a joy ride. I have killed people for less" I was hoping Ella didn't hear me as I never want to see that side of me, but she turned to the kid and said, "He is serious."

It was nice seeing the blood leave his face. I am sure the kid will also catch a little buzz from the remnants of the joint. It was kind of cool as you walk in, and they ask for the name the reservations are under. "Doctor Gabriela Mattina." "Very good Doctor Mattina, nice to have you back with us again."

The maître'd of course eyes me up and down and is not quite sure what to make of me, or is it that the good doctor would be out with a long haired half breed like me. I give him the death stare, fucking goof. But I did keep my cool. I also have never been in a restaurant where your server puts this cloth napkin in your lap. Kind of freaked me out to be honest. I would have stabbed him with a knife but wasn't sure which knife on the table I should use. He handed me the wine list and I said show it to Ella, I am a beer and shot guy. This made Ella smile. I don't know much of her dating history, but I am willing to bet there are either successful Italians or professional people. Dinner conversation was good; she never acted any better than me. She laughed at all my silly stories, or she went really deep with full attention paid when I talked about Mom and Pam's death. Especially with it being the same week a pregnant Natasha told me she was leaving me. I have had some sincere female friends over the years. Charlene was solid and caring but Ella was different. Hard to describe exactly. She had her shark; I did the usual Filet Mignon and Lobster tail. I did try her shark, it was all right, not sure if I would order it on my own. One of the most interesting questions she did ask me that night was whether I was a 49er or Raider fan. "Raiders of course, you?"

"I actually have no choice but to cheer for the 49ers."

"Of course, you have a choice, why would anyone cheer for them? Ugh." I did a little snicker until she told me her Dad Tony Mattina, make that *Doctor* Tony Mattina is the team's head physician.

It appears her whole family is high end professionals. Her oldest brother Anthony is an orthopedic surgeon in Los Angeles. Her older sister Lisa is the head geriatric Doctor at this hospital in Palm Springs. Then there was Frances who was a year older than Ella, he was just a priest, man talk about the failure of the family ha ha! Ella was the baby of the family. If things get serious, wait till they get a load of me. After dinner we hit this dance club in San Jose. Now not sounding arrogant but I have pretty good foot coordination from karate, kickboxing and jumping rope. And I am also a pretty good dancer. But this club didn't play any rock at all. I asked what this so-called music is. "It's disco, Mitch. Where have you been?" she said laughing as she dragged me to the dance floor.

Normally on a first date I can't wait to get the chick out of a bar and back to my place to fuck her silly. Tonight, I just wanted out of here. I truly have to corrupt this girl and take her to the dark side. I think a drive up and down the coast listening to Black Sabbath, Led Zeppelin and Uriah Heep and a lot of weed should help. But I also want a second date and even more. So, I just pretended I was back in the jungle and in a fire fight with Charlie. No surrender. And once we finally left the club, by the way, my little Italian firecracker was pretty bombed, I slapped in some Aerosmith for the ride back home. "Oh, I love the song Dream On. Oh, Mitchell this has been the perfect date, thank you so much."

She just smiled straight ahead, did the odd giggle, and held my hand. After about twenty minutes or so Ella fell asleep. See I knew that disco music was not good for the soul. Time for me to do a little subliminal therapy. While she was sleeping, I kept saying over and over disco sucks. It will make you feel sick. Perhaps I had a little too much control of her brain as she woke up about five minutes from her apartment saying she has a booming headache. I looked at her as I wondered whether or not this was her way of saying "Had fun, but not enough fun for you to come up and fuck me, now go home." But her eyes were beet red and I know it wasn't a show she was putting on. My next fear was that she would get sick in my car; don't care how sexy you are that doesn't go over well at all with me. Yeah, she was quiet, but I kept asking if she was ok, like a trooper she said it was the wine and too much dancing. It took a lot for me not to say it was the music. We pulled up to the front of her building; the doorman came out and opened the car door for her. She thanked me, gave me a kiss, and said she had a really good time. I asked if she wanted to do it again, she smiled and said of course. She went to walk inside the doorman when I got out of the car and said,

"Hey doc, take a couple of aspirins and call me in the morning." She laughed and said good advice. I drove home feeling pretty positive about the date; I may not have gotten laid. Joseph would have been proud of me. I came home and Oscar had some moaner in his bedroom, fuck she was loud. At least one of us scored. I turned on the stereo, smoked a couple joints, and had a couple more beers so I wouldn't hear Miss Moanalot when I finally crawled into bed. What I did hear the next morning was the phone ringing. I looked at my alarm clock and it was just after nine, this better be important.

"Morning Mitch it is Ella, I would like to say thanks for a great date. I am sorry that I passed out on you, and I would like to make it up to you right now if you are interested?"

I had to wait a second to shake the cobwebs still formed in my brain. "You mean this morning or another time?"

She laughed and said, "Right now silly, come by."

"Sure, let me grab a shower and I will be right over."

"You can shower here; don't make me start without you." No cobwebs left now. I burned those fuckers.

"I will be there in ten unless I get a speeding ticket along the way." I had a glass of orange juice and brushed my teeth; I have a feeling I will need my energy and nothing worse than bad breath to spoil the mood.

As I left the washroom I heard the phone ringing, I wonder if it is Ella wanting me to bring some weed over.

13

"Hey baby, talk to me."

"I am not your baby, Mitchell, I am your boss. Listen, the Redmond twins found one of the brothers we are looking for in Texas, Chuck is keeping an eye on him now. Donnie will be at your place in thirty. Get a hold of Oscar and I want you guys in the air as quickly as possible. Pack lots of ammo and weapons, going to be a shit show, lad." I looked to Oscar's door and it was shut, which is a good sign even if I don't hear miss Moanalot going off like some whore. I told Joseph I will call him back, let me see if Oscar is around. He told me to be quick about it. So, I knocked on the door and I heard the whore say go away. This is my house, who the fuck does she think she is? I opened up the door and walked in, I told Oscar to wake up. This cunt sat right up and told me to get the fuck out right now. So, I did. I walked right into my room, pulled out a 9MM and stormed back into Oscar's room and pointed the gun right at her.

"You open that fucking mouth of yours one more time and I will blow your head off, you stunned fucking cunt." She was now scared shitless; Oscar was now wide awake. I told Oscar to get her out of here, the Irishman wants us in the air, Donnie is on his way over. He looks at the twat and tells her to get her ass in gear. She is now starting to tear up, Oscar gives her a smack and reminds her she is just a play date. She leaves the apartment bawling with her shirt on inside out. I start to pack and break out all my weapons. Boxes upon boxes of ammo. About ten minutes later the doorbell goes, it is Donnie. He comes upstairs and asks if all is good. I say yeah. The phone rings and I answer it. It is Ella asking where the hell I am, I totally brain cramped. God, time to think quick.

"I am so sorry; I was just going to call you. I have a confession to make Ella, I just don't work at the bar and own the t-shirt store. I am also a bounty hunter, a job that I want kept under wraps as most people see us as bad people going after worse people. My boss just called and this guy we have been tracking for months was just found in Louisiana. He raped this teenager and skipped his bond. I really want to bring this bastard to justice. I have to leave right now as I have a plane to catch. I promise I will make it up to you." Donnie and Oscar just stared at me as I had dead air on the other line.

"Please be careful, Mitch. And yes, bring him back for justice. Call me once you are home, and thanks once again for last night. And yes, I will still make up to you for bailing on you last night."

"Thanks Ella, I really appreciate that, will make sure I am back quicker than ever now." I hung up the phone and both Donnie and Oscar shook their heads.

"You think quick on your feet, Mitch." Said Donnie.

"If you think about it, we are hunting for these brothers, so I am sort of telling the truth."

"Never really thought about it that way, and we are bringing them to justice Seamus "The Shark" Finn style." Donnie turned to Oscar and said we need to fly in as close we can to Laredo Texas without drawing the eyes of local or federal law enforcement. Oscar nodded his head yes and broke out this book and set of maps.

"I know a private airport named Lewis about forty minutes from there, let me make some calls. It will cost us to land there." Donnie said that was fine, make the calls. Donnie then looked at the map and said to me perfect. I asked what else we needed to know about these three brothers as Joseph didn't really say too much.

"Paul, Jim, and Eddie Murdoch. Real bad asses, they move dope back and forth from Mexico to the states. If I know Seamus, he doesn't like dealing with others, never gets his hands that dirty, I am sure the Murdoch brothers didn't know who they were ripping off. Paul is being held in a jail in Laredo awaiting a bail hearing. We will put up the bail and then snatch him up. Get info from whatever means possible as to the location of his two brothers. Seamus wants all three dead."

"How do we prove we have killed them?"

"We bring their identification back with us."

Oscar got off the phone and said it will cost us two hundred dollars to land there. Donnie said that is not a problem. He asked Oscar around what time we will be landing. Oscar got out a pen and paper and did some math. "We need to stop in Nevada, Phoenix, and Laredo for fuel. We need a good head wind; I would say nine hours." Donnie then pulled out his little black book and made a couple calls. First one was to Sean Quinn, I heard him give him my address.

I asked what was up. "Joseph wants all hands on deck for this one. We will be outgunned down there, Mitch." The second call was to Candice, he asked if there were any new changes with our person of interest. He said good to hear, he also told her where we are landing and be ready to pick up four of us. He also told her if he makes bail to kidnap him and hold him until we arrive. The doorbell rang and I went downstairs and there, wearing a set of combats was Sean Quinn, yeah nothing says heat score like a monster of a man wearing combats, carrying a rifle case and army duffel bag.

I asked him to come upstairs as we are almost ready to leave. "Nyah is outside; she is driving us in my station wagon." My heart sort of dropped, so many wrong scenarios racing through my head right now.

"I will go out and tell her to come up also." Fuck I just wanna make sure she drove here without any direction, the less dear old crazy dad knows the better it will be for me and her.

"Let her stay in the car Strongbow, the less she knows the better it is for me, and all of us." Nyah looked over and saw me talking to her dad. She smiled and waved, I smiled and waved back and swore I heard Sean growl. As we walked upstairs, I asked Sean why he brought his rifle upstairs, why not just keep it in the car.

"Donnie said one of the bounty hunters is looking for a FN C1, if Donnie thinks it is in good enough, they will buy it. I don't think him looking at it on the sidewalk would be cool." Sure, as fuck as soon as we got upstairs Sean took out the FN and showed it to Donnie. He opened it up, checked out the sights, pulled back on the breach and said perfect. Chuck will take it. He also pulled out a Uzi, Donnie once again checked it out and said Candice will love this. Sean then looked around the apartment. Like really scanned it. All I kept thinking was fuck I hope Nyah left nothing here like say a personal hair clip. Oscar said we better get moving as the plane is being filled as we speak. We all came downstairs carrying rifle cases and either duffel or gym bags. Nyah got out and opened up the back of the wagon, she gave Donnie and I a hug.

Oscar asked Nyah where his hug was; Sean got into his face and said, "NO hugs for you." I patted Oscar on the back and said let's get in the car. Sean drove with Nyah in the front while Donnie, Oscar and I jumped in the back. I whispered in Oscar's ear that Sean is overly protective of Nyah and he will kill him like he was an ant at a picnic, nothing more than a nuisance. Speaking of nuisance, Nyah popped in a Jackson 5 eight track. And of course, she had to sing. I asked Donnie if he had any ear plugs, Sean turned around and shot me the dirtiest fucking look. Yeah, we couldn't get to the airport fast enough. Once we got there, Donnie and Oscar got out and handed this guy an envelope of cash. The guy then walked and told us to pull up beside this hangar. We unloaded all our gear. Nyah wished her dad happy hunting with a long hug. All of us now look at him.

"Thanks, baby. Hopefully the deer in Montana don't hear us sneaking up on them." She tells all of us to take care of her dad; she shakes Oscar's hand, hugs Donnie, hugs me and whispers, "We are fucking once you get home, mister". That totally cut me off guard as I got a hard-on and dry mouth. I am tongue tied and blush, or at least it felt like it. I couldn't look over at Sean and Donnie gave me the one eyebrow up look. Fuck, you would think it was Joseph. We then heard a plane come out from the side of the hangar. At first, I thought it was just a four seater single prop plane. But it wasn't. It was a Dehavilland DHC 6-100 dual prop plane. It was huge and sounded bad ass.

"How the fuck did you ever afford a plane like this Oscar?"

"High stakes poker game in Montreal, I was moving blow at the time into Canada. This owner of an iron ore mine and I were the last two at the table. I put up twenty-five keys of coke, he put up his plane. My straight flush beat his four cowboys and a deuce" I remember in San Quentin he was one of the best poker players I ever met, you don't get lucky winning, but you do get lucky that no one kills you while taking their cash or in this case, their plane. While we loaded up the plane, Oscar checked all the shit on a plane that a pilot needs to check. He then got in and told me to jump in the front and handed me the maps we would need. Donnie asked him when the last time he flew was.

"About two years ago, but it is like riding a bike. The biggest difference is when you fall off your bike you get back up. In a plane, you crash and die." Oscar then asked the tower for clearance for takeoff. He told all of us to make sure seat belts are on really well. Within a couple minutes he heard back from the tower and approached the beginning of the runway. He revved up the engines, let out a big *woo*! and he was flying down the runway full speed until we were airborne. I still get a rush taking off into the great wild blue yonder, for Oscar he was all ear-to-ear smile. I guess for him it is also a sure sign of his prison freedom. You know in his next life he is coming back as a free bird not a caged one. One the first leg of the journey he asked if I wanted to fly the plane. I said sure, Sean piped up rather loudly and told Oscar if he wants to teach me, do it when he is not in the plane.

"Are we a white-knuckle passenger big guy?" Oscar then did a quick nosedive for a couple thousand feet before pulling the plane up. Sean was swearing his head off and heading to the cockpit with a gun in his hand.

Donnie stopped him and reminded Sean that if he kills Oscar then we will die for sure. I told Oscar that Sean has zero sense of humor and Donnie, and I can't contain the big man if he gets into the kill zone. Oscar said he was sorry and will fly the plane normal. Oscar also said we will have to all get out of the plane when it is being refueled. Nevada and Arizona were no problems at all. But when we landed in Laredo, we had this nosy wanna be cop snooping around the plane as it was being filled. He was a whiny little man, early thirties maybe, short and stocky. He asked what are we doing in Texas, Donnie took charge and told him we were going hunting. He then asked if we had permits to hunt here. When Donnie said no, he said we are going to be in big trouble then. Stupid fuck, didn't even see Sean land a punch that knocked him cold. We just looked at each other as Sean carried the knocked-out mouthpiece into the plane. That was our cue to get our wheels in the air as soon as possible. Sean taped the guy's hands together and tape over his mouth, Once we leveled off, Oscar looked at Sean and said now what. "You fly the plane and be ready for a pressure drop, boys put your belts on."

The guy was now starting to come around, Sean pointed at him and said, "You nosy little fucking wanker, see what happens when you poke your nose in where it don't belong, funny you where telling us we are going to be in trouble, who is the one in trouble now?" Sean looked out one of the windows and grabbed the guy by his shirt towards the door.

"Oscar, you have a hold of that steering wheel thing?"

"I do, but don't do anything stupid." Sean said fuck you, opens the door and then threw the guy out of the plane. We did another nosedive with the pressure of the door being open. Sean struggled but managed to close it. Oscar was eventually able to get a hold of the plane. He looked at me and just shook his head no.

I just put my finger to my lips and shook my head no. I have heard rumors how ruthless and unforgiving Sean can be, they left out plain fucking nuts. He could have killed all of us. We landed at that private airport. Donnie gave Oscar an envelope full of cash for them to store our plane. They all knew Oscar, which is good. If all hell breaks loose we will want out of Texas as quick and secretly as we can.

Donnie spotted a black cargo van with someone waving at us. He smiled and told us to grab our gear and start walking towards our ride. With the van running and it being nighttime the headlights blocked who our ride was, all I could see was the silhouette. Donnie then said, "Candice, you sexy angel, give me a hug." Candice was tall and solid looking, at least five ten and about a buck seventy, killer ass that stuck out in her tight jeans. But when she turned to me as Donnie introduced me as I was taken aback how fucking beautiful she was. Not *girl* beautiful but solid chiseled facial features, killer tan, thick lips, doesn't look like no bounty hunter I ever saw. And when she hugged me, she was strong, that too caught me off guard.

God bless Texas!

Donnie then introduced her to Oscar, but she just stared and smiled at me. She made eye contact with me the whole time she hugged Oscar and then Sean. She was like a Goddess, a Goddess warrior, total turn on. We put all our gear in the van, Donnie told me to sit in the back as he wanted all of Candice's undivided attention. He could tell there were sparks just a flying. "So, please give my guys the whole low down on these brothers."

"They are the Murdoch brothers. Three of them in total, Jim the drunk, is currently being held in the Laredo city jail on a five-hundred-dollar bail for busting up a bar.

14

His two brothers Eddie and Paul managed to escape before all the cops arrived. More than likely, they fled to Mexico. Paul is the ringleader, an arrogant fuck. Eddie is sly and the most violent brother. They are small-time thieves and drug dealers. They rip off local tourists, will rob them and any small-time dealers smuggling across the border. They will take their dope and kill them. They know better than to go after any of the cartel smugglers, they are basically like vultures."

Sean then asked Donnie what happened with Seamus guys and these scum brothers. "Word on the street is that these boys are originally from Gloucester. They have done odd jobs for Seamus and his crew in the past. They had to leave the northeast as they had become heat scores, large heat scores for their reckless actions. They contacted one of Seamus captains and said they came across ten kilos of pure uncut coke that they couldn't unload locally. Sounds to me as if they robbed someone they shouldn't have. Seamus sent some guys to do the deal, not sure what happened next but there was a gun fight with the Murdoch boys, and one of Seamus' men was killed and another wounded. And here we are kids. Seamus wants them all dead and if possible, makes them suffer first. Personally, I would also like to find the ten kilos of the coke, a bonus for us. As Donnie was telling us the events that led us to be here, Candice kept looking in her rear-view mirror at me. I am glad Joseph is not here as after we kill these bastards; I am going to fuck the shit out of her. She drove us to this hotel that was right across from the police station. Chuck her brother was up there sitting on the balcony with a pair of binoculars.

"Donnie how are you?" said Chuck. "I am good brother, how are you? Let me introduce Sean, Oscar, and Mitch"

"Quite the fucking United Nations crew there, Terek. Welcome to Texas, boys." As we all went to shake Chuck's hand it occurred to me this is the first time I have been in Texas since Lucy and I were here, what a fucked-up adventure that was. Chuck handed us three photo mug shots of the Murdoch boys, he said don't ask where I got it from. He said let's just say not all cops are fans of them. I studied the pics really closely, and without being told who was who, I banged them all off. The twins and Sean all seemed impressed. For me it is a God giving talent if there was a God. Donnie asked how long has Jim been locked up for and how much is bail?

"He has been in custody for three days now and bail is five hundred bucks."

"I don't think his brothers are cheaping out on the bail, I think they know they are wanted men and gave up Jim, fucking losers. I think we should post bail. Sit back and see where he goes, the odds are he will lead us right to his brothers." Now for the next issue and yes, it is a problem, which one of us is going to post bail? Oscar and I are fresh out of San Quentin, Donnie is a full patch with the Hell Hounds so you know the cops will have pics of him, and Sean is more than likely an illegal immigrant. Chuck is a bounty hunter so the odds are someone might know him. What about Candice wearing a wig and a dress, yeah, they won't recognize her.

She was a little reluctant at first as she is a cowgirl first, jeans and boots not a dress. She did look at me and asked if I wanted to see her in a dress. I really wanted to answer naked would be my first choice, but pretty sure her brother wouldn't appreciate that. "I think you would look amazing in a dress, go for it."

She smiled at me and said done. She asked me to go with her and pick it out. Oscar smiled, Sean frowned, and Donnie shook his head as did Chuck. I said sure. As soon as I got in the hall, Candice pulled me in and started to neck with me. We are talking hard core tongue wet sloppy kisses. I whispered we should get away from here. She agreed so we held hands going down the stairs and giggled like school kids with their first crush. We necked a little bit more before she started the van and I thought we were heading to the dress store, but she had other plans and within a couple minutes I knew exactly what those plans were.

She drove us out of town to a secluded area. We pulled off to the side of the road and before you knew it, we were in the back of the van necking once again and undressing each other. Fuck, this was hot. She was stroking my cock as I started to finger her really hard. I knew she liked it rough. Once she was thoroughly soaked, she told me to fuck her hard. I did as instructed and showed no mercy as I slammed her as hard as I could, I was biting her nipples, the more rough I was becoming the more excited she became. Surprisingly for a first time fuck I held back longer than she did, she had a couple solid orgasms before I felt my ejaculation build up.

I asked her where she wanted me to cum, she said in her mouth. Fuck, that excitement made me shoot a monster load and a half, right down her eagerly awaiting throat. That was so hot; fuck, I felt like a teen sneaking a quickie in. Candice took my whole load and swallowed every last drop. It was also a hot day, so we were both drenched in sweat. She hid all aspects of us having sex, the sweating will have to come up with an explanation. I am just so happy Joseph didn't come along and supervise this whole mission as I would be sitting in the hotel room with a hard-on only fantasizing about her. We drove back into town just smiling at each other, I am still in awe over what just happened. We did find a dress shop and beside it was a Harley Davidson shop, perfect as I grabbed Donnie and I t-shirts from there. I walked back into the dress shop and there was Candice, is this white sexy summer dress, no bra, jet black wig looking like some silver screen actress. Betty Paige, or Jane Russell came to mind. "You look beautiful, hon."

"Why thank you, Mitch. Yeah, I do look not bad if I do say so. I would fuck myself." The sales lady looked at her as if she had a huge turd in her mouth. Chicks swear, get over it. I paid cash for the dress and asked for a receipt which I will give to Joseph. We drove back to the hotel room and all eyes were turned at Candice as she walked in the room.

Oscar the horny bastard said, "You look like Helen of Troy; your face could launch a thousand ships." She liked the attention, Chuck, not so much, as he shot Oscar a look, I wonder what Chuck would shoot me if he knew I just fucked his sister, not just a look, I am sure a .308 shell from the barrel of FN C1 he just bought from Donnie. Donnie told her only one more thing would look better with that dress, curiously she asked what? Donnie went into his duffel bag and passed her the Uzi submachine gun. Her eyes and smile lit up like it was Christmas. She looked ten times hotter than Patty Hearst. Donnie gave her the cash to go down and bail out Jim. She will say she works for a facetious bail bond company whose name they have used in the past.

She will leave a note for Jim saying, "You know where to meet us, P & E." She is then to head to her van where Oscar and I will be waiting for her. Donnie and Sean are with Chuck in his car facing an opposite direction waiting for Jim to leave. We will follow him and see exactly where he goes. I am really hoping the bogus note leads us to his brothers. We can kill them all and then I can take another round or ten out of Candice before heading home. It had to be at least 110 degrees, we were not in the shade, and I was really starting to sweat. About thirty minutes after Candice posted bail a red Ranchero with black racing stripes and a blower sticking out of the engine hood pulls up in front of the police station. The sweat is burning my eyes and I can't really see the driver, I just see them wearing a cowboy hat. Within two minutes Jim leaves the police station, he looks in all directions of the street before getting in the Ranchero. They drove past us as we all ducked down. Candice started the van and we started to follow them through the streets of Laredo. I was also shocked just how big Laredo is. All the traffic did help us blend in and not be spotted. Chuck would take lead, and then we would take lead following him. We really didn't want them to realize they were being followed as I can't see him giving up to us so easily. The real question is does he have any firearms in the Ranchero. After about eight blocks the car pulled over and Jim got out and used a pay phone. Whoever he was talking to you could tell it got a bit heated as Jim slammed the phone down and punched the phone booth. He took off again, Donnie headed right to the phone booth, he motioned us over and said to follow him and he would catch up. So, we did as instructed. The car now seemed to be driving more erratic, does he know now that they are being followed. I said to Candice if they get to a straight away on the outskirts of town, we won't be able to catch them. I could tell the driver of Murdoch's car kept looking in the rear-view mirror; yeah we are spotted for sure.   She looked at me and said decision time.

"We get to a dissolute place Candice ram them. Oscar, you take the driver, if he puts up a fight put a bullet in him; I will take Murdoch and throw him in the back of the van. Candice, you back us up with your Uzi. Once he is inside, we will cuff him and tape his mouth. Remember we need Jim alive." For the next twenty minutes it was a cat and mouse game through the streets. Candice drove like Richard

Petty, every time the Ranchero had a straight away and you thought they would escape she would cut them off. Lots of metal was being slammed and I knew they had no weapons as they would have fired by now. I did however have my silencer and once we were in the industrial part of town, I shot out both rear tires. Sparks were now starting to come from them driving on the rims. Candice saw we were fast approaching a set of railway tracks, so she drove past them and cut them off. The car was trying its best to back up but was hung up on the tracks. Go time, we all jumped out. Oscar as instructed made a beeline to the driver, Candice opened up the vans side door while I chased Jim who was now on foot. I told him to halt, or I will blow his head off, he kept running. I even fired a shot into the ground just ahead of him and he didn't stop, fucker! After about two hundred yards I was close enough to tackle him. Note to self, *more cardio at the gym*. I jumped and grabbed a hold of his shoulders and bulldogged him into the ground face first. He was almost knocked out when I flipped him over and gave him a head butt and sent him to dream land. I threw him over my shoulder and carried him back to the van. The driver was not one of the brothers, he looked Mexican and was beaking off at Oscar and Candice saying he is going to come back with his boys and fuck us up.

While still holding Jim over my shoulder I raised up my handgun and fired two shots in his head. Yeah, that shut him up. I told Oscar to check the vehicle for any info on the whereabouts of the other two Murdoch brothers. I threw a knocked-out Jim in the back and told Candice get him cuffed and tape then we need to get as far away as soon as possible. I helped Oscar and found not a fucking thing; within two minutes we were mobile. I told Candice we can't go back to Laredo, cops will be looking for us. "I actually have some solid people in Asherton; it is about seventy minutes from here. A ranch where we can deal with this guy. Chuck knows to call there if I go AWOL, it is like our designated safe house for this job."

The ranch was off the one back road by at least half a mile. Really secluded, perfect. We stayed in the van as Candice walked to the front porch, she was pretty fearless as all kinds of dogs were barking at her, big mean looking dogs. I thought I might have to jump out and shoot a few if they started to attack her. Eventually this very solid guy came out wearing an army combat coat, black t-shirt and carrying a 12-gauge shotgun over his shoulder, he had a long beard and even when hugging Candice didn't really smile. He also kept his eyes on us in the van the whole time.

The two of them started to walk towards us and I picked up him wearing a set of dog tags, yeah, they matched his cowboy boots, the kind with the silver toes and spurs. He was also chewing a wad of chewing tobacco. "Mitch, Oscar, I want you to meet my friend, Josh Green." We both shook his hand and I asked where he served. He spit out some of the tobacco and said, First Marine Recon." This guy doesn't smile and doesn't fully open his mouth when he talks. He eyed us up and down again and asked if we served.

"We were both 506 infantry, 101st Airborne, 75th LRRP, 5th Special Forces Group and eventually SOG." This brought a smidgen of a smile to his face; he just nodded and then spit out some more tobacco juice.

"We have someone in the back of the van, Josh. The boys here are going to try and get some information from him. Chuck and the rest of their crew will be calling and asking for us. Let them know we have the package and to come here. We will make it worth your while."

"How much worth my while?"

"Two hundred bucks worth your while, Josh."

"That's almost worth my while. Three hundred if I have to bury his body. And you two will be doing the digging." I stuck out my hand and Josh said deal. I could the way he shook my hand with that extra force he and Candice were lovers at one point, definitely pissing on my leg. Josh said to bring Jim out to the barn and chain him until the rest of the crew arrives. Jim was still out cold so chaining him was easy. Oscar was the newbie, so he stayed with him while Josh, Candice and I went inside the house to wait for the call from Chuck. The ranch house itself was old, really old. But it was not neglected at all. Josh gave us both a beer and asked what Jim did. I looked at Candice as I am pretty sure Donnie really doesn't want me telling a complete stranger our mission down here. She nodded yes but I can see Donnie's mug shaking his head no.

"I must respectfully decline. I am not at liberties to discuss why. Now, when my boss gets here you can ask him, not saying he will answer you, though." Josh just nodded his head yes and then looked back at Candice. By the time we were finishing our beers, the phone rang, Josh answered it and said yep, just a minute as he handed Candice the phone. She said we have the package here to drop by. Candice said Chuck, Donnie and Sean will be here in about an hour. Josh told Candice she looked really nice in that dress she was wearing. He looked at me and told me to wait outside in the barn with

Oscar. Well, I am pretty sure the fee now involves him and Candice getting it on. I asked Josh if I can bring a beer out for Oscar. "I am curious, what nationality is that guy first off?"

"He is American, but born in Syria."

"So, he is not a Jew or south American right?"

"Not at all."

"Yeah, bring him a beer. Don't come back in till I tell you." I brought Oscar out a beer; Jim was still passed out. We sat in a hot barn and listened to Josh fucking Candice, it may have been good for Josh, but it got silent after not even a minute, quick draw McGraw. Oscar said he would fuck her for an hour straight and give her a shit load of orgasms. He asked if I would fuck her. "I already fucked her when we were dress shopping."

"You cocksucker, Strongbow. Good for you brother, any good?"

"Yeah, she is very aggressive, took my whole load in her mouth so she didn't come back dripping cum through her dress." Oscar started to laugh and said he wants a go with her also.

"Fuck, man; that is up to her, by the way Josh is kind of fucked, and Chuck seems pretty protective. So, time your move when we are away from here. Something tells me Josh has buried more than one person out here." Oscar finished his beer and I said let's see if we can wake this guy up. Couldn't find any water, Josh said no going back in the house, so I whipped my dick out and started pissing on Jim, flashbacks of Herschel's wedding. Oscar was laughing so hard he said he had to pee now, yep all over Jim who was now coming around. His face was a bit of a mess from me headbutting him, nose was busted, and he was moaning trying to come out fully from his knockout slumber. Oscar said he is moaning longer than Candice did. I couldn't stop laughing and I told Oscar that I have to get my mean face on, stop it. I also knew I had to trick him and let him know we had no plans on killing him. He was, after all, knocked out cold when I killed his driver friend.

"Jim, do you know why you are here?" He said fuck you two, and spit at me. Wrong move, I threw a solid left hook right into his sternum. You heard the wind leave his lungs. He was gasping for air, I put my hand on his windpipe and asked if he wanted to die.

His eyes watered, showed fear as he shook his head no. "Then tell us where the coke is, and you will live."

"What coke? I don't know what you are talking about, honest." I gave him another shot in the gut.

"Do you think I flew three thousand miles to hear bullshit? Every time you answer me wrong you will feel pain. In Nam I did this for days at a time when torturing VC Officers. And right now, we are not even into the torture aspect, fuck Jim, this is just foreplay before we fuck you really hard, understood? Now, once again where is the pure uncut coke that you boasted to the stupid fucking Micks up north."

Jim looked confused when I said this, my plan is working. If he thinks Seamus sent us he knows he will die, now he is not sure. "You don't work for him?"

"Not at all, you have my word, I am half Sioux and half German, Oscar here is Syrian." Jim now looked at Candice who was headed our way.

"And she is a bounty hunter from here in Texas. We are just mercs working out of Long Beach. Our boss just wants the coke, that's all. I know if we kill you then there goes the chance of us getting the coke. Now my boss is on his way over. He is one sick son of a bitch. He will rip out your toenails one at a time to get the info, he is one sick, twisted, demented fuck. You won't wanna deal with him and his anger issues." Candice asked if he is talking, I said not yet, let's go for a walk. I told her our game plan, she said it was smart, he is a drunk, offer him a beer.

I told her to grab three, tell Josh I will buy him a case. "Please tell me I am a better fuck than him?"

"He has never had wind or stamina, always let's loose in under two minutes. Fuck, he is like a twelve-year-old boy. I need you to fuck me again Mitch, you know Oscar is a good-looking guy, maybe I will take you two both on, what do you think?"

"As long as our balls and dick don't touch, I am cool, Oscar is a sexual machine, he will be in, maybe we can spit roast you?" Candice did this huge smile, "I knew there was a reason I got wet the first time I saw you, Strongbow."

"You better go and get us the beers before I start jerking off right here and now, baby."

"Such a smooth talker, Strongbow." Candice came right out with three beers and following behind her with once again no enthusiasm was Josh. I noticed Candice has now undone the buttons on her dress top so you can see her nipples. She took a sip of a beer and spilled some down her exposed chest, her nipples popped right out. Jim's mouth now dropped wide open. She smiled and lifted the beer can to his lips and told him to drink. He drank the whole can back in one large and long drink.

"Jim, tell the boys where the coke is, and I will personally give you a case of beer. Blindfold you and drop you off near a highway."

"I don't have the coke, my brother Paul does."

"And where is Paul right now Jim?" said Candice. Before he could answer, the dogs started going crazy. Chuck's car was coming with the rest of our crew. Jim showed fear once again. He started to shake as his eyes were now glued on the upcoming car. Candice tried to reassure Jim all is well, he totally zoned out on her. It was like the grim reaper was about to make an appearance, in some respects, he would be right. I even found myself staring at the approaching car. Josh walked towards it with his shotgun over his shoulder once again and ordered the dogs to halt and head to their pens. Fuck, they all did, impressive. Chuck got out and shook Josh's hand and gave him a hug. Then the dark wings of death got out, Donnie was on the passenger front. And the big Irishman, Sean Quinn got out of the back. Josh pointed towards the barn, and I heard Jim say *God help me* and he was now trying to break free of his chains. Yeah, whatever confidence has been built up, is now gone, long gone actually. I told Oscar to keep a close eye on Jim as I wanted to tell the boys what I have been doing so far. All liked it but Sean, well he didn't really say anything, just growled. I asked Donnie what the deal with the phone booth was.

"I got the operator and said I was Texas Ranger Butler and I needed to know the last number called. She gave me a bit of a hard time until I told her, and escaped murder convict just used the phone. Then she gave me the number and town. It is in Mexico. Cloete, you know it Josh?"

"Yeah, it is an old coal mining town, not that far from here. Maybe an hour if we do it legal, an hour and a half if we want to sneak in."

"I will pay you, Josh. We just need to know whereabouts both brothers are at" So, the five of us headed back to the barn.

"Jim, this is my boss, I told him how you have been helping us, which in turn, helps yourself from being hurt. We just need to know who has the coke, which brother?" Jim looked at Donnie and said, "You will let me go?"

"Yeah, I will let you go. I just need to know if they are both in Cloete and the addresses of them?" He was totally stunned. We knew that one or both were in Cloete. It had him turn white.

"Are you going to kill them? They are all I have left in this world."

"No as long as they give us the coke without a fight." Once again, he was having second thoughts. He started to shake his head no. Donnie reminded him that we are the ones who bailed him out of jail.

"Your brothers were going to let you rot in that jail, Jim. I think we are being more than fair. When we leave here, you will be free."

"I think you are bullshitting me. You are all here for revenge not just the coke. They are family. I would rather die than give them up." As we were all looking at each other, Sean Quinn said fuck this twirp and went into his duffel bag. None of us knew what he was going to pull out and use on him, and what he did next shocked all of us. He pulled out a propane torch and lit it.

He told me and Oscar to hold him still. He now stood over Jim and said, "You wanna be loyal to those two bastards and die for them, then it will be a painful death, last chance wanker, give us where they are at." Jim was crying and shaking his head no.

Sean was pure evil, "This is how we would get the English to rat at who was betraying us. Old school IRA truth serum." Sean went right for Jim's crotch with the lit torch. The screams of pain coming from Jim were deafening. And the stench of burning skin, clothes and pubes almost made me sick.

"Now tell us where they are, or I will burn every inch of flesh on your body." As Sean headed back to his groin area with the torch, Jim gave up his brothers. Donnie asked him who all might be in the house, weapons everything we would need to know including where the coke is at. After Donnie was satisfied with the answers he asked if he could now be set free, Jim said he would find his own way to a hospital.

Sean said, "I will set you free, free in hell to join your brothers also.' Sean pulled out his 9MM and popped three rounds into his chest.

"Let's bury this bastard and track down his brothers." Donnie looked at Josh and asked if he could help us get across the border undetected.

"First off, big man, that was fucking brutal, I loved it. Yes, I can, and I do know that town. Perfect spot for someone to hide. It was a coal mining town. Lots of rough boys and Mexican gangs run it. No cops or soldiers, it is like something from the old west. I do have some contacts there also. We will leave around midnight tonight."

He looked down at Jim and said, "I will show you where we need him buried." Donnie told me and Oscar to give Josh a hand. We threw Jim's lifeless body on the back of a pickup truck, Josh said to grab two shovels and a bag of Lyme he keeps for such an occasion. We drove on his property for about five miles from his house. Dug the grave, threw in the body, and poured Lyme over it. Threw dirt on top of him and then headed back to the house for a couple well warranted cold beers. Josh said he just slaughtered a cow that morning and would we like the freshest steaks we ever tasted. All of us like our meat so he threw a couple bags of coal in this half oil drum. Poured some gas on it and then fired it up. Even the spuds he wrapped in foil and the corn was all from his land, I was impressed. Candice made up a salad for us. All of us like our steak the same way, medium rare. As we were at the dinner table, by the way, no grace was said. Josh told Donnie they have worked together in the past. Donnie looked at him and said he looked kind of familiar and to refresh his memory.

"I would say three years ago a couple guys from your motorcycle club were murdered and robbed. The killers delivered a pair of heads, that were Hell Hounds in a gym bag to George Payment. That's who hired me to help you guys look for the killers." Holy fuck my stomach flipped, I was that robber and killer they were looking for. Your breathing becomes all fucked up. Is this whole Seamus Finn robbery a rouse to get me down here and kill me on Texas soil? Now, I also know to follow conversation without getting my two cents in and drawing attention to myself.

Donnie then pointed to me and said, "George married Mitch's cousin, Val." That is not what I thought was going to be said next. I am fucking dying to know what all was found out about these killers, but how? After dinner, Josh asked if we all had phony identification in case we do get nabbed. We all did, including the twins. I was a little hesitant that Candice would be coming with us. But Donnie said nothing makes people drop their guard than a hot chick. Donnie suggested it has been a long day; we should all grab some sleep. Of course, Oscar and I were relegated to sleep in the barn. Before I closed my eyes, I had visions of me beheading both Hell Hounds and setting them on fire, but the visions were like from a movie. To me it didn't seem real, that whole heroin addiction rampage with Lucy was anything but real, a total nightmare at times. What I wouldn't give to hear her voice one more time.

I closed my eyes and heard in a very soft whisper, "Mitch, Mitch." The ranch was dead quiet, my heart was now beating out of my chest, what the fuck? Were the mushrooms around the steak of the magical variety. I then felt a tug on my pants that was real. Then Candice's head popped up with a big smile. She put her index finger over my mouth and undid my pants. She started to play with my cock until I was nice and hard. She then gave me a wink and got on top of me.

As she was starting to ride me, she undid the buttons on the top of her dress to fully expose her breasts. I have this feeling she likes to play rough. So, I started to twist her nipples, her eyes lit right up, and she started to ride me even harder, I knew it, I fucking knew it. Next thing I see Oscar's head pop up; he goes, "Fuck Strongbow, I thought you were jerking off at first."

"I am busy, you heard Donnie, get some rest." He looked at Candice, then me, laughed and then he disappeared. She rode me hard, full thrusts, the girl has a lot of power in her hips. And when she comes, she has the most intense look come over her face. Not sure how many times she did cum, but when I finally came, fuck, I passed out cold. Donnie woke up me and Oscar just before midnight. Josh had this 1963 jet black Jeep Wagoneer. It had nothing silver on it at all. Nothing that would or could reflect under the light of the moon. And just like on a special ops mission us too had nothing that would reflect. Josh even had black face paint for us to wear. You would think we were back in Nam, well except the fact we have a hot chick tagging along. Josh told us we must worry about bandits and the army when sneaking under the cover of darkness. When it comes to bandits, can't deal with them, just kill them all and when it comes to the army; most of the officers are corrupt. We will try and buy our way in and if not, just like the bandits, kill 'em all, Currahee!

It was tight quarters, but I have been stuck in the back of an APC full of sweaty dirty grunts, so things have been worse. For the next two hours everything was an off-road adventure. I couldn't really see too much, but Josh knows these back road twists and turns, through rivers, totally trippy to say the least. He only stopped once. "As soon as I drive ahead, we are in Mexico, we are illegally crossing and could all be sentenced to the rest of our lives in a Mexican prison. Everyone willing to go ahead?" I almost started laughing, he was so serious, what the fuck? We had to all say yes before he would put the vehicle in gear. For the next forty-five minutes all eyes were on everything to the front, side and rear of us. At least as far as a visual goes. This is also the first time I have been back in Mexico since I killed Janssen's. I can still hear and visualize him raping her. She was never the same after that. And a part of me also died that day. I truly hope that fucker is rotting away in hell with no dick, and one hell of a headache where I stabbed him. Lucky in a way for us there was only a sliver moon showing. We eventually made our way to this older dirt road. Josh said to take off all our war paint makeup off our faces. We get pulled over by the local cops, all act cool. Say we crossed at Laredo. And like the army they too can be bought and if they get stupid, we will kill them and drag their bodies into a ditch off the side of the road. We got into the outskirts of Cloete around three in the morning. Josh found us a motel for us to crash at until the morning. He and Donnie would then try and get some info on the remaining Murdoch brothers Paul and Eddie. I was sharing a room with Oscar, we both took turns killing cockroaches, spiders and making sure no snakes were ready to strike at us. The place was a total dump, you slept with your clothes on and a handgun under your pillow. Dump or not, I slept solid. Candice drained whatever energy I had on reserve by fucking me almost till the time we had to leave. The twins, Donnie and Josh took off looking for info, so Oscar, Sean and I went looking for food. Found this greasy spoon that was still serving breakfast. Sean looked at some of the plates of food going past us as we looked over the menu. I understood some Spanish, Oscar and Sean knew fuck all. In fact, Sean said he has no interest in eating Mexican mystery meat. With Oscar and I being in Special Ops, we have eaten all kinds of Southeast Asian forms of meat that slithered, had hooves or beaks and claws. I told him to order some huevos rancheros which he did. Oscar and I both ordered beans with spuds and some mystery fried meats. Just seeing Sean look at his plate full of food put down in front of him and the look he gave, fucking classic. He tried one of the eggs and the whole time he was eating it you would think he had shit under his nose. We left the diner and headed back to our motel. Josh's truck was back; let's hope he has info for us so we can take care of business and get back home. Well, they did get the info that was the good news. Bad news is that Paul and Eddie for a fee are staying at the local police chief's house. What better protection than a corrupt cop with power.

We thought of everything to try and get at them including a diversionary tactic that included blowing up the local gas station. But that would be too obvious, and they would hunker down inside the house with the head copper attending the explosion. Have one of us try and disguise our voice and say we are Jim, and we need help just outside of town, but nothing seemed logical enough for them to lower their guard. Eventually Sean said fuck that, it was hot, and he needed a pint of ale. He said we was going to the saloon in town. Donnie told him not to go by himself. So, I said I would go, Candice of course said she would come as well. It was about a fifteen-minute walk to the saloon. Candice was all lovey dovey wanting to hold my hand all the way there.

Sean looked at me the same way he looked at his breakfast this morning. I even kissed Candice as we were walking, yeah watching the big man shake his head made me laugh inside. The saloon like everything else in this shit town was a dump, but they did have cold American beer and tequila. Sean loves his beer and drank a Bud straight back in one gulp. He burped and did a little bit of a smile, still could have been gas, not sure. We had a couple beers into us when Candice said she had to use the washroom. I told her to squat not sit, she looked at me and said she is a Texan, she knows all about the horrors of Mexico, lord knows she is not the only one. Candice's white dress broke me free of the hatred vision I was having. She just passed the bar itself and then stopped. Her eyes got big, and she made them go left. I had no clue what was going on. Then she headed to the bar and started to talk up this guy. He wasn't there when she first headed to the bathroom; he must have come in when I was zoned out. Sean said my girlfriend is acting like a whore with her hands all over this guy, laughing it up and even has the nerve to look back at us.

"Sean, I don't think she is acting like a whore. I am going to the washroom. If the guy she is hanging off goes to leave, have a good look at his face."

Sean sat up straight now, his ice-cold steel eyes now focused on Candice and the guy. I got up and made sure not to look at them heading to the washroom. I did go piss, nothing worse than scraping on a full bladder, or course it seemed to be the longest piss in history. I came out of the washroom and looked at the guy; fuck me, it was Paul Murdoch. I sat back down and told Sean to go head back and get the guys as it is Paul Murdoch. Sean didn't argue, he got up and headed back to the motel. In hindsight maybe I should have gone back as I can move a hell of a lot faster than him. Two minutes later Paul went to the washroom, Candice came over and asked now what. Time to think quickly.

"Wait another twenty minutes, keep him drinking and flirt with him. I will go outside and tell the boys to go wait for you two in the alley. Once the boys are here, I will come up to the bar and ask for a shot of Mescal, which will be the sign. You tell him you wanna suck his cock. Take him in the back and the only head he will be getting is a broken head."

"You are evil, Mitchell Strongbow, I love you." Candice went back to the bar, undid a couple buttons on her dress. It took me about ten minutes to finish my beer, I went outside and waited for the boys. As soon as they pulled up, I told them the game plan. Josh and Chuck were concerned for Candice's safety.

"Guys, she will tell him to drop his drawers, he will be so fixated on her he won't see you guys coming." I told Sean to come back in with me. Josh was going to stay in the truck. As soon as he drops his pants, Donnie and Chuck will tell him at gunpoint to surrender to us or die. He will be handcuffed, tape over his mouth and a pillowcase over his head. We will then take him back to the motel and get him to talk his brother Eddie into leaving the captain's house. Seems easy enough. Sean and I went back in, I walked up to the bar and ordered two shots of mezcal. That was the cue for Candice that all is in place. Well, Candice certainly started to turn up the heat on Paul. She took his thumb and put it in her mouth and started to suck on it. She then started to rub him through his pants, now this guy had this stupid look on his face to begin with, now he seemed to stick his chest out and suck his gut in. Candice then started to nibble on his ear and must have said that magical word "Blow Job" as his eyes got big, he smacked her ass and grabbed her hand and started to walk out of the saloon. I just looked straight ahead and paid no attention; I think Paul was so fixated with her he wouldn't have noticed anything. After two minutes we downed our shot and then headed to the alley. We sneaked around to the back and pulled out our weapons. Then dear sweet Candice put on a show; fuck, I think I am the one who now loves her. She undid Paul's pants and told him to pull them down along with his underwear. Once his pants and underwear were around his ankles, she started to belittle him.

"You fucking call that a cock? My four-year-old nephew has a bigger cock than you." Paul called her a fucking cunt, bad move. She threw a left jab, right overhand and kicked him in the nuts. He hit the ground hard and was starting to moan in pain. We all rushed in as she started to lay the boots to him. Donnie taped his mouth shut while Chuck threw on a pair of handcuffs and then a pillowcase over his head. Sean signaled Josh to pull up with the truck. We threw Paul in the back and then off to our shit motel which I am sure has heard its fair share of screams over the years. We pulled up; Sean went to the front desk to make sure the owner didn't poke their head out. Looked around and once the coast was clear we carried Paul inside. While still blindfolded Donnie uncuffed and then cuffed him to a chair. Donnie told Chuck to sit out front of our room and watch for any signs of non-friendlies approaching, you just never know. Then it is time to get info on the remaining Murdoch brother and hopefully score the five keys of pure coke would be a huge bonus

Donnie removed the pillowcase from Paul. His nose was a mess, Candice broke it for sure. His eyes were swollen and turning black already. Those swollen eyes also showed a lot of fear.

Donnie turned to Candice and asked her to plug in the iron. "Why? Because I am the only female in the room?" was her response.

"Yeah," was Donnie's answer. He looked at Paul and said he is going to remove the tape from his mouth.

"Mitchell, stand beside Paul with your knife, if he hollers for help, cut his tongue out." I did as instructed and pulled it out from my boot. I also grabbed the notepad on the table beside the bed. I tore off a piece and paper and cut it with the knife.

"See Paul, Mitch keeps his knife's razor sharp. He is Sioux and is pure lethal with that knife."

Donnie pulled the tape off his mouth and said, "All we want is the five keys of coke. You give us the coke, you live, and we go back to Boston."

"Where is my brother Jim?" said a terrified Paul. Donnie looked at him, shook his head and grabbed Paul's Adam apple. Paul started to turn red in the face as he was being choked.

"First off, we ask the questions not you. But if I had a brother, I would ask him the same. Your brother sold you and Eddie out. He is being held by associates of ours back in Laredo. Once we get the coke and head back home, he will be set free.

Now each time you interrupt me, that iron that the beautiful Candice has heating up, will sear your skin. And just in case you think I am bullshitting you, or don't realize just how much this hurts, let me give you a sample."

Donnie put the tape back over his mouth, grabbed the iron and walked over to a squirming Paul. Donnie with the most intense yet calm look pushed the iron to the inside of his thigh. I thought Paul's eyes were going to bulge out of his head. He screamed and then started to cry like a baby looking for his mama's tit. Donnie then pulled the iron away, looked at Candice who said I know, plug the iron back in for round two.

"Paul once again we just want the coke, if we wanted you dead, well you saw how easy it was to get you in a secluded area, you would be dead and left for the buzzards in the desert. Now, once again I am going to remove the tape, same as last time, Mitch will slice your tongue out, you will more than likely choke on it and die, so no yelling right?"

Paul nodded his head yes and Donnie tore the strip of tape off his face.

He was looking rough, he is ready to spill the beans, I know it.

Donnie then went over and talked to Josh in the bathroom for a couple minutes. They came out and Donnie asked Paul once again where the coke was. His voice was trembling as he said Eddie had it.

"Good boy, Paul. Now was that hard?" He shook his head now as he cried.

"And Eddie is at the cop's house right now correct Paul?"

"I think so, I am not sure." Donnie then took me aside and told me to steal a vehicle and sit on the house.

"Mitch, the coke is a bonus. That's a huge bonus for us. But I don't fully trust these Murdoch brothers. I am going to get Paul to call Eddie and tell him we are doing a switch. Paul's life for the coke. We are going to tell Eddie to meet us at this abandoned mine about ten clicks out of town. If Eddie leaves the cops house with anyone else, just kill him right then and there. We will kill Paul and throw his lifeless body down an old shaft." He asked me to go to the office and get a couple maps of the town and surrounding area. I did as instructed and came back with three maps. Josh showed me exactly where the cops house was. Where the switch with Paul for the coke is going to happen. Next was the call to Eddie. Paul sobbingly asked for him and then said someone wanted to talk to him.

"WE have Paul. Friends of ours have Jim tied up in Laredo. If you want both of your brothers to live, give us the coke." There was a bit of silence, so Donnie told Candice to bring him the red-hot curling iron.

"Listen to your brother scream as I burn his flesh." Donnie pressed the searing hot iron into his other thigh, he screamed long enough for Eddie to hear him and then re-taped him up.

"I am not a person to fuck with, you have ten seconds to make a decision, the coke, or you will be an only child." As Donnie counted out loud, he got to seven when Eddie finally said fine. He gave him the location and the time for the switch. As soon as he hung up the phone. Donnie took me into the bathroom and told me to steal a vehicle and sit on the cop's house.

"Keep the vehicle close and once you see him leave alone, wait about five minutes then head to the sight. Mitch, sit in the weeds and get a good sight for a clear shot, and once the switch is done. Shoot them both dead. If he leaves with anyone else, kill him right, then and there. If all of a sudden, all these cops show up you know he has called for help. Look for the right time and kill him and head to the location switch and we will head home."

In the regular army I never disobeyed an order, they programmed you that way. But once I got into Special Ops you become your own man. So, I looked at Donnie and said, "I think it would be better if I headed to the switch site at the mine."

He looked confused and asked why. "If I were them, I would make sure I have people in place, so my enemy is walking into a trap. Fuck man, this is Mexico, *corrupt* Mexico. There is no way he will hand over the coke without a firefight, crooked cops, they don't have to answer to no one. Send Oscar to the house, I will watch for anything out of the ordinary, and if I do see cops or bandit's I will take care of them." Donnie smiled at me like my Dad would when I did something special.

"I know you will take care of them. Yes, that works." Donnie told Oscar to head to the cops' house and keep an eye on Murdoch and anything unusual. Before I left, Donnie said once the switch is done and the coke is good, both brothers will be killed.

"That goes without saying." I told them if I do see anything, I don't like during the switch, I will do a hawk call. I grabbed my M-21 rifle, both 9MM handguns, told the boys to be safe and I will see them around midnight. Today's vehicle of choice to steal was a VW Bug, so many to choose from, powder blue seemed like the grooviest one to take. I took the route that Josh showed me to the mine. Got out, walked to the highest point to see if any enemies had beat me here. As I looked around, I had this eerie feeling, this has basically become a ghost town. So many buildings and zero forms of human life. I can almost sense how much energy this place must have had when the mines were running full out. Now just snakes, scorpions and lizards are living in this abandoned town. I saw no human life form, so I surveyed what is the best place for me to set up and wait for any unwanted guests. I also know there will be no air extract and we are in their turf; they truly have the hometown advantage. If Eddie does decide to bring the cops in. they will know where to set up for us when we leave. I think taking the main road out will be wrong, ambush wrong.

So, I went back up as high as I could go, looked around for any old roads not on the map I was giving I noticed a pattern with this rock formation that was at least twelve feet wide, had to have been an old oar road for their heavy equipment, so I jumped in the VW and decided to see just how far it went. You can tell it has been a long time since anyone has been down this road. I drove for about thirty minutes and ended up on the outskirts of Villa Union, a small town.

When Josh shows up, I will see what he says, if you have a hot LZ and this will be hot, you always know another way to get back to base. As soon as I got back to the mines, I rechecked for any unwanted guests and wished I had some C4 explosives. I think a big explosion with some of these old buildings collapsing behind us would help us disappear into the night and take out our enemies. I know methane gas kills miners every year, just not sure how to use it for our advantage; fuck, should have paid more attention in science. So, I went to the top of this tower where I had a perfect view of everyone coming from all angles for miles and miles. I also put my home-made silencer with a muzzle flash on my M21 sniper rifle. You can't help but daydream in the barren waste land how many special ops missions I found myself with a rifle and waiting for the enemy to arrive. And Mexico is just as fucked up as any jungle, or city in Southeast Asia. Around eight or so I saw this big old boat of a car headed my way. It left a trail of dust from the desert's unspoiled sand. It stopped and three men got out. All of them carried rifles and they certainly weren't guys I flew down with. If Donnie sent reinforcements, he would have come with them. I need them all out in the open. The sun is now in their eyes as I line up my rifle. Two of the guys have their rifles hung over their shoulders while one has the rifle in his hand, he is the biggest threat.

I have my scope on him, come on boys get away from the buildings. Of course, that would be easy. The two guys with the rifle are now checking buildings and have disappeared while this guy is now in the center of the mining town looking around. I start to control my breathing and take the safety off my rifle. I refocus my scope and put my finger on the trigger. All looks good; I gently squeeze the trigger and watch his head explode as his body hits the ground. Fuck, do I leave the safety of my snipers' nest and get rid of the body or sit and nail the other two? Well, because I am not sure the layout of the buildings and where they are. I will stay here. It took five minutes till the next guy appeared. He still had his rifle slung over his shoulder, fucking stupid Mexicans. This guy was wearing a hat and it was fucking up my scope sights on him. So, I re-aimed for the center of his chest. Controlled my breathing, squeezed the trigger and watched his whole chest explode. Okay, two little piggies down, where oh where is my third piggy? My head was on a pivot looking for any movement at all. Eventually I saw his shadow in a building. I am in no hurry, come out and play my piggy. I then hear an old creaky door open, and I see him exit a doorway and walk onto the sand. Feeling kind of ballsy, so I made a pig squeal call. He stops cold in his tracks, looks around for the noise. Sees the guy whose head I blew off on the ground and runs to him. He gets about halfway there and realizes what has happened and hits the ground and is pointing his rifle looking for anything. I control my breathing, refocus the scope and nail him between the head and shoulder.

An explosion of blood now flies into the air. He is not dead, as the shot has him now on his back, screaming in pain. Really annoying my piggy. I stand up from my kneeling position and once again control my breathing, finger on the trigger; I have the scope on the top of his skull.

I gently squeeze the trigger and my third piggy is now silent. I am sure the birds will come and eat his brain matter that is now strewn across the desert. I now come down from my sniper's tower, I put my rifle over my shoulder, but I have one of my 9MM pistols in my hands. One by one I empty out their pockets first and then grab a hold of the little piggies and drag their lifeless bodies to an open mine and put their bodies in just far enough, not getting a hernia for these fucks. I kick around the blood-soaked sand from each of them and finally I head to the old boat which turns out to be an early sixties Caddy and move it to the rear of the buildings and onto the road I think we should take out of here. What a solid looking car. I can see keeping it. I then go back to my sniper's tower and go through all their wallets. The one guy had a cute wife, one was better off that I killed him and the third had just cash in his wallet, I am willing to bet he is the one who had his rifle ready all the time. I am willing to bet he is a contract killer for the local Mexican mob. I took the cash and put it in my wallet. Put the caddy keys in my pocket.

The rifles were two M16s and one Heckler Koch G3, major score. I love the 7.62 grains of mayhem. The only other action was watching the buzzards fly in and eat whatever body parts or brain matter I didn't bury enough in the sand. As soon as the sun went down, I felt alive once again. The adrenaline let down after the kills was causing me to drift off for minutes at a time, but now I have butterflies knowing the shit show is coming soon. Around twenty-two hundred hours, I saw a single vehicle headlights headed my way. I had my rifle scope zoomed in on the vehicle the whole way. Once it stopped and the lights shut off, I heard Donnie yell *Strongbow*. "Donnie, I am at twelve o'clock, there is a ladder for you to climb."

No way am I coming down and losing my sight of everything

headed our way. Donnie looked puzzled at the other weapons I had and asked where I got them.

"Looks like Murdoch sent three guys over to ambush us."

"No shit. Where are the three guys now?" said Donnie checking out the HK rifle.

"They are dead lying at the mouth of the mine shaft on the left."

Ear to ear grin came to him. "Good boy."

"Listen, I am going to call Josh up as I found a back-door escape route, see what he says." Josh came up and I told him what I found and where I ended up.

"That actually works out well. We came in not far from there."

I told them both I have two vehicles on the west side, a Caddy and a VW bug.

"Donnie I would also like to rig something explosive wise so we can disappear into the darkness of night. I have no doubts that there is a welcoming party waiting for us the same way you guys came in."

"Sean brought a half dozen hand grenades actually, I agree with Mitch. I have a few ideas." So we went over a few ideas, all were brilliant and will work for sure. Time to get prepared for the switch and the whole shit show. Candice and Chuck stayed with Josh's truck the whole time. Paul was cuffed and had on the pillowcase and mouth tape in the back of the truck. Sean was busy booby trapping our escape route. Josh and Donnie were going over the game plan as to how everything was going to go down. I was still in my sniper's tower. Around 23:30 I saw a flashlight in the distance doing Morse code. It has been a while, but it came back really quick. I told Donnie what I saw and what it was saying. It spelled Currahee. It had to be Oscar. I wasn't going to give away my position, so I asked Donnie if he remembered it. He didn't so I told him the dot and dashes to send. I wanted to make sure it was Oscar, so I asked what cell block we were in. As soon as I saw the right answer come back, I told him to come in.

I told Josh to guard my post as my gut told me things aren't good. "Listen guys, they sent three guys up earlier in a black Caddy. They will be waiting in the bushes for us."

"That's all-right Oscar, Mitch met them, and dealt with it, and it didn't end very well for them." said Donnie.

"Good as there are at least two more station wagons headed our way. They pulled up to the house and I split as soon as I saw that. These guys look hardcore" With Oscar, Donnie, Josh and myself being Vietnam Vets and Sean being involved with wars regarding the English and the Orangeman back home, it was agreed that we are going to be out gunned so our key surviving and getting back to Texas alive is speed and the element of surprise.

"I know we are outgunned but do you remember what they did in Beau Geste? I see three dead Mexicans joining our ranks. Let's put them in positions for them to take fire as we are hauling ass through the darkened desert." Everyone liked my idea, so we pulled all three out from the mouth of mine. Not sure why I was being punished. But I had to carry one of them up the ladder and into the sniper tower. I made sure I chose the lightest one of the three. Sean did in fact bring with him some C-4 and hand grenades. Oscar gave him shit for bringing it onto an airplane, and then thanked him. So, all of us went over a game plan that Donnie and I came up with. Now there are always variables, let's just hope we can overcome them. I went back up to my sniper tower. Oscar was about a quarter mile down the road; he would flash us when he saw movement come our way. He was also to stay there, and once the second part of our plan was initiated, he was to take out all secondary vehicles. The shots would be for the radiator, driver and if he could, the drivers then haul ass back to the Caddy and Josh's jeep. That is where Candice and Chuck are waiting the whole time and making sure no one snuck up on us from the west. Donnie and Sean were to do the Paul for coke switch with Eddie, while Josh would be the rover making sure nothing came at us from the north.

The VW was used as a blocker and rigged with hand grenades. As soon as you open it, anyone within fifteen feet will be critically hurt. By twenty-three thirty we were all set up and ready for the remaining Murdoch brother and their associates. Your heart is starting to speed up. You go over the plan many times, too late now if you forgot anything or if you decide to change anything major. Like a beacon in the valley of death, I saw Oscar's signal of a vehicle approaching.

I yelled out the key words, "Remember the Alamo" which means trouble is just around the corner. I didn't focus on the car that was approaching; I was looking for any other forms of life. Once the car was stopped by Sean, and then searched, did I point my rifle on the driver and any other movement. Sean told the driver to get out. He walked towards Donnie, Chuck and Paul who was on his knees and still had on the mouth tape and pillowcase. Donnie asked Eddie if he had the coke. Eddie said he did and asked if we could take the pillowcase off of Paul's head. Donnie told Chuck to take off the pillowcase. Man, even though I am at least thirty feet away you could feel the anger coming off Eddie.

Donnie told him to get the coke. He just stared at Donnie. "I am not playing games, get me the coke now or I will tell my boys to put bullets in your head right now. Mitchell, you have him in your sights?"

"Of course, I do. Say the word boss and I end this fucker's life right now." Eddie was now looking around. Is he wondering what happened to his three scouts he sent up earlier. He looks pretty fucked up right now. He reluctantly said the coke is in the glove box. His head was on a pivot and my spidey senses were starting to get really uptight, things aren't right. Donnie told Chuck to grab the coke. I kept my rifle on Eddie, he tries to bolt. I know the car is going to explode as soon as the glove compartment box is open. Fuck it, I tell Donnie something ain't right. He now looks around; backs up and puts his handgun on Paul's head. But he didn't tell Chuck to stop. Chuck goes into the glove compartment, reaches for something. Stands up with a package and says all good. Not good as Eddie hits the ground. I hear a rifle go off and then I see Chuck hit the ground. He is now gasping for air as a barrage of gunfire is fired upon the guys below me. Donnie screams cocksuckers and blows Paul's head right off. I now catch Eddie in the ass as he is trying to crawl under his car. I look out into the darkness and see flashes of gun fire going back and forth. It is too dark for me to see anyone. It also appears that Eddie has hidden a gun under the car chassis and is firing from under there. He catches Sean. He falls down to the ground; he is cursing and screaming and then throws a hand grenade under the car.

Donnie yells out, "Eskimo Pie!" which means retreat to the vehicles out back. I wait for the three second delay with the hand grenade. It goes off and the whole car explodes. The whole night skies lit right up, it also shows at least a dozen guys firing and coming to our position. No way can I leave Oscar out there. I yell out to Donnie to get everyone out of here, leave me some C-4 and Oscar and I will meet you at the designated LZ. I now start to take aim at those that I can see. Oscar knows exactly what I am doing allowing him to make his way to me. As soon as I see Oscar getting close enough, I slide down the ladder and hit the ground. I can hear Eddie screaming as he is being burnt alive. I grab the C-4 and attach it to the tower. As soon as Oscar made visual with me, I lit the fuse and we both hauled ass to the Caddy. We jump in and I can see in the rear-view mirror approaching headlights. I put the gas pedal right to the floor and hear the huge sniper tower explode.

The headlights that were fast approaching are gone. I continue to drive with the headlights off and within a minute the night sky behind us erupts in another ball of flame as the VW we had bobby trapped has now ignited. For the next couple minutes, I keep looking behind us and I see nothing at all. Oscar asks if everyone is good.

"Chuck was shot somewhere in the upper body; pretty sure he is dead. Sean was also hit, that is all I know." We caught up to the rest of the crew at a gas station in Union City. As I suspected, Chuck was dead. He took a bullet in the throat. Candice was a fucking mess. Sean had a good size gash in his right leg, he was in a lot of pain, but he would survive. Right now, we have to keep moving and get across the border. Josh said it would be best if we put Chuck's body in the trunk of the Caddy in case we do get pulled over. Candice wanted no part of that as shock has now set it. Donnie told her in no certain way we either put him in the trunk or leave his body in Mexico. Candice said do what you have to do and said she was driving with us. So as soon as our vehicles were full, we headed back to Texas. It was a long ride that seemed to take forever. The whole time you keep looking in your rear-view mirrors for any sign of being pursued. A bawling Candice was curled up in a ball in the front seat with me. All I kept thinking was the greed of this elusive coke almost got us all killed. Yep, fucking greed, man. We have killed all three brothers and been home by now.

It seemed like an eternity for us to just cross the border. At one point Candice sat up, looked out the side window and said, "He is all I have, no mom, no dad and now no brother." Time for me to open up a few wounds, "My dad was killed in Vietnam in 1963, four years later my mom and oldest sister were killed by a drunk off duty cop and a couple years after that my only brother was murdered in San Quentin prison. I honestly feel your pain, hon. The only thing I can say is that the pain never really leaves, you just learn to cope. The nights are the worst, hon. And my mom and sis were killed on their way to see me, so yeah, guilt is a ruthless cocksucker." Candice didn't say anything. Fuck, I am not even sure she heard me. Oscar patted me on the shoulder though. We pulled into Josh's farm just as the moon and the sun were doing shift change. I was mentally and emotionally drained. Yeah, opening up to Candice certainly brought back the worse memories of my life. Even getting out of the car every single injury I have suffered in my twenty-six years on this planet seemed fresh. Candice didn't get out of the car. She just sat there still looking out the side window.

Josh walked over and asked if she needed anything. "I want my brother to be alive, that is what I want," said an angry Candice. Josh told us to bring Sean inside. He is a big man, and it took all of mine, Donnie and Oscar's strength. Josh said he will call this vet to have a look at Sean's wound. After he hung up the phone Josh stood and looked outside at Candice who still hadn't moved from the car. He walked to this cupboard and grabbed a bottle of Jack and headed outside. Human nature is to look outside and see how this all goes down. Yes, all of us were looking when Sean lost it.

"For fuck sakes, someone better find me some fucking whiskey." So I went to the same cupboard that Josh pulled out the bottle of Jack, grabbed him a bottle of tequila and said sorry this is all I could find. Sean shook his head and started to drink the bottle. Josh came in a couple minutes later with Candice and walked her to his bedroom. They were in there for a couple minutes before he came out alone.

He came over to us and said, "Candice has agreed to bury her brother here at my ranch. And I can see today hitting over a hundred degrees. So, I think we should start digging his grave now before he starts to cook in the trunk of the car." We all agreed to help out except Sean, he asked Josh for the bottle of Jack. Josh headed to the barn and brought out shovels for us while he went back in and started to build a casket for Chuck. We were almost finished digging when this car pulled up in the driveway. I went and got Josh as his dogs were going a little more strange than normal, a huge red flag for me. Josh said that is the vet to look at Sean. I was confused as to why the dogs would go crazy over a vet until Josh said he is not a war vet but a veterinarian who has fixed all his dogs, you get your nuts chopped off, you too would remember them till the day you die. I started to snicker at the thought of a horse doctor taking care of Sean and this I had to see for myself.

When we walked in Sean was singing Irish songs, the bottle of Jack was empty, and he was drunk off his ass. The doc looked at the wound, asked how he got it, but Sean was slurring so Josh told him a hunting accident. He cleaned the wound, stitched him up and said to stay off his feet for the next little bit. Donnie paid the vet and once he left, he went into his bedroom to talk to Candice. All you could hear was his voice talk, then a couple minutes later she followed him out of the bedroom. Her eyes and cheeks were fire red. She was slouched over and had zero energy in her. Josh went to get her a shot of Jack, but Sean also drained that puppy. He told her to grab a shower and get changed as her dress was full of Chuck's blood and we would come back and get her. Josh then told us guys to give him a hand. He and Oscar carried out the homemade casket. It was put beside the grave we just dug and on top of two sets of thick ropes. Josh said let's lift him out and put him in the casket. I opened the truck and Chuck was a mess. The bullet went right through his throat. So, we grabbed his legs and arms and carried him over to the casket. I said to Josh I think we should nail the lid shut. If it was my brother, I wouldn't want my last vision of him like this. Josh agreed, we grabbed his hammer and nailed it shut. We went back in the house and washed down a couple beers and waited for Candice. Josh looked at Donnie and said, "I don't want to seem like an insensitive dick, but I think right after the burial you guys should leave."

"Tell you what, we have all been up since yesterday. Let's bag a couple hours sleep and then we will head out once the sun has gone down. Oscar has to call ahead and get his plane ready to fly back. Yeah, I also don't need Oscar fallen asleep while flying." Josh said fine even though you could tell he wanted us out of here as soon as possible. I am thinking he wants to be the hero for Candice.

Fuck, maybe with me being over tired I am looking into things also. About thirty minutes later, a showered Candice came out with a change of clothes and said she was ready. So, all of us except Sean who was now passed out, headed to bury Chuck. Fuck me and call me delirious from the sun and lack of sleep but my body did this almost jolt action when Josh pulled out a bible and started to read quotes from it. And when he asked all of us to bow our heads, I just looked at Donnie and Oscar whose eyes were as big as mine. So, out of respect for Candice, and a fallen brother in arms Chuck, me the atheist bowed my head. And the more he talked the more you could tell Josh was totally into this. Certainly are some fucked up people in Texas now, aren't there? After about twenty minutes, Josh said it is time to lower Chuck's body. Thank fuck. It took a lot of strength, but we were able to lower him without dropping him. Then all of us including Candice helped to fill the hole with dirt. I asked Josh if there was any chance I could grab a shower before we left.

He said it has been a dry summer and his cistern is low on water. He did make us some egg salad sandwiches all the while making sure Candice didn't bother with me too much; yeah, jealous for sure. Once again Oscar and I were relegated to a hotter than fuck barn to sleep. And you know now no way would Josh let Candice sneak out and see me. Feeling a little paranoid, I made sure to have my 9MM beside me as I laid down in the hay, but you know what? Within thirty seconds

I was out cold, pardon the pun, but dead to the world. Donnie came in and woke us up, by now the sun was starting to set. He said he pulled the carpet out of the trunk of the caddy and that is what we will be taking back to the airport with us. If I didn't feel so beat up physically and mentally, I would drive it back home and keep it.

Josh made us some sandwiches for the flight home. We all thanked him, and Donnie paid him for his services. He also gave Candice some cash and said sorry the way things turned out. I was the last person that Candice hugged. Josh was of course hovering, and she told him to give us a couple minutes. She did a partial smile and thanked me for being caring to her. "No bullshit Mitch, you do learn to cope?"

"No bullshit you do. Now there isn't a day that goes by that I don't miss all of them, and yeah once in a while the death of my mom and Pam fucks my head up. But I have a pretty solid inner circle who keep things positive for me."

She then put both hands on my cheeks and rested her forehead on mine. I felt a tear roll from her eyes to my cheek. I gave her a kiss, walked over and gave her my home phone number and the Pamdora's business number and said I am always here for those fucked up days, or if she wants to head out my way for a vacation. She thanked me, one more long hug and then I jumped in the back of the caddy with Sean and off to the airport we went. We weren't even out of the driveway and Sean asked me if I had relations with Candice.

"You mean fucked her, Sean?"

"Yes Strongbow, did you fuck her?"

"A couple times, why?"

"Its little punks like you why I keep a gun ready when Nyah tells me she has a date." I was dying inside with laughter, if only he knew. I stayed up front with Oscar for most of the flight. All aboard were quiet. And all of us yanks that had served in Nam, were used to brothers being killed in action. But this seemed different, seem to hit home really hard. Does being back stateside, and now a civilian make us all soft, lost our edge, and if so, does this make us not as lethal? Oscar picked up on me being not only being quiet, but deep in thought.

"Strongbow, Candice break your heart? You are anywhere, but here brother." I took a sip of beer, looked at Oscar and said, "She was fun to play with, nothing more, nothing less. I keep replaying how Chuck was killed. What could we have done different? Even the big gorilla in the back being shot, that could have been you, Donnie or myself.

We were Special Ops, none of us should have got a scratch on us. I felt slow physically, and mentally. I am normally thinking three moves ahead, this time I struggled, not good, man."

"Strongbow, don't be so hard on yourself. Those were not some Mexican street gang members. A couple of them were wearing the OG107 boots, yep same kind we wore in Nam, and their weapons were high end. They were fucking mercs, maybe even ex-special ops like us. And as far as you go, listen man, you moved really fast back in Nam. I would say you're what, 80 pounds or so heavier, and I think you are even faster now, sure as fuck are a lot stronger. Chuck's number was up. Not sure why he would put himself in such a vulnerable position, we wouldn't now, would we?"

I just shook my head no.

"Just like in Nam after we lost a brother, we need some serious R&R once we land, you in Strongbow?" Everything he said made sense, crystal fucking clear to be exact. I wonder how many more mercs are now in our line of work?

It seems to be the perfect fix for us adrenaline junkies. Our war in Southeast Asia may be over, but the battles back home are just starting.

The Mitch Strongbow Series

Book 1- Santa Dies Once Again

Book 2- Summer of Love, Fall of Hate

Book 3- A Jungle is Still a Jungle

Book 4- Criminology 101

Book 5- Chasing Dragons, Slaying Demons

Book 6- Inside Looking Out

Book 7- Freedom

Book 8- Diablo Returns

Book 9- A Fool's Betrayal

Book 10- The Ghosts that Haunt Me

Book 11-Forbidden or Worse

With more Strongbow Revenge to come in the series!

www.pandamoniumpublishing.com
pandapublishing8@gmail.com